How far can he bend her before she breaks?

MIND TO BEND

STOLEN OBSESSIONS
BOOK ONE

AURELIA KNIGHT

MIND TO BEND

AURELIA KNIGHT

Copyright © 2023 by Aurelia Knight

All rights reserved.

No part of this book may be reproduced in any form or by any electronic or mechanical means, including information storage and retrieval systems, without written permission from the author, except for the use of brief quotations in a book review.

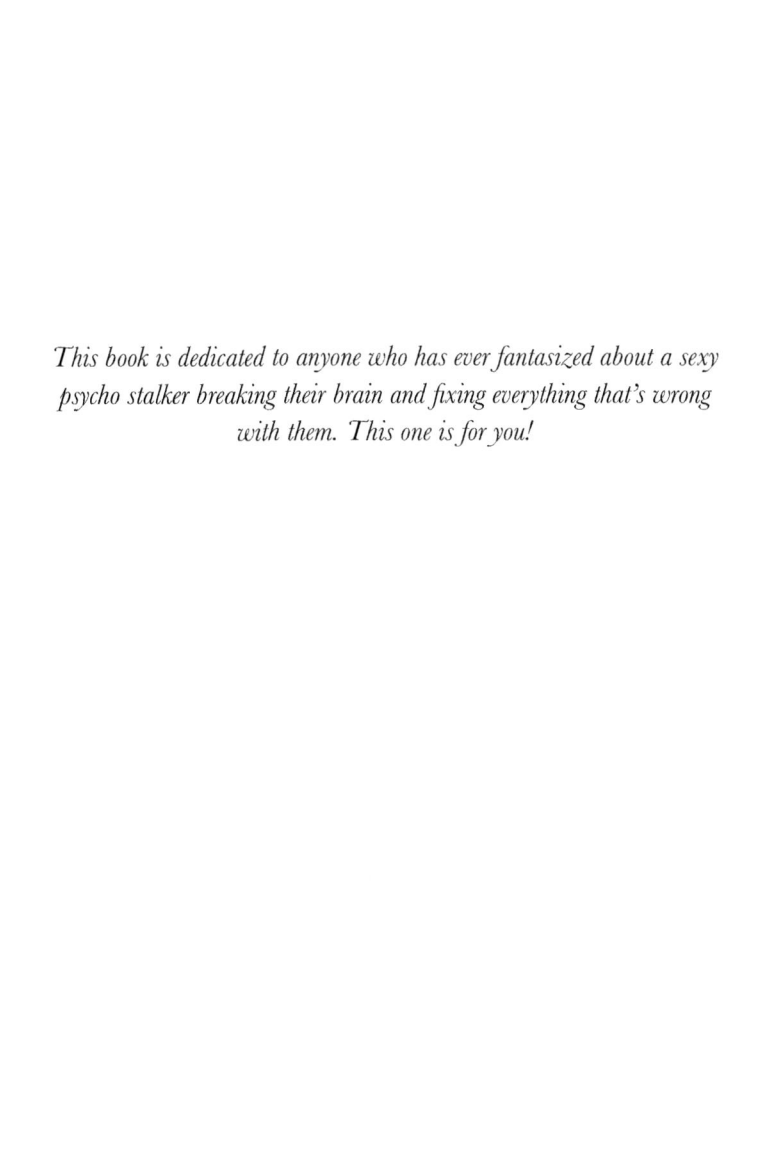

This book is dedicated to anyone who has ever fantasized about a sexy psycho stalker breaking their brain and fixing everything that's wrong with them. This one is for you!

WARNING

Mind to Bend is a dark romance with dark themes throughout. This book contains graphic, violent and sexual content that may be upsetting to some readers. The following lists some, not all, of the potentially sensitive subjects included. If you have a specific concern please reach out on www.AureliaKnight.com or in Aurelia's Facebook group Aurelia's Illicit Library.

Dub-con, murder, breath play, manipulation, stalking, abduction, hypnosis, cheating (not between main characters), dissolution of a marriage, religious abuse (historic, off page), spousal abuse (both emotional and physical on page)

CHAPTER ONE
SERA

"This isn't my fault, Tim." My hands tighten on the steering wheel, taking the worst of my aggression out on the leather. I stow the rest of the heat simmering beneath the surface. I don't have many options left, and none of my standard problem-solving techniques have stopped my husband from being a jerk these past two weeks.

Why give up your lost cause now? A sarcastic voice asks.

The light on the side of the road flips to red, and I press the brake. Tim makes a noise of displeasure, and I'm unsure if it's because of my driving or the conversation. A mechanical arm drops across the road, keeping us out of the railroad crossing while the flashing yellow lights warn a train is approaching. The first car hasn't passed yet, but I can tell from the sound that it's one of the long freight trains overflowing with construction materials and tanks of liquid rather than a passenger train. We're going to sit here for a while.

My gaze slides to Tim, and my heart clenches a little. It's like yearning, and I hate feeling it for my husband. His blonde hair drapes around his sky-blue eyes, and I have a knee-jerk reaction to tell him to cut it.

I know that judgmental voice is not my own, and like I often do, I push my father's opinion out of my head.

My father is a hateful person, and so is Tim's. On days like this, which is every day, I genuinely despise the man for the hatred he tried to sow in me, all in the name of his God. Most of the time, I'm not sure I believe in God at all, certainly not my father's definition, and other days I believe as fervently as he does. And *that* is when I hate God even more than my father or myself.

Tim's weathered band t-shirt clings to his abs, making him look forbidden and alluring, as does the general distaste for me radiating off him. I crave his approval so badly I could scream. I would crawl on my knees and beg for it if that wouldn't turn him off more. He's my husband, and we're young. This is the part of our marriage where things should be *easy*—they are anything but.

My gaze drifts over the brick buildings surrounding us. This area used to be the state capital, but that was a few hundred years ago. Now, it's run down, mildly impoverished, and crumbling away in places. The discolored red of the buildings sits in stark contrast with the blue sky, and I wish I could tell Tim how beautiful I find the world. But, unfortunately, I can't because he hates it when I do.

Tim's eyes prowl over the sidewalk. Despite knowing why he's so hyper-vigilant, I can't help the stabbing in my heart every time he monitors our surroundings. Rationally, he knows we're far from home, but somewhere inside, he always thinks anyone could be watching the pastor's daughter and the town drunk's son.

Violent alcoholism did not preclude Timothy Baker senior from attending church or hinder his relationship with my father, the Pastor. In fact, the mean bastards are the best of friends, joined by their self-righteous indignation. Though they can't find us here, I shiver at the thought of that possibility.

Tim and I married at twenty-two, fresh out of our local state college, though we had tried to do it at eighteen. The day after high-school graduation, we intended to elope, but his father got it into his head that Tim wanted to marry me because I was pregnant. His father beat him so severely that we needed to hold off, wait for him to heal, and attend the local college. I stayed by his side through all that.

Marriage was the only way for Tim and me to get free without our fathers trying to stop us after the first terrifying debacle. Once it was proven that I wasn't pregnant, his father started to back our relationship. I believe as an admission of guilt over what he'd done to Tim. But whatever the case, they would have never let us leave the state alone, and our marriage was necessary. Regardless of the rather bumpy start, I *thought* we married for love. I believed we wanted to enjoy our freedom together.

I still *do*, but I'm not so sure Tim ever did.

The last eighteen months together haven't gone as I hoped. Our persistent unhappiness was the last thing I expected when we moved east. The house we bought was supposed to be our dream home, a much-needed fresh start and the beginning of something good. Those expectations have gone so well that I'm headed to marriage counseling with a man who hates me and sees his father in every older dark-haired man we pass.

The metallic shaking of the tracks and the screaming whistle make conversation impossible, so I inspect the deep lines around Tim's eyes and jaw as I wait. The ever-present flush in his cheeks softens me, de-escalating my anger. I've always wanted to make his life easier, not more complicated. He deserves peace, and what we currently have is so far from it.

My father "whooped" me or beat my bare butt with his belt when I did something wrong, but Tim's father is a worse monster than mine. Memories of Tim broken and bleeding fill my mind, and I blink hard to clear the gathering tears. What are a few white lines scarring my backside compared to broken bones, tee—

"I know you think it's *my* fault." I strain to hear Tim's words over the noise.

Mercifully, he's oblivious to the direction of my thoughts. I'm grateful he's not thinking about why we left home or what his father did to him. My heart aches for Tim and has done so ever since we were kids, but his anger is wearing me thin. His words have sharp edges, and even the mild ones sting. It's been *two weeks* since I walked into the bathroom and found him doing the thing I'm too embarrassed to say.

I'm not even sure why *he's* so angry. Before I even made this appointment, he was furious that I opened an unlocked door. But no matter how much I want to lose my mind, I am a peacekeeper at heart.

I wait for the caboose to pass before I answer, "I don't think it's necessarily your *fault*, but I am not the one being mean. You are." I sniff back a tear as I turn onto the highway that leads to the fancy new medical complex on the outskirts of town.

"I'm being *mean* because you're making us do all this. Why can't you get over it?!" I'm not surprised he can't say what *it* is. I don't think I can either.

"Do not yell at me. We have been married for eighteen months, and—" The tears on my lashes cloud my vision making it hard to drive. "You know exactly why I can't let it go, but please, let's just talk about this when we get there. It's not safe to get emotional behind the wheel."

I grind my teeth, realizing my father's words slipped out.

"Fine," he agrees, hearing what I did.

I pull up outside of the all-glass building. More and more of these super medical complexes have been going up lately. This space used to be a strip mall. When we first moved here, I cried in the dressing room of the discount clothing store because I felt like such a worthless whore wearing one of the outfits I loved and longed for. I still bought it, even though I've never worked up the nerve to wear the ensemble. My chest twinges uncomfortably, bringing me back to the present, and I refocus on the tower now standing in its place.

I pull the car into a spot and turn the engine off. Tim won't look at me as I face him. "Is this how it's going to be now? I thought you *loved* me." The words are sad, manipulative even, and I know it. Still, his rejection stings as much as his betrayal because, despite our situation, I have always loved Tim.

"I *do* love you. I'm just…" He drops his handsome face into his hands and hisses in aggravation. "Let's see if this guy can help, okay?"

"Yeah." A brief flare of satisfaction sparks in my chest at him yielding to me, but it dies just as quickly.

We walk inside at a respectable distance. It's an old habit to "leave space for the lord" between us. Since we left home, we have worked hard to dispel old hang-ups, but this isn't about those so much as our current issues; the discontent in our marriage runs deep. I reach for his hand, and I don't let the hurt show when he pretends not to notice. Tim already thinks I'm pathetic.

The spacious lobby sits almost empty. The glass ceiling

matches the building exterior, arching dramatically into the sky and letting the soft spring sun pour in. The desire to sit in a comfortable chair and stare at the sky floods me, but the only seats available are a pair of austere benches beneath the giant directory mounted to the gray wall. Under the heading *Sunrise Mental Health Services* is the name Shane Nelson MD. We find the elevator and hit the button for the third floor.

A pop song with a sexy beat plays softly in the background, and my skin prickles. The fear that I'll get caught listening and get in trouble is still deeply ingrained in me. In addition, I'm shivering from the early spring air and the draft in the lobby, and the combination has my teeth rattling. Part of me hopes that Tim will wrap an arm around me and offer me some comfort or warmth, but I'm not surprised when he doesn't. Affection has never come easily to us.

The elevator opens to another empty room. It makes sense that there isn't a secretary everywhere we turn, but it feels ominous to be so alone. This building is so massive I doubt doctors occupy even half the offices, and with the population of this city, they probably never will, but I am surprised we haven't seen *anyone*.

Unlike the board downstairs, this sign holds more empty spaces than filled ones. Sunrise Mental Health and an osteologist top the otherwise empty list.

This place is creepy.

We head left. The hallway seems to lengthen and narrow in equal measure increasing my anxiety, like in one of those old cartoons I watched with the older kids behind my parents' back in the church basement. Tim's footsteps thump unnaturally loud. Is he trying to increase the tempo of my racing heart, or is he being petulant?

By the time Tim pulls the door back, I'm second-guessing every life choice that's led to this moment. Should I have let what I saw go? Or endeavored to do the same thing myself? I try my hardest not to think of the one time I did and how improper it felt.

A pretty young woman sits behind a desk in the center of the simple office space, and while I'm relieved there's someone besides Tim and me in this building, I'm embarrassed to meet her eyes with those thoughts so fresh in my mind. An intricate bun sits in a spiral on her head, brown curls hang artfully near her temples, and I resent my plainness by comparison.

The office is simply, if not sparsely, decorated. The cream walls soften the glaring fluorescents. Had they been white, the place would have looked like an asylum, and I kick myself for the thought. *That's a flattering way to think of my psychiatrist.* The receptionist smiles at Tim a moment too long before greeting me.

"Good morning. What can I do for you?"

"Good morning," Tim answers for the two of us out of habit. He doesn't believe that he owns me or that being a man makes him superior, but that doesn't change the fact that he often acts that way. Old habits are hard to break. "I'm Timothy Baker, and this is my wife Sera. We have an appointment with Doctor Nelson."

"Of course." Her brow raises in mild disbelief as she judges us as a pair and decides that *I* got lucky. Maybe I did since my husband *is* hot and a good provider. I imagine we could be great if it weren't for that *one* thing. "The two of you need to fill out a little paperwork, and Shane will be with you shortly."

My lips purse at her calling the doctor by his first name. Most doctors I've known insist on being addressed by their formal titles, and I can't say I blame them. If I spent that long in school, I would want people to call me "doctor" too. Tim doesn't touch me but guides me toward the chairs he likes with the force of his presence. I *hate* that I understand this subconscious communication and that he still uses it.

He hands me the paperwork, silently claiming he's no good at it. I know that's not true. He doesn't *want* to, but I don't complain and fill in the information in silence. Every bit of personal information he *should* know, I remember for him. My chest twinges as I write his birthday.

Tim turned twenty-four last month. *That* was an uncomfortable gathering. I don't even think his friends knew he had a wife before then. I certainly didn't know any of *them*. Being only three months behind him, we'll be the same age again soon. *I* won't have a slew of secret friends at my party because they don't exist.

I'm finishing up as the girl behind the desk says, "He's ready for you."

I stand awkwardly, feeling out of place and insignificant, as I try again to take Tim's hand, and he ignores it. This time, we both know that he saw. He waves for the secretary to lead the way, and we follow her. It's hard to miss Tim watching the sway of her hips. Does he watch me like that? I wouldn't know because he would be standing behind me, but somehow I doubt it.

She leads us down another long hall, and I swear it's only so she can shake her ass for my husband. I gasp slightly, placing my hands over my parted lips. I'm not usually this type of person, and my jealousy surprises me.

Tim's eyes censure me with his disapproval, and I can hear his unspoken demands, *What is wrong with you? Shut up.*

The look I give him conveys my apology, and I once again hate this unconscious dance we're trapped in.

I turn back to the plain walls, trying to focus on anything else. The decor is bland, with a few more landscape portraits and nameplates on the various doors. There are more doctors in this practice than I realized, but it's so quiet that I wonder where they all *are*. She knocks on one before opening it.

There's a gust of cool air as we step inside like the air conditioner is set to high even though it's not yet summer. The rich smell of books and leather wraps around me, calming my fried nerves. I don't know who I expect behind that door, but it's *not* the God I see.

CHAPTER
TWO
SERA

Doctor Shane Nelson *occupies* a leather armchair in what appears to be a comfortable sitting room. There's no other way to describe how he seems to take up every inch of space and molecule of breathable air.

I can't guess his height from his sitting position, but his limbs are long and muscular, powerful. He has to be over six feet tall. Worst of all, he's so goddamn handsome it's painful, and he's smiling at me.

Breathless and speechless, I know I will have to say something soon, but my brain short-circuits. Tim doesn't catch my reaction as he speaks for me again. Doctor Shane responds, smiling easily at Tim, but then his eyes flick back to me.

The casual set of his lips freezes in place as if he didn't see me correctly the first time and now recognizes me. His warm expression turns into something forced. His deep ocean-blue eyes remind me of the chilly wind blowing up my spine, and I must be feeling an echo of that now. Simply looking at him can't be enough to pebble my skin.

A brief look of confusion crosses *Shane's* face before a strong hand shakes my shoulder.

"Earth to Sera!" Tim grunts, finally drawing me out of the spell Doctor Shane cast on me.

Guilt floods my stomach as I drift back into my husband's sky-blue eyes. Eyes that appear dull when compared to the oceanic depths of our doctor's. I don't believe in love at first sight, especially *not* for married women, but I do believe in evil, and the Devil himself plopped this man in my path. Temptation and sin incarnate.

Doctor Shane recovers quicker than I do. "Why don't you two have a seat, and we can chat a bit?" He waves to the couch and armchair opposite him. The cozy cluster of seating reminds me of a living room. "It's our first session, so this is nothing more than a warm-up, a way for us to get to know each other as doctor and patients and ultimately get an idea of what type of work we need to do."

"Okay, Doctor Nelson," I gulp.

"Please, call me Shane. Doctor Nelson is my father," his voice wraps around my skin, smooth and deep, encouraging another wave of goosebumps.

"Shane," I agree, cursing the blush rising to my cheeks.

His fair skin contrast with his ink-black hair, and his blue eyes shine even brighter between the two. Before I notice the strength of his shoulders or how soft his mouth seems, my pulse is racing. I thank God I'm seated and take a steadying breath as I realize Tim has never made me feel this way—not once.

As if to cement the thought, Tim sits in the armchair rather than beside me on the couch. He gestures toward me.

"Sera is the one who insisted we come. So, she can *start*."

My eyebrow lifts in question. Tim's aggravated because he's embarrassed, and while I understand, this is not my fault. He thinks I won't be able to stomach telling this doctor what happened because of our intense religious upbringing, and that the words themselves are so weighted and burdened with shame that I'll balk. Well, he's wrong. As hard as it was, I turned my back on those beliefs, and it's time for the rest of my life to catch up.

"I caught him masturbating." There's not an ounce of shame to be heard in my declaration, but that's not a true reflection of the storm brewing in my heart.

I'm mortified.

A moment of tense silence surrounds us. Tim's shock thickens the air as it attempts to shove my words back down my throat.

"Okay." The doctor's tone is neither dismissive nor shocked. "I gather from your tone you find that unacceptable within the agreed-upon terms of your marriage. Is that correct?"

I flounder. My cheeks burn bright red, and Tim watches me with a self-satisfied smirk. He has been against this from the start, believing the damage our upbringing did to us is enough to keep us from speaking about our burdens and feelings ever. He thinks our baggage is too dark and heavy to let free in front of anyone.

He also can't explain why his friends seemed shocked when I corrected them about me being his wife rather than his girlfriend, and I think there's more to his aversion than he wants to let on. So for once in my life, I won't let things go.

"That's not the problem exactly. We've never discussed whether we're okay with that or not. Tim and I had a very..." I hesitate as I try to think of the right way to say it, "*conservative* upbringing. So I can't pretend I'm entirely comfortable with *masturbation*, but I think in other circumstances, I might not mind so much." I run my finger along my bottom lip as I think.

"So, you would be okay with what you saw after a proper discussion?"

The doctor's gentle gaze probes me.

"I don't know if that's true. Is lying to a therapist a sin? I wasn't doing it on purpose." My eyebrows crease as I navigate my thoughts.

He laughs softly, "No, there are absolutely *no* sins in therapy. Well, at least not when it comes to you working through your thoughts."

The gentle sound of his amusement warms my insides. The idea of thought and speech without sin sounds titillating. I want him to show me what that could be like.

Tim sits completely aghast, staring at me like he's never seen me. I suppose it's true that I'm usually quiet and, up until now, I never dared to utter a word like *masturbation*. Hell, just thinking it makes me sick and a little hot. But I'm not sure why he's looking at me like he's seen a ghost.

"Part of me does feel like *masturbation* is dirty, but I don't truly *believe* that," I admit, hating that my father's lessons have taken root, even when I know he's wrong.

"Cognitive dissonance, Seraphina."

When Doctor Shane says my name, my insides melt. Usually, I hate my full name, but the way he says it does something to me. I want to hear him grunt it like he's both angry and pleased with me, like in that one video I watched the first night I tried to touch myself.

"Sera," Tim corrects, disliking the use of my first name more than I do. Any reminder of home is too much for him. We fought for a month when we first moved away because he didn't understand why I wasn't comfortable going by Sarah.

"What?" I ask Shane, like Tim never spoke, feeling as stupid as I sound.

"Cognitive dissonance. Holding two opposing beliefs at once. It's one of the more interesting parts of the human condition." Judging from his smile, the *human condition* fascinates him more than anything, and I think I like that about him. "But that's okay. Talking about these difficult topics is a great way to make sense of them. So, you caught your husband masturbating, and while you intellectually comprehend that's not bad, you're having trouble believing it?"

The question in his voice is to be polite. Shane carries a calm efficiency that tells me he believes wholeheartedly in his ability to fix our problems and anything else he sets his mind on. I envy his confidence with a burning flash in my stomach that shocks me.

"There's more to it than that," I argue. "It's not that I'm some prude who can't accept that my husband has needs. We, we—"

Tim's face burns scarlet as he barks, "Go ahead and tell him, Sera! *You* made us come here."

He's not *always* an asshole. He's not, but this whole situation embarrasses him and makes him feel like less of a man. I'm hurt but not heartless. I'm not sure what's been happening with him these last few months, but I love him.

Shane's deep blue eyes level on my husband. "Tim, I think it's best if both you and Seraphina take your time. As I said, today is more about getting—"

"We've never had sex." I don't know why it's easier to say when they're distracted, but it is. "We're virgins." The truth flows, bringing an intense sense of relief. I laugh at the lightness in my chest, the utter freedom of the moment. "And his friends had no idea we were married. He didn't even want me at his birthday dinner." I drop my face into my hands, letting the pain he's caused crush me. I'm still laughing even though it's agonizing.

Thank God, Tim doesn't say anything. But again, I'm not sure what to expect from Shane. From what I've seen of him, I anticipate level-headed neutrality, and that's what I get. *Kind of.*

"Okay. I understand you've been married a while, so that's a little unusual, but unusual isn't bad. I'm interested to hear Tim's opinion on both subjects."

That's what the doctor's lips say, but his eyes bore into mine like he's reading every sinful slutty thought I've ever had right out of my soul. Why does Dr. Nelson, Shane, make me feel like he's done more to me with his gaze than Tim ever has? My nipples harden, and I die a molten death as I watch his eyes flick to them. He licks his lips, and no matter how innocent I am, my center throbs at the promise implicit in his action.

"We've been married two years, Doc," Tim snarks after a moment's thought.

"Eighteen months," I correct. "If we get to two years and still haven't done it…" I don't even want to think.

Tim grits his teeth.

"Do you have any idea why it hasn't happened yet?" There's a note of caution in Shane's voice, and I wonder if he can tell how *close* Tim is to an outburst.

"Not a fucking clue!" He shouts, even more embarrassed than when I caught him masturbating.

"Seraphina," Shane's gaze swivels back to me, and I swallow hard. "Do you know why the two of you haven't been… *intimate*?" He tests the word, but a crazed part of me wishes he said something much more vulgar, *offered* me something much nastier.

I know precisely why we haven't had sex, and they aren't easy words to say under the best of circumstances.

Here, they *should* be impossible. But Shane's presence is so magnetic I can't resist speaking the truth.

"He can't get hard for me."

"What the fuck, Sera?! That's not fucking true!"

"Yes, it is, Tim. When we tried to have sex, you couldn't get hard for me, but when you were watching Pornhub in the bathroom, that was plenty for you. We've been together since we were sixteen, Tim, and that was the first time I have ever seen you hard!" Tears stream down my face. I try to scrub them away, but they're coming too fast.

Tim slaps the leather. "You know what, Sera? The last time someone thought I fucked you, I got my legs broken. *This* was your idea. You stay for *therapy*."

With that, he pushes up from the chair and storms out of the office. The door slams shut behind him, causing me to jump. My tears pick up in intensity, and for a painful moment, I don't realize I'm alone with Doctor Shane. Tim can't get hard for me because he associates it with bone-breaking pain. Something deep inside me shatters because as much as I love Tim, I have no clue how to fix this. I don't think we *can* fix this. I stare at the door long after it closes.

"Seraphina," Shane begins softly. "Are you okay?" Now that we're alone, his voice sounds deeper, smokier, and even more tempting than when Tim stood between us. The pain still ricochets through my body, but Shane has grown more prominent in Tim's absence, somehow taking up the space Tim occupied rather than leaving it empty between us. I'm losing my mind because I'm sure he's filling my lungs next, and I hardly want him to stop there.

"No."

That single word is so insignificant in the face of my pain and the intense attraction to the man across from me.

I know I don't love my psychiatrist. I love Tim, but the connection between Shane and me is so intense it makes me ache for everything that Tim and I aren't and perhaps never will be.

Shane's eyes are so blue they feel like an act of God. Like the ocean far away from shore where the depths plummet halfway to the Earth's center, untamable white caps crashing on top of pressure so intense it could easily crush you. They meet my own, and I swear he sees every emotion crushing my insides, everything I've ever felt. The charge between us draws him out of his chair and across the room.

I don't know much about therapy, but I'm sure his next move goes against a few ethical codes. Strong arms band beneath my legs as he hoists me out of my seat and into his arms. He takes the spot I'd been sitting in and nestles me into his lap, holding me against his chest. I'm tense at first, so stiff it's almost comical.

I'm not sure why Shane is doing this. For a split second, I think I've lost my mind out of a sheer, intense desire for this man. I know I should protest, but I don't want to. Has anyone ever held me so tightly?

"Relax, Seraphina," he speaks against my ear, and the subtle vibrations of his voice send a shiver straight to my nipples and the spot between my legs. No one calls me that anymore, and I'm more than a little alarmed by my reaction. I *should* be tense, but instead, I relax into him. His hold on me warms me, an intimacy I can barely comprehend.

Maybe I knew a little of it once, but it's so far in the back of my memory that I can't scrounge it up. My mother's affection felt like home, and *this* is more than that. Except it can't be because Shane isn't anyone or anything special to me. I'm so starved for physical affection and intimacy that I must have gone insane.

"You can cry if you need to. Everything is going to be okay." His words are my undoing, and the tears I was sure I could hold in spill over my cheeks. Rubbing circles onto my back and stroking my hair as I cry into his incredible-smelling chest, he doesn't say anything else for the rest of the forty-five minutes of our session.

I settle eventually, tears drying on my cheeks, then his shirt, yet I still don't climb off. The sculpted muscles of his chest are under my palms, and I desperately want to run my hands over them, test how firm they are beneath my fingertips. Instinctually, I know where I can lead this, but that's so wrong I can't believe I'd even think of it. I hate myself for not getting up the moment he placed me in his lap, and I hate myself more for not being able to pretend I regret it.

Instead, I sit stock still, terrified of the most incredible excitement I've ever had in my life ending, and terrified for it to go any further because I have no intention of cheating on my husband. I may have let religious extremism go when I ended my relationship with my father, but I don't believe adultery is okay. Plus, I haven't suddenly stopped loving the man with whom I've spent half my teens and entire adult life.

I love Tim. I love Tim.

I chant those words in my mind when one of Shane's hands stops just above the curve of my butt; I shudder as I force myself to think of the word *ass*. I tell myself I feel his struggle, how badly he wants to drift that hand further. But in reality, I only *feel* how badly *I* want him to drift that hand lower and dig those strong soothing fingers into my round flesh.

"Our time is up, Seraphina," he finally says,

removing his hands and leaving my skin aching for more. Heat floods me at his words, both from my arousal and embarrassment. The pain the end of this session brings is akin to crushing and grinding my heart beneath a millstone. He's right when he says our time is up, and this whole thing has been a disaster. My entire life *is* a disaster.

"I intended to set up individual sessions with you and Tim today and make your appointments for next week. Is that something the two of you are interested in pursuing?" He lifts me from his lap as firmly as he placed me there and sets me on my feet. He stands in front of me a second later, close enough that if I leaned forward a fraction, I'd press against the length of his body. I might have if not for what he just said.

Instead, my mouth hangs open as I process the question. There has to be more to say than that. Shane sounds so normal, like nothing at all happened.

I clear my throat, "He will be. I'll make him."

"Okay, that's great. I think there's a lot of work for us all," he says as he guides me to the door.

Shane leads me down the hall with his hand on the small of my back. The point of contact between the two of us is subtle after the time we spent cuddling up, but the intimacy of this gesture vibrates in every part of me. I stare at him out of the corner of my eye, and I think he sees me because he wears a crooked smile that makes my heart race. Tingles zip along my skin, radiating from where he touches me, and at that moment, I have forgotten that Tim is outside, mad at me.

The thought of going to hell crosses my mind when I glance over at the crotch of his pants, trying to glimpse if Shane's shameful arousal matches my own. But, unfortunately, I'm not skilled in the art of noticing a well-hidden erection. I've only seen two live penises before and one belonged to a flasher when I was twelve.

Seeing Tim hard for the first time was... Well, it was hot but also heartbreaking. I've wanted to see him that way so many times, and he's left me feeling beyond rejected for so long. It's complicated with Tim. Every damn thing is complex, but I don't care as I notice the thick outline in Shane's pants. He *is* hard for me.

Someone wants me. Shane wants me.

Undeniable heat floods my lower belly, and moisture slicks my thighs. I thought I had experienced arousal before. I thought I was hard-up and desperate to know what sex felt like, but I was wrong. I have intellectually and physically wanted sex for a long time, but I have never *needed* a man to fill me, and right now, I do.

There's a stupefied expression on my face as Shane pushes me toward his secretary. "Tasha, Seraphina here needs to make a few appointments for next week."

"Of course, Shane." She smiles in obedience at him as he leaves us with a friendly wave.

We arrange the appointments, and I leave the office, doing my best to keep my face straight as I head out and look for Tim. My heart sinks as I find he's not out front or in the space we parked the car. I check my purse for my phone, sighing loudly when I come up empty.

I'll have to call a cab if he doesn't come back for me. After a few minutes of hoping and procrastinating, I head back inside, planning to use the phone at the reception desk in Doctor Shane's office. I'm embarrassed to be heading back there so soon. After what happened between us, it feels like an excuse to ask him to do all the sinful things I scarcely understand swirling around in my head.

When I get there, no one is sitting at reception. I consider just using the phone, but I don't know the number of any cab companies, and there is probably a code to dial out. So I head back to Shane's office with my heart slamming the entire way. The hall seems longer than when Tim and I followed Shane's pretty secretary. I'm somehow even more nervous than I was before. This is absurd, considering I will only ask him to use his phone, not take my virginity on one of his small couches.

I swallow hard at the thought of him doing just that. Finally, I stop and take a few deep breaths, forcing away the lump in my throat. I'm aware of the bright flush coloring my cheeks, but I hope he interprets that as me being upset about Tim leaving me here. That is reasonable, a hell of a lot more understandable than being physically affected by my doctor so intensely that I'm dripping and palpitating.

I take one more breath before I knock. I hear nothing but muffled noises, then the word "Yeah,"

I take it as permission to enter but am shocked to find that he didn't expect me.

Shane sits at his desk. The light pine finish blends into the tan walls behind it, so I didn't see it when Tim and I first came in, but it's impossible to miss now. Shane sits behind it like it's his damned throne. One elbow leans on the desk, and his chin rests in his hand. He must be the Devil because I immediately imagine him with a crown around his head, a dark prince.

His dark slacks are open. His belt buckle catches the light, resembling a jewel pointing to his erection. He's gripping it so tightly in his hand I swear it has to hurt. Beyond how delicious he looks, my first thought is how thoroughly he puts Tim to shame. He's huge, but his length isn't what scares me: it's the circumference.

Watching his strokes in fascination, he thickens further as he works himself, his brow furrowing in concentration and his white teeth pressing into his plush pink lips. I can't help but notice how similar his lips look to the gleaming head and how his white teeth match the pearly substance bubbling up invitingly at the tip. I have the wild urge to suck that lip into my mouth and bite it harder than he is. Then proceed to lick up his mess.

I make a noise, something hungry and a little feral. Shane's gaze flicks up, meeting mine.

He groans, "*Seraphina,*"

Cum spurts out of him, thick and white. His face is intense as he stares into my eyes and empties himself. I watch each pulse, each twitch, as he empties. The deep slit in his head spills into a river of thick white, but his hand continues to pump his shaft. The occasional spurt launches into the air to celebrate the sexiest man alive finding his release.

I want to drop to my knees and taste him so badly that my hand falls from the door I still held open. I need to get away. The door swings closed, slamming so hard between us that I jump in surprise. I'm not thinking about anything other than escaping and the taste of his orgasm as I run away as fast as I can.

I go the wrong way down the hall and take the stairs instead of the elevator, not caring how I get home anymore —it's only a few miles, so walking isn't a big deal. As I'm convincing myself this isn't one of the worst days of my life, I come face to face with Shane's receptionist. She's leaning against the wall on the landing between flights and wearing a stupid smile as she types on her phone. The sound of my stomping feet makes her jump, and her wide eyes shoot to me.

"*Sera?*" she asks, and her gaze flicks nervously back to her phone.

"I'm fine!" I squeak as I continue past her, down another flight, and through the lobby.

The whole way home, I work to dislodge the feel of Shane's body against mine and the heat that watching him come stoked in me. Did he say my name because I was there? Or was he thinking of me? And why am I enough for this man I just met when I am not enough for Tim?

CHAPTER
THREE
SHANE

TWENTY MINUTES EARLIER

I LEAVE SERAPHINA WITH TASHA TO MAKE HER appointments. With my fingertips blazing at the memory of her skin, I'm buzzing at the inevitability of seeing her again. How I wish it wouldn't be odd to stand beside her and encourage her to take the next available appointment because I can already feel the separation from her like a physical loss.

Heading back to my office, I have to stop myself from glancing over my shoulder, hoping to see her juicy ass. Thoughts of her ass are only making my pants tighter and my walk less comfortable. Conjuring up Seraphina's stunning yellow-green eyes and pretty petal lips in my mind doesn't exactly calm me down, but thinking of something else is impossible. So this will have to be enough.

My thoughts wander from her eyes to the last hour. I need to go over all the things she said and learn from what she shared. It's a shame *he* was there for our first meeting, but fair enough for him to be present for the last moment she belonged to him.

None of this was what I expected when I checked my calendar this morning and found that I had a new couple to counsel. Upon seeing Seraphina, a zip of lightning ran straight from the base of my brain through my heart and to my cock. I don't believe in soulmates or magic, but I know damn well what belongs to me, and that woman is mine. I bite my knuckles until I can put myself into some semblance of control and let myself into my office.

Typically, I dread new patients, but given the fact that I've not been in this office for three months yet, they're *all* new. Although that feels no more than a blip of time, my old life and city are far off in my rearview—where they belong. My family has no reputation here, and that's exactly what I need.

Even though it's necessary, I still don't particularly enjoy this part of my job. Getting new patients and building relationships with them is tedious and time-consuming. I prefer the stable portion, where I can guide them toward the best versions of themselves, all while getting the profound satisfaction of knowing *I* control their lives. Lives I *could* break if I so choose.

Couples counseling is more interesting in some ways. I like the spectator sport of mediating disagreements. People who've been in love, stayed together for years and had children, have more pain and baggage than I can imagine. But I'm not a sadist, and their pain isn't satisfying to the hungry thing inside me. Once they mend fences or divorce, they're usually out the door, and only a select few stay on as my patients.

I'm so fucking hard now it's disgusting. Thoughts of controlling every aspect of Seraphina's life run rampant through my head, and I can't take it. My cock leaks as I imagine her flushing under my praise, flourishing under my instruction. I realize with a smile that I was never going to fix their marriage. I shut the door behind me and lean against it before going to my desk.

After my initial reaction to meeting Seraphina, her beauty, innocence, and bravery only charmed me further. I'm nothing if not rational, and I would happily ignore my response to her if she weren't also *perfect*. Revealing the painful details of their relationship must have been close to impossible between her hangups and her fear of Tim's anger. She didn't outright say she fears him, but that's what her body language told me. I'm not yet sure what to make of everything she disclosed. Did she feel free to speak because she felt safe with me? Or is my girl so desperate to get free she's willing to take the risk?

Either way, I don't like it.

I work my belt buckle loose as I sit and lean back in my chair. I quickly unzip my pants, get my cock in my hand, and shiver like a virgin as I wrap my fingers around it. I guess that's fair too, considering my Angel's inexperience. I wonder if she knows how delectable she looked and felt in my arms. If she could feel how badly I wanted her, how desperately I needed to trample the lines between us... The idea that she doesn't know how desirable she is enrages me as much as it turns me on, and I take my frustrations out on my cock.

I replay the memories as I squeeze and pump myself, rolling my thumb over the leaking slit at the image of her long blonde hair and overly plush lips. I want to bite those lips, suck them into my mouth, and gnaw at them. Lap up her tears, sweat, and cum. The urge to taste and know every inch of her is damn near impossible to deny.

I picture myself turning over every stone in her mind along with every secret and thought, like panning for gold.

I want to mix her up thoroughly, and I want to drown in her.

Despite the mom jeans she hid herself in, she has a fantastic ass. Irresistibly round and biteable. I wish she wore something more revealing, not because I'm concerned, but because I want to know her *now*. Does she have a freckle on her thigh that tastes as sweet as she looks? Maybe a few scars? I want to know them all, taste her secrets. I'll listen intently to all of her stories and trace every line that makes her.

Accepting her past with Tim will be incredibly simple. I will free her by snipping the remaining tethering threads one by one until she doesn't even remember the man she used to call husband. Given my position as their psychiatrist, I like my odds. I will take her for myself regardless of who Tim is as a man. He could be a saint who donated his life to charity and the poor, and I would still take and taint her. But she wouldn't *be* mine if she wasn't better for having me. Seraphina needs me as much as I need her.

From ignoring her and regarding her with disgust to stepping over her, Tim is a big part of why Seraphina thinks she's trash. The permanent slump to her shoulders takes an inch or more off her height. She cowers, looks down, and shuffles through life like a show dog awaiting her next beating, and I can't help but point fingers at the man holding the leash.

The thought fucking pisses me off, and I grip my cock too hard. My balls tingle in response to the overstimulation. I loosen my grip but speed up my tempo, thinking about the satisfaction of fitting my impressive cock in her tight cunt.

She's a virgin. He's never touched her.

Her scent still clings to my shirt and skin, teasing me with how close I was to her. Every inch of me aches with the need to correct her virginal status. I don't think fucking makes someone more or less valuable, but the fact that she *is* a virgin only confirms what I knew the moment I saw her.

She is mine so innately that the man who married her has never claimed her. Mine on every level to the point her pheromones make his dick soft. I'm so close as I imagine filling her with my cum until the scent of my ownership seeps out of her.

My mental image of her tits and pussy remains nondescript. I don't want to disgrace my future wife, the mother of my children, by imagining some other cunt between her perfect thighs.

A soft noise startles me out of the moment, and my eyes snap open. Realizing I'm not alone, pale green and yellow eyes meet mine. Seraphina's plush lips part in surprise, the perfect opening to tease the head of my cock into. Her nostrils flare, and I hope she's equal parts scandalized and turned on. Her pupils blow out, and I'm sure I've gotten my wish.

"Seraphina," I grunt her name as I come all over my fucking hand.

I'm not sure what I plan to do, but I'm getting to my feet with my cock still out, my hand coated in my cum. Seraphina is already gone, the door slamming shut behind her as she races away.

"Fuck!"

I grab some tissues and clean myself off. My cock hangs heavier than usual, already hardening and preparing to drive me insane with my need for her. I shove it into my boxer briefs, pull up my pants, and follow after her.

I am *not* intending on dragging her back here, holding her down by her pretty throat, and fucking her until she's taken multiple loads of my cum, but tell that to my raging erection.

I do my best not to get caught running as I fly past the reception desk, where my secretary Tasha is, to my surprise, absent. I race to the elevators, knowing I'm behind Seraphina. There are two, and I hope I'll catch the one she didn't use. It comes quickly, and as short as the ride is, I still can't find her on the ground floor. I keep looking, even though *no one* is here. Why did she come back, and where is she now?

That's not a question I intend to leave unanswered.

CHAPTER
FOUR
SHANE

I sit at my computer and pour over everything I can find on my soulmate. She and Tim live in a house not far from here. They own it, no mortgage, and I'm stumped by how they afford it. He works as a landscaper, and while he makes decent money, he's undoubtedly not raking it in. Buying a house in cash at twenty-four doesn't come from a six-month-old landscaping business.

Seraphina doesn't work, which is bizarre given the disparity between the house and Tim's income. She also doesn't go to school or have social media. However, she has a bachelor's degree from a state school out west in *theology*.

Tim has a degree from the same school, but he's not working as the engineer he trained to be, and rather than advancing his degree, he's currently enrolled in a bachelor's program at the local state school, business management. *And* he has social media. It doesn't take me long to figure out there's more to this situation than Seraphina realizes.

On Tim's Instagram, nothing is damning, but there are no pictures or mentions of his wife. When I click the profile of one of his frequent commenters, however, I see multiple images of him hanging on scantily clad women. None of these pictures prove anything since he's not kissing or groping, but they speak volumes. I can't imagine Seraphina out with her arm slung around other men. At that thought, I decide against showing her these pictures. There are plenty of ways to get rid of Tim without causing her more pain.

"Well, well, I wonder if his dick works for them."

I save the pictures to a file and continue looking through the information. There's a virtual tour on the real estate website from when they bought their house, and I can see the layout. The primary bedroom walks out to the backyard and overlooks the inground pool. A row of neat hedges lines the sliding doors on either side. It would be an excellent spot to watch her if they haven't changed the landscaping much.

I close my computer and head out, satisfied I have enough to get close to her. I tell Tasha to cancel my one appointment in the afternoon as I walk past, not allowing her to respond or question my decision. She gapes at me, but I hop into the elevator with an easy smile on my face—I'm going to see Seraphina. Tasha will probably leave as soon as she's sure I'm gone. The truth is, I don't care that much.

My steps eat up the tile as I head toward the parking lot and my car, a dark blue Mercedes sedan, safe, nondescript. I didn't buy it to stalk women, but I can't deny how well it works for that purpose. I've never needed to follow my prey before. This wolf has always been invited in.

I click the fob, the beep letting me know I'm one step closer to where I need to be. I climb inside and settle into my seat. The push-start hums to life, and I pull out of the lot. The incessant beeping won't stop until I buckle my seatbelt. I curse, *you win this time,* and snap the belt into place.

It hasn't been long since I've seen my little Angel, yet I'm itching to be close to her. My skin is practically turning inside out with the need to connect with hers. I know I can't do that tonight, but there's no reason I can't watch her, and catch a glimpse of what she's hiding beneath those boring clothes.

I'm not used to this tiny decaying city, and each time I pass through it, I take it in with interest. I grew up in a different sort of place. How does this depressed little slice of life look to Seraphina? Is it big or small compared to her home? Does she like it here? I find it hard to imagine she does, but I may be letting my own misgivings color my worldview.

I drive into their neighborhood, quickly finding the house, a big blue colonial with white shutters and a red door. The first time I pass, I don't even slow, quickly taking in the blue truck in the driveway. Two lights illuminate rooms on opposing sides of the house. The rest is dark.

On my next pass, I slow and turn on my left-hand blinker. The empty street seems lucky, but people looking out of their windows could still see me. Appearing lost is a lot better than the truth, and I observe their home while pretending to read the numbers on the left.

The light in the primary bedroom and the den are both on. I park a few blocks over on a quiet street with other cars—my black jacket clings, the panels and stitching nondescript. I don't cover my face. Skillfully hiding it is much more effective than a mask that immediately draws attention. I prefer no one to realize what I intend to do.

Thankful for the lack of streetlamps and the dim moonlight, I cross the lawn and stick tightly to the house. I'm almost sure I'm going to trip a motion detector, but no lights came on as I leisurely cross the backyard. This wouldn't be a bad place to raise our children. Seraphina will decide once she sees her options; with my trust fund, she has many of them.

I peek into the den window, checking if either is inside. Tim sits on a couch, his head in his hands. His phone lies beside him, open to a text exchange. A bottle of beer rests haphazardly on the arm of the couch, begging to be knocked over. Guilt pours off him, and I wish I could see what the fuck those texts say.

I use his distraction to move past the window, not even bothering to be quick about it. Instead, I think about Tim and Seraphina as I slip through their backyard. What has their married life been like? Do they use this patio furniture, and does he touch that silky soft skin of hers? He's married to her, so he must have kissed her at least once.

Filled with murderous rage, I'm thankful for the cool night air that seeps the worst heat out of me. I'm holding the last straw of my emotional control when I come to the sliding glass doors of the primary bedroom. They're uncovered, letting light pour out. *Why shut the curtains when your bedroom faces the backyard?*

Unable to see her at first, my heart races at the movement in the fluffy nest of blankets. I'm not just excited by the thrill of being caught or the wrongness of my actions. Even with the glass and her marriage between us, her nearness exhilarates me. My stomach is full of butterflies, and I can honestly say I've *never* felt like this. Seraphina lays on the bed, her golden-silk hair fanned out, and she's crying.

My cock is hard in an instant, the urge to go in there almost wholly overwhelming me, but I don't. I plan to marry this woman, and that kind of thing can't be rushed. *Because* she's crying for a reason, and her pain stirs something tender and violent in me, I'm torn between comforting her and murdering him.

I'll kill him if I *have* to, but not tonight and not before I've exhausted my options. He'll be easy enough to manipulate, an asshole and a macho man who always thinks he's better than others, if not for his looks, then his good standing with God. I'm handsome too, but I *never* felt godly or pure. Tim's ego will work against him. As will his obvious and desperate need for male approval.

Seraphina rolls over in bed, drawing her knees against her chest and wrapping her arms around them. Her panties peek out from beneath her oversized nightshirt, revealing the incredible curve of her ass. I get so close to the glass my breath fogs it. Each cheek is full and round, soft. Long legs splayed over the bed make me desperate to see what lies between them, but I still can't see her tits. I hold in a frustrated noise at being denied her nipples. Despite my baser nature, I don't spend *too* much time looking. I'm so fucking hard as it is I don't need to make the situation worse.

Seraphina is so tiny in that position my urge to protect her overwhelms me. It's as strong as my need to bury myself inside her tight, untouched cunt. I watch as her breathing evens out, and she falls into a deep sleep. I continue staring at her until I'm sure she's dead to the world. Even as I stare at her, I can't explain how I know she's mine, but the thought alone rings true in every cell of my body. Maybe she isn't intended for me, perhaps I'm crazy, but that doesn't fucking matter, and it never will because I *won't* let her go.

It takes all my effort to pull my gaze away from her, but ogling is not the only reason I came here tonight. Returning to the den, I find Tim asleep on the couch beside his phone. *Perfect.*

I quickly decide to enter through their bedroom door rather than the front. A single decorative rock sits beside the sliding glass. They may as well have engraved it with "spare key," and a flash of fury fills me. How can she be so flippant about her own safety? I haven't seen any cameras either, but I'm hopeful they have one on the front door. The pane moves easily beneath my hands, and I worry the chill will wake Seraphina. I close it quickly, but my Angel doesn't seem to notice the drop in temperature.

God, she is breathtaking.

Exercising restraint like never before, I stand stock-still, *needing* to be near her but knowing I can't. I hardly trust myself not to spread those pretty thighs and take her. I have *never* considered such barbaric behavior before. Even when I've played with my patients' emotions for my amusement, I've never felt the urge to take from them physically. But *Seraphina* makes me crazy.

Walking toward her on silent feet, I sit carefully on the edge of the bed. I wait until her breaths are deep and steady before my fingers twine in the lengths of her hair. It's just as silken as I remember, and a charge runs up the base of my spine. I want to touch her more thoroughly, but I don't know how deep of a sleeper she is *yet*.

I'll know that and everything else because Seraphina will love me so much she will need me to breathe, and I'll love her the same way. I'm not entirely crazy; I'm well aware that lust is what I currently feel for her, but I'm also confident that I'm headed for a short, hard fall.

Her pretty lips part, and a single word escapes her, "Please,"

I have no clue what she's dreaming about, what she's begging for, but because I'm selfish, possessive, and covetous, I pretend I know what she wants. I lean forward, kissing her so fucking sweetly. It's soft and brief, but she sighs into my mouth, and her tongue darts out just once to taste me. She's velvety and luscious, and her tongue against mine is an indulgence that makes my cock leak in agonized anticipation. I pull back, practically killing myself in the effort. The gentle kiss will have to be enough for now.

I stand and head to her bathroom, where I find her still-wet towel from her shower and the panties she wore today lying on the floor. When I pick them up, I find the crotch wet. Shoving them against my face, I inhale her scent. *Fuck*, she smells sweet. Popping the fabric into my back pocket, I continue into the den, where Tim sleeps.

Aware of the unnecessary risk, I go to Tim's phone, an older iPhone with a fingerprint scanner, and gingerly press his finger to the glass. Sorting through the contents, it doesn't take me long to find evidence that he receives a lot of nudes and sexts, but nothing so far confirms he's actively fucking around.

That's okay. Conversations with these women will clear up any questions I have about Tim. I forward everything vital to myself and then delete the messages. It's not a high-tech solution, but he'll never think to check.

Heading to Seraphina's room, I look at the pictures on the walls. I'm in better control of my anger now and am at no risk of taking it out on Tim tonight. It's dark, so I can't make out many details, but I notice a stark lack of family. Some people might consider that odd or sad, but I find it comforting. Our family will be her *only* family.

I take one last look at her.

"He won't be making a fool of you for much longer, Angel," I whisper to her before kissing her ever so gently. Then, I slip out the way I came, wishing more than anything else to stay beside her.

CHAPTER FIVE
SERA

I WAKE IN THE MORNING BEYOND DISORIENTED. MY MOUTH is dry, and my lips tingle. I must have fallen asleep with my jaw hanging open, except that doesn't explain my filthy dreams or why my panties are so wet and shoved between my labia as if my hands wandered in my sleep. *Oh, Jesus.*

Tim's pillow remains untouched, the blanket on his side still tucked beneath the mattress, and I decide not to care about that. My attempt to confront him last night was met with a door slammed in my face, so that didn't end up in a productive conversation. It's probably for the best, as I was so guilt-ridden I would have just sobbed and confessed everything. *That* would have been a terrible idea, especially because I didn't *really do* anything other than let Shane hold me. I'm not wrong for walking in on a private moment—rude, yes, but not wrong.

For once, God or the universe seem to be on my side; Tim never came to bed. I need space from him and all the ways I'll never be enough. Plus, the couch in the den is old, shitty, and about a foot too short for him. An uncomfortable night of sleep serves him right for leaving me to walk home. I don't even bother feeling ashamed about my petulant thoughts. I've always tried to be the bigger person, but he's making me petty.

I walk through the house, hearing that he's already getting ready for work, which is another good thing. His temper tends to come out during his morning routine—aimed at me, of course—and I don't think I can take it right now.

I pause outside the hall bath where he is showering and toy with the idea of saying good morning. If things were the way they should be between us, I could climb in and help him get dirty and then clean. That's the spontaneous kind of thing husbands and wives do, isn't it? I'm not even sure, and that's a stab to the gut. Deciding against saying good morning, I head to the kitchen to make coffee and breakfast.

The coffee Tim prefers sits on the top shelf, and I stretch to get it, knocking a dish over. It clatters to the floor, and I pick it up, glad I switched to composite materials that don't break. My father beating me over breaking plates stuck with me, and a full-blown panic attack is the last thing I need any time I drop something.

Next, I scramble his eggs the way he likes them, even though he's a jerk and made me walk home last night. Given the state of my marriage, I shouldn't feel so guilty about letting another man hold me, at least not so much that I'm kissing up to Tim. What I saw in that office wasn't my fault, but I can't get the images out of my head, and I can't stop how my muscles clench in hollow agony each time they do.

That terrible guilt twists my gut even harder as heat pools in my lower belly. The image of Shane biting his lip and coming while he said my name has my insides trembling and twitching, clenching at the desperate hope to magically find him inside me. He won't, and he can never be. The remorse makes me hotter, and I'm so alarmed my hands tremble in sync with my insides.

I'm still unsure if Shane was coming to the thought of me or if it was simply too late to stop himself and he said my name in surprise. The timing was unbelievably close, but what do I know? Maybe that's what he does on Tuesdays at two. Even if it's only an illusion, feeling wanted is intoxicating.

It *had* to be a coincidence because I *don't* want to stop seeing him as a doctor.

Shane seems to understand my predicament, and I like how easy and open he is about these sensitive issues that make me squirm. I need that to get through this. Tim and I need help, and I cannot stand having to explain to another doctor what's going on between us or risk them not understanding. Tim already hates me. There's no way he'll accept doing this again. Aside from that, there's no way I can explain why we would need to.

No, I'll forget what I saw and stop getting wet whenever I think of it.

Tim walks into the kitchen, the stern look on his face softening when he sees the care I put into breakfast. It's still not warm, just less hostile. He thinks I'm trying to apologize for yesterday. That only makes me feel worse because I'm *not* sorry about anything that happened before he left —or after, for that matter.

I'm sorry for wanting another man more than I've ever wanted you.

But instead of lightening my burdened conscience, I smile and eat in silence.

"Good eggs, Sera," he murmurs as he scrapes the last bite into his mouth. He doesn't put his plate in the sink before leaving the kitchen, and while I knew he wouldn't, it stings that he doesn't even try. I get on with washing the dishes as he finishes getting ready.

Tim heads to work shortly after that, and I'm thankful for his absence the rest of the day and late into the night.

Usually, when he calls to say he'll be home late, he upsets me. Now, having more space from him is a blessing. I used to worry about what he was doing with jealous, paranoid thoughts. But now, I couldn't care less. On the other hand, that's not how I feel about Shane. I twist the simple wedding band on my finger as I repeat my newest findings to myself.

I don't care what my husband is doing right now.

As I lie alone at night, I consider touching myself to Shane. I'm getting desperate. The hot and needy feeling between my legs has no chance of fading when the animalistic part of me demands I seek some release. Sadly, she's not strong enough to overrule the nervous majority, resulting in me lacking the confidence to take care of myself.

It doesn't matter how many articles I read or instructional videos I watch, reaching down there and bringing myself to orgasm still seems innately wrong and sinful. Every time I touch my wet, sensitive flesh, I shrivel, and so does that heat. It doesn't help that I'm as bad as a cliché teenage boy poking around for the first time because I don't think I've *ever* found my clit. My few female friendships have been surface-level, even in college, I never felt close enough to someone to ask for advice.

Tim comes home and gets into bed beside me sometime during the night, and I stiffen from head to toe. His proximity disturbs me to the point of nausea. I'm surprised to find no longing or desperation to touch him, only affliction and the hope that he'll give up and leave. After an hour, give or take, I convince myself he's going to chicken out, and that's enough to get me to pass out.

I succeed in gaining a few tense hours of sleep. My body must know Tim's beside me since I hardly move an inch, but I'm still surprised to see him when I open my eyes in the morning. Sky-blue eyes watch me, and I'm both unnerved and flattered by his attention.

"Morning, beautiful," Tim's voice is smooth and sweet, not as deep as Shane's but pleasant and familiar.

At his compliment, warm tingles dance between my thighs, and I fluster at my body's response. I didn't realize I still wanted that from him, considering he's left my heart in shreds and I can't stop thinking about Shane.

Approval. The rational part of my brain whispers, and it's right. That's what I'm responding to.

"Morning, Tim. Did you stay out all night?" For once in my life, I mean the venom in my tone. Who does he think he is to roll into bed with me at any odd hour?

He shakes his head, and there's a sad expression on his face. "No, I slept in the den again until about three."

"Why?" I don't want any of this. I want *sex*. I want a *marriage*. Why does it seem so impossible to have that with my own husband? I'm so sick of him treating me like an annoying sibling rather than a partner.

"I'm not sure how to be around you." The open sincerity he regards me with equates to a sharp knife to my already bleeding heart.

"All of this because I want to have sex with you." The heat from his fleeting compliment still burns beneath my flesh, revealing the degradation of this moment.

He pauses. His brow furrows, and he lets out a whooshing breath like I've hit him in the stomach. "It's not that." His bottom lip trembles like a small boy's. I can see the little boy he once was inside the man, and I'm not sure how I can feel all the things I do for him.

"Then what is it?" I snap, tears streaming down my cheeks. I don't want to hear what he has to say, I can't take it, but we can't live in denial forever.

"I want to have sex with you too, Sera. I swear to God, I *do*, but every time I get too close, I think about my legs breaking under a fucking baseball bat, and I can't do it."

He sobs, actually sobs. I have never seen Tim cry from anything other than a beating.

I suck in a sharp breath while the world, my world, is falling around me. Is Tim leaving me?

"Is that it then? You let me love you all these years, and now you tell me you're done with me!?"

He scoffs. His hands scrub his tears away but more fall. "No, Sera! That's not *it*, but we need to work through this *together*. Not with that creepy fucking shrink."

"He's not creepy," I shout back as I leave the bed and stalk toward the closet, shaking my head. I need to get dressed, start my day, and find any excuse to get away from Tim. I think he knows we cannot work this out together and is terrified of what Shane might uncover, as well as how drastically our lives might need to change.

"Don't shake your head! I told you the truth, okay? I admitted what my damn issue is, and if you think you're going to get more out of me through that guy, you don't know me at all, Sera!"

He's following behind me, dragging the duvet onto the floor without giving a shit. I feel his shouting in my bones, and now *I'm* crying. I want to crumble at his feet and let my submission beg for forgiveness on my behalf, but I'm done being his doormat. This discontent has been a slow-growing thing, but I've had enough of being treated like half a person.

"What is your problem?" I square my shoulders and face him. "Do you think we can deal with this together? You can't even *bare* to touch me, and I'm *agonized* by loving you!"

Not waiting for a response, I turn my back to him and dig through my dresser for a box of tissues. Even though Tim already knows I'm crying, I don't want him to see my tears. For some reason, I feel possessive of them, like they don't belong to him.

"Oh, come on!"

He slams the closet door shut behind me, trapping me inside. The closet is technically a walk-in, but I'm claustrophobic, and it isn't spacious with the two of us in here. Tim knows how afraid of tight spaces I am, and he smirks at me like he knows what he's done.

"What was that guy even talking about? Cognac Disconnect? He's probably drinking that shit before his sessions for all the brilliant garbage he came out with! And the way he was looking at you…"

Powerless to breathe due to his puffed-up chest pressing against me, I'm overwhelmed by his display of jealousy. But what does he have to be jealous of? He doesn't even want me.

"Cognitive dissonance, Tim," I spit back, letting the budding anxiety from being trapped color my voice with rage. "If you had paid any attention in school, you might have heard the term before."

Anger flickers over his features. "I know the term, Sera. *I'm* just not an intellectual snob who thinks I'm better than everyone. I never thought *you* could be impressed by someone like that."

His words smack me. I never wanted to go to college at all, let alone again, and he's throwing that in my face.

"No, that's not why *you* think you're better than everyone, is it?"

"That's a load of shit!" he shouts, stepping forward and pressing me into the built-in drawers.

I'm about thirty seconds from having a panic attack, so rather than respond to his accusation, I ask him what I truly want to know.

"How *exactly* was he looking at me that you're this mad?" I sound angry and accusatory, but I'm thrilled Shane's attention was noticeable.

"Like *he* wanted to be the one to *fuck* you!"

His square jaw clenches at the same time the veins pop along his neck.

"And *that* upsets you?" I laugh in disbelief.

"Don't be stupid, Sera! Of course it upsets me."

Tim's as red as he was that day I caught him in the bathroom, and I swear he's telling the truth. That only makes this hurt worse.

"So you left me alone with him without a ride home when you thought he was trying to *fuck* me? You're disgusting, Tim, and if *you* don't want to, someone else will!"

I push past him with all my might. At first, he stands in my way, looking down at me with a superior expression. The walls are collapsing in on me and panic flares in my eyes. His malicious face drops, and he lets me go, surprised by his own rage and desire to hurt me as if those intentions belong to a separate entity. I'm running from that as much as I'm running from him.

I've never said the word fuck aloud in that context. I've said it several times to prove a point as an expletive but never a verb. The look of rage and disgust on his face is plastered inside my mind as I run through the house toward the guest bedroom, where I can get dressed in the hopefully-matching clothes I grabbed. I regret my words, but there's no taking them back now, and I can't pretend I didn't mean them.

I hear Tim a few minutes later, his angry steps and the banging door resounding as he goes. His tires scream, announcing his departure.

CHAPTER
SIX
SERA

Tim doesn't come home, and I'm left distressed and relieved by his absence. The fight took a lot out of me, and I'm emotionally exhausted. Being stuck inside the house is unpleasant, but I'm miserable with all of Tim's things around to remind me of his absence and our failing marriage. For the millionth time, I wish I had a job.

How many times have I wanted to volunteer, and how many excuses has Tim made for me not to? I replay them as I work my aggravation out on the grouting of our kitchen floor. Each of his lines grows thinner than the last until I'm sweating and fuming, unable to understand why I *listen* to him.

I'm using Tim's toothbrush to scrub the grooves spotless, and while I like to think I'm getting some vindictive satisfaction, that's not true. I don't have the guts to leave it where he could use or discover it. When I finish, I will throw the used-up plastic away, and replace it with one of the spares in the cabinet. He'll never notice.

Scouring the rest of the house into spotlessness takes less than a day. Of course it was already clean, but I've gone the extra mile on every front, including making some baking soda lemon concoction for the oven.

I'm finishing the oven and snapping off the oversized yellow gloves as the doorbell rings. For a second, I'm nervous it's Tim, but even if he forgot his key, he wouldn't ring the bell since we have a secret key hidden in the back.

Before I greet my visitor, I rinse my hands quickly and dry them on my pants. They shake as I slide open the latch on the peephole. I'm surprised and relieved to see a familiar brunette woman from around the neighborhood. Pulling the door back, I put on my best smile.

She looks me up and down with only the slightest haughty tilt to her lips. Up close, I can tell the woman's a few years older than me, thirty tops. Her hair hangs over her shoulder in a braid, revealing the round diamond stud in one ear. The same bright stones wink at me from her engagement-ring-wedding-band combo.

"Hi?" I mean to be polite and welcoming, but I don't do a lot of social interaction, and I've never spoken to her before. My overalls are too big and hang off me, making me feel even more like a little girl. The scent of cleaning products wafts off me, and I'm sure my appearance doesn't sing my praises.

"Hi, Mrs. Baker?"

She reaches out a hand, and I take it a second too late, shaking a little limply.

"Yeah, Sera," I correct, pushing a stray lock of hair out of my face.

"My name is Kimberly Shaw, and I'm the head of the neighborhood watch."

She's staring at me like that should mean something. I blink a few times before I manage to say, "Oh? Uh, can I help you?"

"Do you mind if I come in a minute?" she's speaking a little slow, and I give her a tight grin as irritation floods me.

"Oh, of course!" I step aside, and she walks right in, confident in her ability to speak to someone new and enter a stranger's home.

I wave toward the living room. "Would you like to sit?"

"Oh no, that's okay, but Mrs. Baker, I did have some concerning things I wanted to discuss with you. Are you aware of the community bulletin?" At my confused look, she continues, "It's our website." She appears embarrassed for the first time as she continues. "Why don't I just show you?"

She pulls her phone out of her pocket and shows me the screen as she opens an app. I'm loosely following what she's doing. I don't have a modern smartphone, and I'm too nervous about her being here to pay attention to *why* she's here until she pulls up a series of images and camera footage.

"Take a minute to look through them."

My hand closes around her phone, and all I can hear is my heartbeat pounding in my ears as I look at the still photos, which clearly show a dark figure lurking in my backyard. Chills run up my spine as I play the video, and I see the figure skulking back and forth like he's thinking about coming in.

"Police haven't been called yet. We wanted to bring it to you first, but—"

"Thank you, but it's unnecessary." My voice shrills, and I try to tamp it down. "Thank you for bringing it to my attention."

She's taken aback, but not enough to leave it alone.

"Uh, of course. It's my responsibility, but I strongly advise you recon—"

"That's my husband, not some prowler." I interrupt,

unable to remember to be polite when I want her to stop speaking.

Kimberly's mouth pops open, and her eyes narrow into squints. She must have been a popular girl in high school because no one else has this audacity with a stranger.

"Are you telling me the man lurking in your backyard but not coming inside is your husband?"

"He is. His name is Timothy Baker, and he can come inside whenever he likes."

"He's been seen on multiple nights—"

"If that's all, I have an appointment." I'm ruder than she is, but I don't care. I'm about to start crying.

Am I that miserable to come home to?

"Oh, of course." Kimberly's eyes shift to me with an offended slant. She must not be used to being asked to leave. She hands me the flyer, slapping it into my palm and flashing her manicure. "We can always use more members."

"I'll consider it."

I walk her out and thank her before returning to my task, which was already completed.

A few hours later, I'm sitting alone, watching TV and thinking about Tim when today's emotions catch up on me —I'm furious. Does he believe he has the right to leave and not come back, wander our backyard, and convince the neighbors he's a freaking night stalker? I'm so embarrassed that I'm hot around the neck when I hear a sound from outside.

It's a faint shuffling of feet, but I know what I heard. I hop up and out of bed in an instant, throwing back the sliding door of the master bedroom.

"Tim! Come inside. This is ridiculous!" I'm trying not to shout. I don't want to give the neighbors more to complain about, but this is beyond the pale. Whisper shouting, I continue, "You're an adult!"

He doesn't say anything, but I'm sure he's there. That inescapable feeling you get in the presence of another soul creeps along every inch of my being. I'm shivering cold, and I consider leaving him here.

"Tim, please! Please come inside." I'm quiet now, whining rather than demanding, worthy of pity.

But the silence is too much. It's too eerie, and goosebumps break out along my skin. An intense urge to run sweeps over me, like when I was a little girl, and I believed ghosts were watching me. My certainty that it was Tim standing in my yard feels foolish now.

Tim doesn't care enough to lurk out here for you.

"Tim," I try, one more time, to assuage my fears more than anything else.

When no one answers, I slam the door shut and lock it behind me. My hands shake, sweating despite the cold. I race toward the bed and throw the covers over myself like being invisible will make me safer. Admittedly, I'm still cold from standing there calling into the darkness like an idiot, but what has me vibrating is the way I stood there begging for trouble.

Why didn't I close the blinds? So stupid, but I'm not brave enough to do it now. Tim isn't here. He's not in the yard, and he's not here for me. These truths cleave my throbbing heart. The things my father taught me about masculinity and femininity were most often wrong. But part of me strongly feels that a man who loves you should strive to protect you.

Am I wrong for wanting that? Or am I wrong for thinking all men should be like that? Maybe my mistake was choosing someone who wasn't that way and then expecting him to be someone else. I must admit that knowing Tim would leave me here like this changes my perspective on our relationship. What is he doing anyway?

In this more exposed state, I sink into that older, traumatized version of myself. How often did I hide in my bed as a little girl, covers over my face, hoping my daddy wouldn't find me? Too often.

I'm disgusted with myself for how much of that little girl still lives inside me and how needy she is. Jensen Shultz may not affect the adult woman I've become, but my father's voice talks directly to that little girl whenever she'll listen.

People who call to demons attract demons.

His phantom hands strike my skin as if they were real. The old pain ripples along my skin, whitened scarred lines from belts and whips searing me deep and shallow. Metaphysical and impossible to relieve, it burns along my soul, and I'm so wrapped up in that old place and terrified of whoever is standing in my yard, that I can't breathe.

That monster becomes my father.

It doesn't matter if it was Tim, a neighbor, a dog, or maybe a squirrel, as far as I'm concerned, whatever moved in my yard was my father, and he's here to finish what he started.

He wants me dead.

How many times did he tell me he brought me into this world and he could take me out? For some parents, that's a joke. For him, it was a fundamental truth. My father believes he owns me, and I'm horrified of the day he comes to collect on that debt.

I get out of bed, ignoring the curtains, and run to the bathroom. I lock myself inside, panting as I lean against the door. It's sturdy; the entire house is constructed well. Moreover, every door is locked, so I should be safe. And if anything, I'd know someone was coming for me before they reached the bathroom door.

When my mind calms, I head to the faucet and run myself a bath. I allow myself very few luxuries, but this is one of them. Soaking in hot water will warm me much more effectively than the blankets in my oversized room. I'm still shaking as I drop in a scoop of Epsom salt and a drop of lavender-scented oil. I turn on my stereo, loud enough to keep me from jumping if the furnace kicks on, but not so loud as to block out an invader.

It doesn't take me long before I'm thoroughly warmed, but the relaxation I hoped for is not there. I'm forced to wrap myself up and dry off when I turn into a prune. I climb out of the tub, wrap myself in a robe, and b-line to the sliding doors. Closing the curtains, I'm sure I see nothing but my room reflected at me. I try to let that comfort me, but I know it's meaningless.

Turning back to the room, I take a few deep breaths. The house is quiet, and there was no good reason to think someone was there, to begin with. On the other hand, all the countless times I have been alone in this very house, I was *never* aware of any danger, and it's getting to my head.

God, Tim is an asshole.

The thought surprises me, but not the sentiment. I really cannot believe he left me in this position. I'm digging through my drawer, looking for my favorite pair of panties, and for some reason, I can't find them. First, I check every one of my drawers, then Tim's, then our closets.

I'm sure about the last day I wore them, the day we started therapy. I know I dropped them on the floor, and I was sure I put them in the laundry, but there isn't a speck of dust left in this house, let alone dirty or unfolded laundry.

So where the hell are my panties?

I chalk it up to the dryer eating them and God being against me as I put on a less comfortable pair and climb into bed. I turn on the TV, hoping the sound will keep the terror and nightmares away.

It doesn't, and I'm once again left wondering why I'm not enough for the man I married.

CHAPTER
SEVEN
SHANE

I count the steady beats of Seraphina's heart as she whimpers through her nightmare. I'm tempted to climb out of my hiding place beneath her bed and comfort her, but she's sleeping so restlessly tonight I'm sure she would wake. I know I'm crossing a line, even for me, but her mournful, plaintive voice calling into the night was impossible to ignore.

"Please, please come inside."
I could never ignore you.

It doesn't matter that she spoke his name. My Angel needs *me* to soften her suffering even if she doesn't know it yet. Seraphina's pain and loneliness only cement what I've known from the beginning.

She's been waiting for me.

I hate Tim for marrying her, but the spineless fuck not bothering to *be* with her enrages me. I resent him even more because of his power in this situation. He could climb up there and make her feel better while I'm relegated to staring at the bottom of a fucking boxspring.

As soon as she closed the bathroom door, I opened that

stupid fucking rock and let myself in. She was in the bath for a long time, and I had ample opportunity to consider my hiding place after I did my best to get a look through a nonexistent crack in the door.

The closet appealed to me, the ability to fully watch her almost too tempting to ignore, but what got me going was the thought of being beneath her. Once decided, I took another tour through their house, much less worried about being quiet with Tim gone and her music playing in the background. I returned with time to spare when the music shut off. The bed turned out to be a wise decision once she came out and searched her room.

The fear of being caught was thrilling, but it worked better for our relationship that she didn't discover me. I wouldn't have been able to keep my hands off her. As hard as it is to hold back, she isn't ready for me to claim her yet. So instead, I watched as she dried off and dressed, only catching glimpses of her smooth legs and occasionally her arms as she bent to pick something up.

Hours have passed, and while I'm uncomfortable, I'm not bored. Seraphina shifts in sleep, her foot dangling off one side of the bed, and her long blonde hair hangs over the other edge. I stifle my chuckle at the position she's found herself in. It's not normal for adults to do gymnastics in their sleep like children. Everything I learn about her endears me further, but I'm equally filled with the need to comfort her.

Without thinking, I reach out and touch the silky strands of her golden hair, willing her to feel the same support I offered her when she sensed the presence of her soulmate and mistook me for Tim. Wrapping the lengths around my fingers, I'm tempted to pull in a show of possession.

The temptation to prove myself the monster under her

bed is almost overwhelming. Would she fight me if I allowed my baser urges to take over and climbed on top of her? Or would she give in to my fingers winding through her pretty hair while my lips tasted hers for the first time? I'm hard as a rock, and I'm so angry over her predicament I want to fuck that aggression out on her.

That isn't what this is about, though. I'm only here as Seraphina's protector and will be back outside before she notices my presence. As a courtesy, I'll put her worthless fucking key back where it belongs.

Though the *neighborhood watch* has nothing on me, I'll double my attention.

She rolls over once more, straightening out and stealing the sensation of her nearness from me. I'm put out, close to rejected, when I hear the most beautiful sound imaginable.

"Shane."

CHAPTER
EIGHT
SERA

One day missing turns into two, then three, and when Tim decides to grace me with his presence, it's midnight on Saturday. Since he's been gone, my life has been both better and worse. During the day, I'm a little freer and happier. But once night rolls around, images of that dark figure in my yard haunt me. I'm sure it's Tim, angrily certain of it, but that doesn't stop the insidious sensation knocking around inside me.

I'm sure I'm paranoid. Either that or Tim is pathetic enough to come home and chicken out every night because I swear someone is there, watching me. Other than the creeping feeling on my skin, there is no way to explain how I'm certain I'm not alone. I've never believed in the boogie man, but the Devil following behind me is a familiar fear. Sure, I'm being ridiculous, but I was raised on faith.

Calling Tim seems like such a simple solution to my problems. In the past, I would have, but if I do, I'll be playing right into his hands. The thought he's intentionally trying to hurt me when I live my life to make his easier crosses a line for me.

I'm past the point of caring what Tim has to say when he comes back. I'm fed up, hurt, and licking my wounds with a cheesy rom-com that plays on the TV. Even more scandalous, I'm eating popcorn, something I was never allowed to do at home and Tim still makes me feel weird about.

The armchair in the living room has always been *Tim's* chair, and I'm taking advantage of his absence to enjoy that as well. Am I being petulant or enjoying the home *I* bought? I haven't decided yet. But maybe I'm leaning toward the former as I wiggle my ass deeper into the cushion.

The handsome, swoon-worthy main character is sweeping the leading lady into his arms for their first kiss when I hear the key in the lock. I shoot to my feet, rolling my eyes at myself as I realize how I snapped to serve him.

I sit back down. Tim has his key, and he doesn't need me to wait on him. His absence changed a lot of things. As crippling as my fear has been, it's taught me that I cannot rely on my husband to protect me. I'm done being Timothy Baker's doormat, and that includes welcoming him home after a week of God only knows what. I'm not in any hurry to see the man, so I let him fumble with the lock and concentrate on my movie. The kiss is everything I wanted it to be, but I can't enjoy it with the anxiety eating up my insides and crawling up my spine.

The door finally cracks open after an unusual amount of effort and jangling. The cold air rushes ahead of him, a chilling omen. I rub my arms, trying to fight off the goosebumps. Boot steps beat an irregular rhythm as Tim stumbles down the hall. I'm sure he's drunk, which is never a good thing. I hold my breath and pray he walks right past the living room and continues toward the bed. The den would be better, but I doubt I'll get that lucky.

There's a crash and then, "Fucking shit, bull fucking shit! You're always leaving shit around. You can't keep a house to save your fucking life!"

The house is spotless, and there's *nothing* in that hallway but a small decorative table that I'm certain has fallen victim to him. I remain seated, quiet, and unsure if he's talking to me or just parroting the nasty stuff his drunk father would spew when he'd fall over his own feet.

My heart pounds, and I think about running as the stench of beer and cigarettes wafts off him and over to me. He doesn't usually drink *that* much, and I've never known him to drive drunk or *smoke*. But that's his truck in the driveway, and tonight he's blasted. His keys dangle from his hand as he notices me in the living room and changes course.

I breathe in a panicked gulp of air. *Of course, God wasn't listening.*

Tim stands in the arched doorway, leaning against the frame. He's as silent as a sloppy drunk *can* be and stares at me for so long that he forces me to acknowledge his presence. My eyes run over his rumpled gym clothes. Was he really wearing the sweaty stuff he had in his car instead of coming home to me? How many days did he wear the outfit he stormed out in before resorting to this? I ask myself these questions and more while the fine hairs rise along the back of my neck.

"Tim, what's going on?" I speak loud enough for him to hear me, but I keep my tone gentle. "Are you okay?"

"You want to know if I'm okay?" His laugh is sharp and cruel. "What's wrong with you, Sera?! Why don't you give a shit anymore?!" he slurs as he shouts, pointing an accusing finger at me. "I've been gone for days, and you haven't fucking called me *once*."

My mouth drops open, stunned again by this man when nothing about his distaste for me should surprise me.

"Me? Tim, what are you talking about? I'm not skulking around our yard, refusing to come inside! I'm the one putting us in couples counseling. I didn't do that because I thought it would be fun! I'm the one *trying*. I care about us. What about you?"

I stand up, unable to stay in my seat like a good submissive wife. He's not listening to me, and I wave my arms in his direction, getting angrier with every passing moment. Tim shakes his head like a toddler throwing a belligerent fit, and with my waving arms and threatening tears, I'm not far behind him.

"Every damn night I'm out, you call and nag me, but not once this week have you bothered me. That's the only reason I never fucked someone else before. You're always goddamn bothering me!"

He tips his head back, revealing his muscular neck and adam's apple. He doesn't care that he just delivered another knife to my chest. How many more of them can I take from him?

"Not once did you call me this week. I want to know if you're fucking someone else," his demands rising to a shout.

Is that why he was in the backyard? Can my expectations of him sink any lower? I thought he wanted to come home and was too cowardly to do so, but he was actually trying to catch *me* cheating on him.

A guilty conscience always tells on itself, Seraphina.

For once, I agree with my father.

"Were *you* with someone else?" I ask the question so quietly I don't think he can hear me, but he's guilty as hell and knows what I've asked from the shape of my lips.

His face falls. First, upset I've come to that conclusion

so quickly, and next, his expression morphs into anger. "Who are *you* fucking, Sera?!"

He takes a step toward me.

"Tim, stop it! I have not been with anyone else! I've never even been with you!"

One more step.

There's rage in his features, anger that I don't understand, and it reminds me of his father.

"You're mad that *I* fucked someone else?"

His voice is deathly quiet, and terror fills me as he reaches out and takes hold of my neck. His fingers wrap around me, squeezing hard and infusing the air with the scent of cigarettes. I only have a moment to realize what is going on before he cuts off my breath.

"I wouldn't have married you *at all* if I realized you were such a little whore."

I look down, trying to see his tightening fingers, but I only see the bulging veins in his forearms as he squeezes. My head is already light, and my brain burns as it begs for oxygen. I'm trying to find or think of any way out of this situation, but it's all happening too fast, and things are getting dark around the edges. I'm horrified to find that, for the first time, he's hard for me and the evidence presses up against my weakening body.

Please, Tim, I mouth, but it's too late, and everything goes black.

I don't know how much time passes until I regain consciousness, but Tim has calmed down. Sitting up, I realize he must have moved me to the couch, and the faded blue cushions squish beneath my fingers. My tingling hands struggle to make sense of the texture, the blood still not fully returned to them. Finally, Tim shoots up from his lying position, big blue apologetic eyes aimed at me.

"Sera, fuck, I am so sorry! That never should have happened."

His voice is rough, like he's been crying. His eyes are red-rimmed, but that could just as easily be from the booze. I don't answer at first, trying to swallow and coordinate my battered throat muscles. I don't know if he thinks I'm ignoring him, but he continues.

"I swear to God I won't fight you anymore. We're going to therapy, and I'm giving it my all. I swear it, Sera. Never again."

My throat burns, preventing me from conveying my doubts. So instead, my hand rubs my offended neck, and we both cry.

CHAPTER
NINE
SERA

The two days since Tim choked me have been bleak and filled with nothing but a slew of random apologies, tears, and small gestures intended to woo me. I resent the apologies and cringe from the tears. The small gestures? Well, they're the worst of all. The gifts he's chosen are for a teenage girl who no longer exists, and it's apparent that was the last time my husband paid attention to me.

My days and nights have been a minefield of stress and pain. All I want to do is curl in on myself and lick my wounds, but I also need to nurse Tim's conscience. I'm sick of being the type of woman who would tell her attacker *it was okay*.

And I did.

I told him it was okay until I was sick of the sound of my voice. Then, I held his hand and prayed to God he would stop crying because our fathers always told us men never cry, and Tim doing so means we're destroyed beyond repair.

I'm so uncomfortable with Tim's apologies that I forget how afraid of him I am until my walls come down in my sleep. Assaulted by nightmares of his fingers wrapping around my neck, I always regain consciousness before he finishes the job. Worse than the night terrors is waking up to find the real Tim watching me with fake soft-blue eyes.

"Sera, Baby, are you okay?"

He strokes me with the same hand that tried to strangle me, and I swallow back my panic.

Please don't kill me.

The first morning I feel alive, Tim and I go through our routines, and he leaves for work. Finally alone, I allow myself to look forward to my solo appointment with Shane. Despite everything that's happened, my psychiatrist has become a safe harbor. My fantasies about him provide moments of relief, moments where I feel free, and I can't deny how attached to them I've become.

Because I know the obsessive way I've been thinking about the man isn't healthy I have the good sense to wonder whether my attraction to him is a response to all this garbage heaped on me, which could be. Or I was wrong about love at first sight and the sanctity of marriage. The cause doesn't matter so much as the effect. And I'm desperate to see Shane, for him to lavish me with more of his gentle touches, to see if he spreads as much light as memory serves.

Tim's appointment with Shane is tomorrow. He made several grand speeches about how seriously he plans to take things from here, but I still don't know if he intends to go. He's always been a big talker when he knows he's messed up. There will be a lot of broken promises to come out of this little fiasco.

Though all the snow has melted, the wind steals any warmth the sun offers, and there's been a lot of that cloying spring rain. I wrap myself up in a thick peacoat giving me the perfect excuse to wear one of my two scarves. I'm stuck between the heavy yarn or the silken scrap of fabric that won't cover the bruises. I *could* use makeup, but Tim doesn't like it, and for that reason, I have none.

I'm not sure what to do about *Tim*. I'm not making excuses for him, but I expected worse sooner. I'm not even sure I'm *that* angry. Hurt and confused? Absolutely! And I've hated every minute of the last two days, but part of me is relieved. Our lives can't get any worse.

I climb into my car, contemplating how Tim's given me more attention in the last two days than he has in years, even though it's skin-crawling and nothing like what I imagined or craved. And as messed up as it is to be happy about it, he got hard for me right before he nearly killed me. He was hard for *me*.

That means this can work.

I shake my head, knowing how wrong I am. My shame burns me up, and the pain is too intense to tolerate without an outlet. I deserve to suffer, so, for a brief and out-of-character moment, I let myself dwell on what my father would say to me about my current situation if given half a chance.

Whore. Jezebel. Witch.

I know my father would wish Tim had finished the job to keep me from embarrassing him further.

I shake off my distraction, put the car in reverse, and head to my appointment. The little white sedan is safe and practical, as Tim pointed out when he ignored my requests for a different color and model. It's not as if I hate it. It's just a car, anyway. I adjust the rearview mirror and wonder why I need to.

Was someone in my car?

I roll my eyes and dismiss my concerns as I imagine Tim spying on me. Did he seriously think I had another man here with me? I'm a twenty-three-year-old virgin, and my husband thinks I'm having an affair. If my situation weren't so pathetic, I would laugh.

My drive across town does little to take my mind off my spinning thoughts. *I'm* not driving drunk, but I'm a menace to myself and others, enough that relief floods me when I pull into the parking lot. Pushing the thoughts out of my head, I steady my breathing and take the elevator up to Shane's office. The thrill of seeing him has me almost swallowing my lungs.

After everything with Tim, I have had nothing *but* time to obsess over what I saw Shane do to himself the last time I was here. I salivate at the thought of tasting what he spilled. I clear my embarrassment along with with my throat as I approach his secretary scrolling social media on her phone. She looks up at me and offers half a smile.

"You can head back."

"Thanks."

She's a lot less cheerful without my husband to ogle at, and I bristle as I walk to Shane's office. Would she be so eager to see Tim if she knew what he did to me? Would she even care? Did the girl Tim screwed care that he has a wife? Did she even know? I set the painful thoughts aside for now, resolved to talk about my issues with Shane and *not* bring up what I saw last time. Regardless of my inappropriate fascination with the man, I need him.

The hallway stays solid this time, and I thank God for small favors as I hold my breath and knock.

"Come in,"

That's a lot more reassuring than the indistinct "yeah" I heard the last time. So I open the door to find Shane seated in his armchair rather than at the desk. I swallow hard as the image of him spilling his release and groaning my name fills my mind. The change of scenery is a small mercy.

"Good afternoon, Seraphina."

His voice is smooth and faultless. There isn't a hint of embarrassment or uncertainty. His bright smile lacks all traces of force, and I'm stunned. For one thing, he's even more handsome than I remembered. For another, he's acting as if nothing happened and what I watched was a product of my imagination. This situation may be *my* fault, and I'm rethinking my entire casual act as I gather the fortitude to speak.

"Good afternoon, Shane," I answer him with only a slight hitch.

"Close the door behind you and take a seat, won't you?" he's asking, but I'm sure I don't have a choice.

"Okay,"

I do as he asks, and he smiles at me. His gaze lacks all heat, and I hear no catch in his words. I must be losing my mind because there's no way I walked in on this guy masturbating. According to my faulty memory, I watched him come like the human version of a volcano, and now he's talking to me as if nothing happened.

Yeah, Seraphina, that happened.

But then I blink, registering how easily I thought all those words and how little shame accompanied them. It could be like that for Shane. Perhaps he's not pretending it didn't happen, but he isn't actually bothered.

I sit on the edge of the couch. It's warmer here than I remembered, and I'm sweating within a minute. Shane wears nothing more than a light button-up shirt and slacks. The blue compliments his eyes, and I'm again startled by the tingle those eyes raise along my spine. Why do I get the feeling I could drown in the depths of his gaze and enjoy every moment until my lungs failed?

It's clear he doesn't share my thoughts as he pulls out a leather-covered legal pad and takes a few notes. I'm his *patient*, and if I behaved appropriately, I would never let him hold me or watch as he *came*. *I'm a voyeur.*

"How have you been since our last appointment? We didn't part under the best of circumstances."

He knows how to style his longish black hair to give him an artistic vibe without being too much, and I want to touch it so badly. His open, unguarded expression reveals the barest spark of heat in the depths of his eyes. My lips part, not yet convinced he's going to talk about this with me.

"I, uh, I—" I stammer.

My cheeks are so hot they have to be bright red. I'm salivating profusely and trying to swallow before I choke.

"Have you and Tim had a chance to talk since he walked out?" he offers, likely to help me form some halfway intelligent response.

Oh, that's what he means.

"We've done a lot of talking," I answer honestly, and I can't manage to keep the disgust out of my tone.

"I see," he says, and I wonder if he does.

His gaze runs over me, and I hold back a shiver.

"Why don't you take off your jacket and scarf? I know it's hot in here—blame the Corporations. I can't even control the heat in my own office." He smiles, but I can't return the gesture.

It *is* hot. I'm sweating, and I will never convince Shane I'm not hot in an eighty-degree office while wearing a coat and scarf. At the same time, I doubt he'll believe my forehead is damp for some other reason. I'm wearing the highest collar I own, but it doesn't cover the worst marks. The only lighting comes from a few mood lamps, so it's not bright in here but hardly dark. I hope

Shane won't look too closely as I nod and unbutton my coat.

Thankfully, he's not watching me. He's looking over our notes from last time, and I see my name written with an artful flourish at the top of the page.

"So, Seraphina, tell me what you want to gain from therapy. I know we started to discuss these things last time, but we were *interrupted.*"

Is he saying that it was Tim's fault? I hope he is, but I don't want to read into things. I breathe hard, trying to work the lump out of my throat and avoid crying in front of this man again.

"Honestly? I don't know anymore." I stand and push my jacket off my shoulders while he's still distracted. "I thought I was coming here because I wanted to have sex with Tim. I *believed* that was my end goal. But everything is messy now, and I don't know what I want."

In a calculated maneuver, I dip my chin and move my upper body, covering my neck with my hair as I lay my jacket and scarf on the couch next to me.

"You *don't* want to have sex with Tim anymore?" his tone is so level, so professional, but I *feel* his excitement.

"I don't know if it's that. I think I still do on *some* level. I *want* to stay married to Tim." I don't bother voicing my fears about the improbability of my wishes being granted. "He's the only person who's ever been there for me."

I drift off, thinking about how pathetic I sound, especially under the revelation of what happened.

"He admitted he cheated on me two nights ago."

Shane doesn't look surprised, and by that, I mean not even a little.

"You guessed," I whisper.

My shoulders sag. How many other people know my husband is disloyal?

Am I that clueless?

"What I guessed isn't important," Shane says, his eyes finding mine. His gaze is kind, and somehow that makes it worse.

For no apparent reason, Shane goes still. One moment he's normal and animated, and the next, he's unmoving with a look threatening violence.

"Seraphina." Goosebumps break out on my skin, my heart pounds, and my palms slicken. I'm terrified and transfixed by his intensity. "*What* is that mark on your neck?"

"I'm not sure what you mean." The lie falls from my lips as I try to readjust my hair, and we both hear it for what it is.

He's out of his chair, approaching me in an instant, and I have to crane my neck to look at him. As I do, I forget myself, exposing the length of my neck for his inspection. He carefully reaches out, lining up each one of his fingertips with the five round bruises.

His eyes hold mine as he asks, "Did *he* do this to you?"

"No," I rush to say.

"Don't *lie* to me, Seraphina. I can see the truth all over your face."

He can see more than the truth. He can see everything I've ever thought, and I need to get away from him before he cares enough to look deeper. Coming here today was a mistake.

"Don't touch me. It's inappropriate."

I try to slap his hand away, but he doesn't budge. He smirks ever so slightly, but the expression is cruel.

"I apologize, *Sera.*" There's an edge to my name, and I'm sure he's shortened it on purpose. "Some patients are comforted by therapeutic touch. I'll note in your file that you're not. Given a choice, I would never *disrespect your boundaries*."

But he doesn't move his hand from my neck.

Besides that little catch when he called me Sera, and his hand still pressing against my bruises, he sounds so professional. I question what's happening right in front of my face, the touch I feel on my skin. Is he trying to make a point about the man I love who happens to abuse my boundaries? The man who choked me until I slipped into unconsciousness? Or is he just another man who crosses lines when he pleases?

I shiver, not moving an inch, aware of how hard it is not to overstep unset boundaries. Shane's fingers trace the bruises once more before he returns to his seat, picks up his notebook, and starts writing in it.

"I'm not used to being touched," I correct his earlier statement.

He cocks an eyebrow at me as his pen stills.

"Is that different from what I said?"

I nod, and he places the pen down, giving me his undivided attention.

"Yes, it's different. I don't *know* if I find touch comforting. I don't remember anyone ever comforting me that way." I wrap my arms around myself defensively.

"Except for *my* touch," he corrects with a look that tells me there isn't any use denying it.

"Yeah, except for yours."

Though the admission excites me, it also stabs deep. *Tim is right. I'm a whore.*

"Did you enjoy it when I comforted you after Tim left our last session?" his perfect professional tone hasn't slipped an inch, but I'm a mess as I answer.

"Yes," I enjoyed it so much I was tempted to masturbate despite being unable to find my clitoris.

"Even though touch is unusual for you?" There's a flicker of heat now, and I'm going to melt beneath it.

"I'm not *entirely* sure how I feel about it, but you asked me if I enjoyed it, and that day I did."

He looks impressed by my bluntness, and while I'm surprised, I don't share his approval. It scares the crap out of me. Is it him that makes me like this, or did Tim break me somehow?

"Did you like it when Tim put that on your neck?"

I stare at him, unable to form a single word. My heart clenches in my chest, stunned by his cruelty.

"Some people have kinks, Sera. That's okay, and you can tell me if you wanted what happened. I won't judge you."

He's still calling me Sera, and regardless of how practiced and courteous he's acting, the reprimand is present in the nickname. Every other time he's addressed me, he's called me Seraphina.

"I *didn't* want it."

I don't know why I say it, given I was trying to deny it even happened, but the words slip out, and the mask he's been wearing falls with them. I see someone vicious beneath it, someone ready to kill, and I'm afraid of what that man might do. He stays in his chair this time, but I sense his desperation to approach me. Perhaps that desire is why he stays in place.

He clears his throat, and with it, the mask is back in place, "Would you like to talk about it, Sera?"

"No," I answer too quickly.

"What would you like to talk about then? It's your time, and I want you to get the most out of it."

The question feels like a trap, as if he's pretending to give me space and plans to work me back around to the topic he feels is most important.

I take a few minutes to consider his words. Assuming he's going to give me what I ask and not back me into a corner, what do I want for *my* time? I don't know how I muster up the courage to say what I truly desire, but something about him makes me feel safe to say anything.

"I don't want to talk. I want you to hold me again."

"Is that *all* you want from me?"

He's asking if I want him to do more. I notice how his fingers twitch like he's desperate to touch me. And God, do I want more from him.

"Yes, that's all I want from you."

Of course it's a lie, but out of the two sins, that's the one I can best live with.

For the second time, my insurance pays this man two hundred dollars an hour to hold me in his arms and rub soothing circles onto my back. I never feel an erection, and he never acknowledges what I saw last time, but it's all I can think about. I'm aching, practically squirming by the time our hour is up, but he never gives me any suggestion he's suffering along with me. Finally, he helps me to my feet and out the door.

"I'll see you in a few days for our group session. We can protect you, Seraphina. Just let us know what you need before then. There *are* resources for women in your circumstances."

I look into his eyes and offer *him* a comforting smile, "I'm a big girl, Shane. I don't need *you* to protect me."

"Everyone *needs* protection sometimes," he leans forward, and I freeze, sure he's going to kiss me. Instead, he leans into my ear and whispers, "even if it's only from the monsters under your bed."

CHAPTER
TEN
SHANE

The night Tim choked my Angel, I got a call from the local hospital as I watched Seraphina. She had been calm, watching a movie, and Desmond, one of my patients, needed me. He had a public episode and was admitted to the psychiatric ward. Every time I have to leave her, I struggle; I hate losing the precious time devoted to her. But that day, leaving Seraphina alone was harder than ever.

I had no choice.

The local psychiatric unit is a disaster, and despite the sometimes immoral nature of my actions, I care that Desmond isn't set back months' worth of progress because of some over-eager assholes who like Haldol too much.

It only took me a few hours to get him into a private facility that would honor my wishes, but by the time I left, it was well past two, and I was exhausted. I drove past Seraphina's home only to check and make sure that she was okay. Sleeping in my own bed would be imperative to recharge after a week of sleeping under her mattress and the mental gymnastics I'd just gone through.

Except when I got there, I was shocked to find Tim's truck. Assuming she was safe, I went home. I don't like being wrong, and I despise when others touch what belongs to me.

Seraphina walked into my office, nervous and off. Her lack of eye contact was evasive rather than shy, making me suspicious but willing to be patient. When she wouldn't meet my eye, I thought they had sex, but it didn't take long to learn that wasn't the case.

How fucking dare Tim touch what doesn't belong to him, marry someone who doesn't belong to him, and then choke her as if she's trash and not the most beautiful of angels? The audacity of his actions stuns me more than the violence in them.

Heading back to my desk, I pull up the folder on my phone devoted to Seraphina, and by default, Tim. I've learned a considerable amount about them, including Tim's client list. He keeps busy, which I appreciate on multiple levels. I can attack on multiple fronts since he doesn't spend much time with Seraphina.

I take my time reviewing the clients he's seen this week, and then check their addresses against maps to find the perfect property. There's really only one that works, but damn if it's not perfect. I pull up the property records and find the owner; a picture and his home phone number are easy enough to find. When no one answers, it's decided. *John Dades* is about to be *very* unhappy with his lawn care.

I clear my throat and adjust my voice until I sound unrecognizable. The phone rings a few times before Tim picks up. I'm full of shit as I ramble about his piss-poor work and how dissatisfied I am. From the well-kept records, I know he's only worked for Mr. Dades twice, so if I don't sound like him, he hasn't noticed. Within a few minutes, he's agreed to meet "me" at the house and fix the issues. I'll give it to the prick, he's likable and good at diffusing tension. But that strengthens the question, why hurt Seraphina when he could leave her?

The answer is simple. The good Christian boy enjoys her pain.

Traffic is tight this time of day, and I do my best to hurry across town to where I directed Tim. His truck is parked on the curb, overflowing with equipment. The faded logo on the side reads "Decker and Son." My research showed he worked for his father's company, but I'm not sure why Tim still has the truck. The question of how they afford their house still hangs in the air. I *will* find out why the numbers don't add up in their household.

The Victorian house has an even creepier vibe than most, and I can guess from the neglect of the structure that Tim spent a lot of time here trying to make the property look this nice. Parking across the street gives me a good opportunity to observe the path to the house. Tim stands with his phone to his ear and his back to the front door.

He's got a fist in his blonde hair like he might rip it out, and his cheeks are burning red. He's realized no one is home, just as I hoped, and he's pissed.

"You're not going to fucking dick me around!" he shouts, and I shake my head in amusement.

An outdoor event must be planned because the house looks uninhabited, though the yard is spectacular. The topiaries are even-shaped, and the bushes and flowers are trimmed to perfection. It's not a stretch to imagine his frustration at being told his work is substandard when he knows he's done an excellent job. But that's nothing compared to being a small woman with an overgrown bully's hand around your throat.

The traffic interrupted my plans. I intended to arrive

before Tim and lay in wait, but that's not an option now. I watch him for a few minutes, trying to decide on the best course of action. He's called the same number three times since I've been here, but the call back I gave him was fake.

When Tim finally gives up and returns to his car, I act on impulse and stride up behind him, glad the speed of his reflex works in my favor. He has no time to glance over his shoulder before I wrap my hands around his neck and squeeze, shoving him to the ground beside his truck. The street is empty. Noise from the highway floats in, but other than that, the only sound is Tim's gurgled attempts to breathe.

Stronger than I expect, he does his best to fight me. Too bad for him, my thoughts are devoted to hanging on and keeping him as silent as possible, ceasing all his grunting and kicking of the pavement. Well-versed in the right and wrong ways to choke a person, I squeeze until he loses consciousness. He's not dead, but he won't be out for more than thirty seconds.

"I like choking women too, Tim. The only difference is when I do it, they ask me to."

I check his right hand, the one he choked Sera with, stretch it out, and make sure it's where I want it. Then, stepping over him and into the cab of his truck, I turn the key and throw it in reverse, pinning Tim's offending hand beneath his vehicle. A wet fleshy snap fills the air, followed by a brief yet chilling silence. Climbing over the center console, I exit through the passenger door. His frantic screams fill the air, and I whistle to myself as a cheek-aching grin splits my face.

It's safe to assume that he won't have any clue who did this when he finally gets free, but one can hope the message will be clear. *I'll do worse to you than you do to her.*

Climbing into my car, I delete the video footage from the homeowner's security app with my own dark web app. Tim is still screaming, and I can't help but think he will be at it for a while. So far, no one on this spaced-out and sparsely inhabited block has heard him.

Driving back to their house, I feel much better than I did before, but the knowledge that he hurt her still sits heavy on me. I want to wrap her in my arms again, kiss each one of her bruises, fuck her senseless, and then leave bruises of my own. Ones she'd beg for, and even if Seraphina didn't like pain, I'd suck hickies into her neck like a teenager to see the way her skin looked marked by me.

The lights are on in her bedroom, the kitchen, and the living room, and it takes me a minute to figure out she's in front of the TV eating her dinner. She looks nervous, as if she's afraid to get caught, and I long to ask her what she's thinking.

She doesn't hear from the police until the wee hours of the morning, and I regret my actions a little when she gasps and repeats, "Five hours?" Not because I think what I did to Tim was too harsh, but because I hate her concern for him, the apparent love behind it. I will never hurt her, but I resent the fuck out of her as I understand the depth of her care for Tim. How, after everything, can she cry and run to his aid?

I stay in their house for hours after she leaves, looking at everything and anything, thinking hard about handling things and the right way to get our lives on track. Tempted to piss on their belongings to mark my territory, and that's when I know I'm losing it and need to go home.

With no sleep and feeling like a zombie, I drag myself into the office. I open my date book and cross out my appointment with Tim for this afternoon. I doubt he'll make it in due to his little *accident*.

Crushing the flirtatious post-it Tasha left on my desk, I watch the way the muscles and tendons move in my hand; ways that Tim's hand will likely never move again. I'm curious to see how he's feeling about that and whether the lesson about touching what belongs to me has sunk in.

CHAPTER
ELEVEN
SERA

Rushing out of the house, I grab the only jacket off the metal hook on the porch as I race to the car. The officer on the phone didn't say much other than Tim had been in an accident, and it had taken five hours for help to arrive. His life wasn't in danger, but I should come as soon as possible. He sounded incredibly grim, and I know full well that being alive doesn't mean you're not in horrible shape.

I'm doing my damndest to drive through my tears while my ears ring like singing champagne flutes, and the squealing makes it impossible to think. What if something serious happened to Tim after everything I'd done with Shane, everything I *wanted*? What if Tim died and all my secrets were left untold between us? If religion taught me anything, it was that the admission of guilt is necessary for absolution, and I'm so guilty I could scream.

I'm unsure where the rational part of my brain is as I berate myself for wanting Shane. I don't take into account how Tim put his hands on me, hurt me, and almost took my life. Instead, I think of Tim, who's broken right now, and I don't know how severe his condition is. Tim, who needs me, who always needed me.

The ride takes a lifetime, and as I screech along the rain-slicked streets, I can't stop crying. I also treat traffic lights as a suggestion and ignore the speed limit. The colossal complex that houses the emergency department is impossible to navigate, and I curse the whole time between finding parking and rushing inside. After showing my ID, the nurse still isn't running to take me back, and my leg bounces relentlessly as I stand there, refusing to take my seat.

Is God punishing me for what I've done? I *love* Tim. I love him, and I wronged him, and I'm never going to do it again. I'll end the therapy appointments. I'll do whatever he wants, anything to keep him from hurting.

The nurse gives me his room number, and the security guard buzzes me in. It doesn't take long for me to find room one-fifteen, and when I pull back the curtain, I gasp at the sight of him. His mangled arm is bruised to hell. He has no cast but a loose set holding his arm in place. Even without speaking to a doctor, I'm sure he needs surgery. He's hooked up to an IV, pumping him full of painkillers.

He looks up at me, and he smiles. My heart blossoms like it hasn't in years. There it is. He wants me, and he *needs* me. We can work this out.

But then he says, "Sera?" His sky-blue eyes blink in confusion. "I don't want you. Where's Katrina?"

Then his lids flutter closed.

I stand there for a long time, watching him in shock—a single question composed of two parts playing on repeat.

Where is Katrina, *and why am I here?*

I don't wait for him to wake up before I leave, and I slip out to the parking lot without saying a word to anyone.

Sleep evades me despite my exhaustion, and I wake

with the manic energy of the overtired. First, I call the hospital and dial Tim's extension. Guilt is my primary motivator, and I can't ignore him when he's hurt. No one answers, so I wait and dial again, nothing.

My next call should be an easy one, but life isn't fair.

"Doctor Shane Nelson's office, Tasha speaking. How may I help you?"

"Hi, Tasha, this is Seraphina Baker."

"Hi, Seraphina," her phony chirp raises my hackles.

I explain that Tim has been in an accident and that we need to reschedule.

Her gasp pops uncomfortably in my ears.

"Oh no! Is he okay? What happened?!"

I swallow the much more genuine distress in her tone.

"He's fine," I answer, only half lying. "Can we move the appointment to next week?"

If she's upset by my evasion she doesn't say anything, and I'm off the phone with her to call Tim again in no time.

No answer.

I don't see him for the three nights he sleeps there. A doctor calls me regularly to update me about his surgery and progress, and I wonder if Tim asked him to do it because he's not taking my calls. The doctor said his arm was crushed, the circumstances of which I'd need to ask my husband about. Except I can't face him.

The nurse calls one last time to tell me I need to pick Tim up at three o'clock the next day. I agree, even though being near him makes my skin crawl. I try to force myself to enjoy my last night of freedom, but I'm anxious and twitchy. I can't shake the feeling someone is watching me, and I barely manage any sleep.

The next day I drive over to the hospital, cursing the lack of sleep and being forced to see Tim. I sit in the pickup line for twenty minutes before a nurse wheels him over to the car and helps him inside. She wishes him a speedy recovery and shuts the door, cutting off the fresh air. I immediately notice the smell of perfume on him. Did Katrina come to stay with him? I'm suddenly sure that's what happened, and I'm having trouble breathing.

"Where were you?" he asks as we're rounding the same railroad crossing near Shane's office. The arm falls across the road keeping us in place.

"You didn't want me there," I answer, trying to keep the tears out of my voice.

Guilt flashes in his eyes, and he says nothing else about the matter.

"What happened to you?"

"Do you care?" He glances over at me with open spite.

"It's absurd, not to mention unfair of you to ask me that when I requested your visitor log."

Of course it's a bluff, but I need him to know I can fucking smell the woman he's cheating on me with all over him. I know he has been wrapped up in her these last two days, and the fact he was too hurt to fuck her only makes things worse. He *cares* for her.

"Someone attacked me from behind, choked me, and parked my truck on my hand," he says the words bluntly, hoping they'll shock me.

I gasp and slap my hand over my mouth because they have the desired effect.

"What?"

"Someone attacked me, Sera. Any idea who?" I look over at him, troubled by how paranoid he sounds.

"Of course not, Tim."

"You wouldn't lie about that, would you?"

"Never. I would never *want* to see you hurt." I steel

myself, "But maybe I'm not the only person upset about your lies."

I doubt he believes me, but he's so stunned by my accusation that he's quiet the rest of the way home. I avoid him as best as I can the rest of the day, but I'm so tired I pass out early. By seven o'clock, I'm wrapped in my blanket and restlessly asleep.

A heavy sense of discontent weighs on me when I wake in the morning. At first, I can't place it, but then I see Tim sleeping beside me. Sweat soaks every inch of my body, and my muscles tense like I'm ready to flee.

I shimmy out of bed, hoping he will remain asleep. The last thing I want is to hear any more of his account on the unbelievable circumstances of his injury.

I grab my shower products and use the bathroom in the hall rather than the one in our bedroom. I need to get away from him, and I need peace. I'm shampooing my hair and thinking about the mess my life is when I hear a noise that I hope is anything but Tim waking in. I'd rather it be a poltergeist or demon at this point.

But of course, there's only one other being in this house. I still haven't asked him for more details about him cheating on me, and I'm not sure I want them. The thought of him with someone else makes me feel many uncomfortable things. The idea of him losing his virginity to someone else doesn't hurt how I imagined it would. I spent years with an over-the-top notion of how we would share the experience. It turns out I didn't want his cursed virginity anyway.

He's standing in the open doorway. I pretend not to see him for as long as I can. The conditioner is thoroughly rinsed, and there's nothing left to wash. Nevertheless, I'm not about to leave here naked in front of him.

"What do you want, Tim? I'm taking a shower." I snap

as I cover my breasts and privates. He can't see through the frosted glass, but I know he can make out my overall outline.

"You don't want me to see now!?" he challenges.

"No, I don't."

I turn off the water and grab the towel from the rack. Tim might have seen a bare bit of something, but I'm trying not to focus on that. So instead, I wrap the towel tightly around myself before stepping out. His eyes flick to the yellowing bruises around my neck and then back up. He swallows, and I say a silent prayer that he won't revert to apologizing.

Tim hasn't mentioned choking me since his accident, and I'm grateful not to be subjected to his sobbing, but I'm worried he's going to crack. His eyes occasionally flick to the bruises on my neck, and he looks like he's licked something unpleasant, though I don't have a clue what that means. At first, he *groveled*, but now I'm afraid of how close he is to another outburst.

Shattered bones...

This situation is very different from the one with his father, back when we were eighteen, but the injuries are so similar I don't want to be around him for fear of further making him associate me with pain. Crushed bones and me, the two things seem to go hand in hand. No wonder he doesn't *want* me.

I wouldn't want the cause of *all* my pain either.

"Tim, how much can you reject a person before they don't want you to see them naked?" I sound nearly as exhausted as I feel.

Tim is rapidly becoming the cause of more of my pain, and I want him less than I ever have. I haven't actually wanted to have sex with him since... That little voice reminds me that I haven't grown self-respect after all this time. I'm just not interested anymore because someone else has my attention.

"I'm not going to keep rejecting you, Sera."

I don't react in any way.

Thankfully, he leaves the room and lets me dress. The man is so hot and cold I wonder if he does it on purpose to keep me desperate. My rational brain knows he will keep rejecting me, but my heart can't help hoping that was a promise he intended to keep. Does he know how pitiful he's made me?

I already had planned to go to our group therapy session alone that afternoon, but I don't tell Tim until I shout from the hall that I'm running errands. Although I'm not lying since I will run errands while I'm out, I need to talk to someone outside this bubble. However, I don't need to dig deep to admit to myself it's not *someone* I want to talk to, but Shane. I must be losing my mind with the oppression in this damn house.

I drive across town, and nervous butterflies assault my stomach. I need Shane to be the rock that Tim won't or can't be. I need someone to be strong for me. Tim has been so touchy I can't breathe around him, never mind sharing my burdens and pain. I've never had anyone to comfort me, but my craving now is so intense I can't stand it.

I don't have any other scarves, and I'm not about to buy one to cover what Tim did. I *don't* work and haven't been out enough to make friends since we moved. So what does it matter if people see what he did to me? Maybe I want them to.

I go to the grocery store once or twice a week, but I don't even need to go to the bank. No one in this city knows me by my name other than Tim, Shane, and his secretary, and whether or not she remembers it when she's not reading her appointment log is iffy. So no one is going to notice the bruises other than them.

What if something happened to me? Would anyone even look?

I drive in a daze, unsure of what's happening to me, but I feel myself slipping into something dark. I'm not sad or hurt but numb, and somehow that's so much worse. I need someone to see it before it's too late. Part of me knows that if Tim wants to hurt me again, I'm going to let him. After, I'll make excuses and hide it again until he kills me because I let him.

Letting the bruises show is a middle finger to Tim and that weak version of myself. But rather than some warrior growing strong enough to defeat the weakling who would lie for Tim, the two parts of me meld into something like cornstarch slurry, a Newtonian substance, neither liquid nor solid.

I pull off the highway into the parking lot, find a spot near the building, make my way up to Shane's floor and greet Tasha with a manic smile—I'm still irritated by the woman's presence.

That feeling intensifies when I say, "Good afternoon," and her eyes flit to my neck, wide in alarm.

My husband doesn't look like a catch now, does he?

She clears her throat.

"Hi, Seraphina. How are you doing?"

There's a note of concern, and I think this bitch might have remembered where she works and how she's supposed to be supportive toward patients instead of gawking at their hot husbands.

A hot husband who cheated on me, choked me, and can't get hard for me!

I'm shocked by the venom in my thoughts, and I blink as I try to answer her. She's seen the bruises and my bizarre hesitation.

"I'm great," I reply. At a different time, the false brightness in my tone would have made me cringe, but today, I'm dead inside.

She forces a smile, and it's not even close to authentic. Instead, her gaze runs over me, and I wish I knew what she sees.

"Okay, well, you can head right back. Shane is ready for you."

She hasn't even called him, and I wonder if he told her he was ready before I got here or if she can't stand the awkwardness of having me at her desk any longer. Either way, I don't care. I'm leaving part of myself on the industrial gray carpet beneath her feet, and although I can feel it's monumental, I don't understand what it means.

CHAPTER TWELVE
SERA

Shane doesn't have that super professional air he's had the other times I've seen him. He seems troubled, and I'm uneasy in response. I sit down without him asking me, and he hasn't said a word as I rub my neck self-consciously. His blue eyes trail over every inch of me, and there's something in them that I can't place. His inspection doesn't feel sexual, making me even more afraid of what he may see.

"Your neck is looking better," he finally says, with a small smile, and a little tension breaks.

I breathe deeply, my lungs expanding properly now that I know he's not upset with me. I wave a dismissive hand toward him.

"Yeah, it's not that bad. I bruise easily, but they'll fade in no time."

His eyes narrow, and he looks so damn displeased with me I want to snatch the words out of the air and take them back. His finger thumps against the desk.

"You caught me off guard. I assumed you would wear another scarf today, a turtleneck or something. You didn't even put makeup on those bruises, did you?"

"No," I gulp, my fingers moving to my throat as the heat of his gaze trails over the marks. I'm shocked when sparks zip through my veins, like the thought of him looking at my bruises turns me on. It *can't*. I'm ashamed of them.

"*You* impressed me, Seraphina."

His deep blue gaze meets mine, those frothy white caps giving them impossible depth. Pride swells inside me so fast and intense I could burst. But before I'm too overcome with joy, I hear the "but" in his tone.

The idea of his disapproval makes me ache before I've even received it.

His lips purse as he scrutinizes me. "I thought a lot about how you might act during our meeting today. I've been thinking about you non-stop since I last saw you."

"You've been thinking about me!?" I squeak like my crush said he likes me.

"I've been weighing the pros and cons of my professional obligations and the personal ones I feel toward you."

His words let all the air out of my expanding chest, and I again feel that I'm losing my mind.

"And what conclusion did you come to?"

"I expected you to do what you're doing right now. I thought you'd sit in front of me, make excuses for *him*, tell me how he didn't mean to hurt you. But instead, you came in here with your head held high. Why backpedal now?"

I struggle.

I'm not afraid of what Shane might say to me, and it's not because he's my doctor.

"I'm not backpedaling. I'm trying to diffuse the situation to avoid conflict."

His eyebrow pops up. "And why do you want to avoid conflict with *me*?"

There's a possessive challenge in his voice, and I

swallow hard. I play with the ends of my hair, thinking about simply not voicing my thoughts, but I know Shane won't allow my silence.

"Because you won't like what I have to say."

"And what *do* you have to say?"

"I'm small, female, and know what it's like to live in a man's world. What Tim did is *far* from the worst done to me, and the truth is, I don't feel as strongly about it as you would like me to."

"Oh no?" his voice is level, but there's something feral in his gaze.

"No," I assure him.

I sigh as I try to gather my thoughts.

"Tim is suffering…" I tell him cryptically, and I know I sound like a mafioso in a bad movie. "I told your secretary he was in an accident, but I didn't say how bad. He's paid for what he did to me."

"I doubt that," Shane levels me a dark look like he can imagine a far steeper punishment.

I'm never contrary. I don't pick arguments or point out the fine details of the point I'm trying to make, but something about Shane makes me want to be understood.

"Well, isn't it convenient that I didn't ask you what you thought of my answer? I gave it, and for your information, someone parked his truck on his hand!"

His brow lifts in shock, and I think it's because the details of Tim's assault are so gruesome. In contrast, his eyes are filled with the warmth of his approval, and that crashes over me as he gifts me with his smile. But then, his expression darkens into something contemplative and melancholy.

"It wasn't enough, Seraphina."

His deep voice is so sure, so even, but I still ask, "Excuse me?"

"What happened to him was not a fair exchange for what he has done to you. But rather than argue over our moral compasses and what we believe the fitting punishment *is* for choking your wife so close to death, why don't we start this session over?"

My mouth drops open. Start *over?* Is this a game for him?

"Let's!" I clap sarcastically, "Good afternoon, *Doctor* Nelson."

He smiles as he looks at his notes. He sees my sarcasm, and rather than resenting my attitude, I've amused him. I want that to make me angry, but instead, I feel warm.

"How are you doing today? Is it, yes, Seraphina?" He looks up at me through his lashes and flashes me a smile. I melt. His teasing demeanor drops, and he continues, "I don't think we need to start from the top, Seraphina, but let's not argue. I know it's been a tough week."

"That's an understatement." I agree as I slump into the cushions behind me, finally letting my fight deflate.

"So help me *properly* state it."

I'm smiling again, and it makes no damn sense when we're talking about my life collapsing all around me. I'm happier than I've been in years even though I'm still wearing the marks from my husband's assault. I think about my answer for a minute and still smile when I speak.

"I'm drowning." *And not in your pretty blue eyes.*

Maybe the fact that he's a shrink explains how badly I want to spill my guts to him, but why am I obsessed with climbing into his arms? That I can't explain so guiltlessly.

"Is that why you kept this appointment today, knowing Tim couldn't make it?"

"He doesn't know I'm here," *And you see me.*

He's quiet. His eyes slide over me, and there's sadness in his appraisal.

"There aren't a lot of places in your life you can turn to for support, are there, Seraphina?"

"No." I shake my head and resist the urge to go to him.

I can't think of anywhere or anyone I can turn to for support right now. I would have said Tim a few weeks ago, but would that have been true? He's been attending school for two semesters now, pursuing a degree he picked this time, forging relationships outside of our marriage that *satisfy* him. He's left me afloat all this time, so why would he care that I've finally gotten exhausted from hanging on?

"Did you feel like talking about your problems would help?" he's talking to me in his perfect professional tone, and a crazy part of me wants to hear his post-climax voice again.

"I thought *you* would," I answer too honestly.

"I'll do my best, Seraphina." He glances at his notebook, writes something down, and looks back at me. "I'd like to try something different if that's okay with you. Leave Tim out of this conversation and focus on you."

"Uh, I mean…"

I run my hands through my hair and push the locks behind my ears, but I don't say anything else, hoping he'll fill in the silence for me. Unfortunately, that's my experience in life. The second there's the slightest doubt, my voice is cast aside. It's as much of a crutch as it is a cage.

Shane tilts his head to the side, like a predator sizing up his prey. "What *do* you mean?"

I sit up straighter, responding to the opportunity to please him. "I'm in therapy to work on my relationship with Tim. I'm not sure how leaving him out of it will help."

"Humor me."

He drags his pen across his bottom lip in a mindless

gesture. His pink tongue flicks out ever so gently, sliding along the plastic.

My mouth goes dry.

"Yeah, okay." *Anything.*

"Are you satisfied with your life outside of your relationship?" His pen taps against the page, but he makes no note of his question. Does he intend to record my answer? Is he even paying attention? The tip digs too hard into the paper, and ink pools beneath the fountain tip.

"My what?"

He clears his throat and sits up straight, simply flipping a few pages back to one that isn't full of ink.

"Your life outside of Tim," he enunciates each word slowly. "Your friends, family, work, hobbies, things in your life that belong to *you*." He tips his head to the side, and I have the most bizarre feeling that this is another test.

"I would have to have *one* of those things to be satisfied or disappointed by them. My life is Tim."

Guilt burns in my gut, and I'm not even sure why. Is it so ingrained in me to be the good little girl who never causes trouble that I can't admit my feelings without shame, even during therapy?

Tim has kept me so fucking isolated, and he pretends he's done it for my benefit, but maybe it's because he's embarrassed by his ties to me. And there is the thought I've been afraid to put into words since his birthday. Not only does he regret marrying me, but he's also embarrassed to call me his wife.

"Seraphina, look at me."

I do, and Shane's gaze reaches the deepest parts of me.

"You don't need to feel guilty for being unhappy."

My cheeks pinken, the heat painful.

"I don't!" I yell, that same guilt stabbing deep. "I *mean*, I'm not unhappy."

I grind my teeth as I correct myself, but it's too late. Shane doesn't respond, just stares like we both know how full of crap I am, and it's not worth acknowledging with words.

"So, you are satisfied with your '*nothing*' outside of your relationship?" he persists.

"No, but the way you're saying it, makes it sound like I'm not happy in my relationship either."

"Are you happy in your relationship?" he asks, ignoring my accusation and staring at the bruises on my neck. Again his tone lacks all judgment, but I can tell he's more invested than he's letting on.

"No," I whisper, and a part of my heart rips at my admission. "I don't even know *what* I like, who I *am*. It's pathetic."

"There's not a single thing about you that's pathetic, Seraphina."

"I'm a grown woman who knows nothing about herself." I look down, toying with the ends of my hair.

His long silence compels me to look up. The broad smile on his face shocks me as much as it thrills me.

"I have an idea. Are you free after this?"

My eyebrows scrunch together. It sounds like Shane's asking me out, but that can't be it.

"I am. Why?"

CHAPTER
THIRTEEN
SERA

Technicolor lights flash overhead while the bass blasts through the industrial warehouse on the outskirts of town. I've never been in a place like this, nor have I ever wanted to be, and I can't remember how Shane conned me into this. The memory of his voice is still clear, and how I felt while it wrapped around me, but what thought process led me to agree was a complete mystery.

People stick to one another in an uncomfortable cluster on the dancefloor. It must be intentional, seeing as how most of them are grinding on one another and appear to be having the time of their lives. To me, it looks terrifying and sweaty. Shane leads me along the perimeter, deeper into the warehouse, and toward the bar.

The air is thicker back here, with less oxygen because of these bodies eating it up. Is there ventilation in here? Unable to breathe, we pause as the crowd grows too thick to pass. Shane trails his fingers along my arm, distracting me from my panic and commanding my attention. I look over and catch the way the red flashing lights play with his blue eyes.

MIND TO BEND

Purple, mystery, I need to taste him.

I don't know what it is about this place, but even with all these people, it feels intimate. Aware of every inch of him, I have to look away before the intensity between us draws my lips any closer to his.

He turns me toward the dance floor and presses my back to his front, his arms snaking around to hold me tight. Before I can question his actions, his lips are at my ear.

"What do you think, Angel?"

The pet name wraps around me and spreads warmth through to my bones. It doesn't matter that my father called me the same, I *like* it on Shane's lips. I realize with an uncomfortable squirm that it's *wrong* for him to call me the same nickname my dad did. And beyond question, it is immoral that I'm turned on by that.

"*Seraphina*," he murmurs, reminding me he asked me a question.

In front of us, a pretty young woman with complicated braids and a sequin top dances with one of her friends. I'm fascinated by the sensual rhythm of their bodies and how happy and free they look. At least, I think they're friends until the girl with the braids steps into the other woman, pretty brown fingers tangling in a crush of blonde curls. She pulls the woman roughly into her and catches her lips in a deep kiss, and of course, every inch of me tenses.

My skin prickles, making me all hot and oversensitive. My nipples scrape my bra, and I twitch at the sensation. I look around, afraid. Afraid because I'm turned on by watching them. What if someone saw that? But no one is paying me any attention besides Shane.

"I shouldn't be here."

"Loosen up," I flinch at his breath sweeping across my overheated neck. "Sometimes people are nice to look at,

Seraphina. It doesn't have to be earth-shattering. Nothing you like needs to be a big deal."

His hand drifts over my shoulder, the touch isn't suggestive, somewhat comforting, but it sets me on fire as much as the slide of those tongues.

When I don't calm down, he pushes me past them with a hand at the small of my back. My overstimulated mind imagines him spinning me around and pushing my hips onto his with his hand on that same spot. His touch feels protective more than anything else, and I shake off the dirty images. Of course he's only pushing me forward to keep me from making a scene. I can't imagine what those girls would have thought if they had caught me staring.

I turn and put up my hands to stop him when I see he's leading me toward an opening on the dancefloor. "This was fun!" I shout. "But I think I should go home now."

I force a smile, and the music swallows up his laugh.

"I'm thoroughly unconvinced. You're scared!"

I shake my head, but words fail me. I am scared and so incredibly far outside my comfort zone.

"Not tonight, Angel."

There's that name again, and I'm buzzing. Have I grown wings? Because I could fly away. I miss the rest of what he said until he grabs my hand and drags me the rest of the way.

"What are you doing!" I shriek loud enough that he manages to hear me over the music.

He turns, pulling me into his arms as tightly as he did on our first meeting, and presses our bodies together. His lips find my ear, and he says, "Teaching you how to have fun."

"I can't do this!" I scream at the top of my lungs and feel his smile against my cheek rather than see it.

"Yes, you can."

His hands move to my hips. He's warm and muscular, hard along his entire body. The smell of man and high-end cologne crashes over me, and my system flies into overdrive. His presence affects me so intensely I forget to fight. Then, he's leading, moving us both to the beat, and we're *dancing*.

"You can dance?" I ask stupidly, the evidence right in front of me rolling against my hips. His eyes meet mine, and I feel something harder than a second before. Does he want me the same way I want him? My rational brain disconnects, leaving space for someone a little more reckless. Maybe someone fun.

My arms find his shoulders first, then his neck. Before I know it, I'm pressed so tightly against him that I can't even begin to imagine getting myself unstuck. He's leading me, teaching me how to move my body to the swells and crashes of the music. My face stays tucked into the crook of his neck. I've never listened to music this loud, never even heard most of these songs. There are people moving and grinding everywhere.

It only takes a few songs to forget everything but the music, the heat of the flashing lights, and the pulsing of electricity on the spots our bodies touch. I'm dying to kiss him, press our lips together and taste him, and whereas he's not discouraging me, he's not encouraging me either. For all I know, he could just be dancing with me, pretending this is the most fun he's ever had. Still, every moment of attention he pays me is worth it.

I've never had someone look at me like this, never felt like anything more than a burden or tool, but right now, I feel like freedom and happiness. I could explode from the newness, and I'm starved for more.

Before I can make a decision that either or both of us

might regret, the music dips, and Shane peels his body away from mine. I frown, but he laughs at the expression.

"I'm going to get us drinks, and you're going to dance to the next song by yourself."

"Why?" I shout back just as the opening bass line picks up. Cold without him against me, it's harder to find the beat.

"Because you never have, and I want to watch you."

I'm still as I watch him approach the bar and order. My hips can't seem to sway without him there to push me. My feet grow roots and plant themselves. When his eyes find me, he acknowledges me with a side nod and raises one brow as if to say what are you waiting for?

I stay stock-still for two seconds longer, but the fear of his disapproval has me moving. I'm awkward, so much more than when it was the two of us. I sway slightly, scared and self-conscious. Looking back at him, there is a similar something in his eyes to the day I watched him come in his office. The desire to see that again is overwhelming.

I close my eyes and let the music in, much like I did with him. I try my best to sway, but I may as well be a board. It only lasts a minute before someone taps me on the shoulder. I open my eyes to find a group of girls, including the two who were kissing when we came in. The blonde is the one who tapped me.

"He said you need girlfriends!" she shouts, pointing to the bar where Shane is watching in amusement.

"I, uh," I don't finish the thought as she wraps an arm around me and pulls me into the group.

"Come on! I'm Sophia, and this is Ava." She points to the pretty woman I watched her kiss. "That's Kat, Kelly, and Faedra."

Each of the girls offers me a wave.

"Let's dance!" someone shouts.

Before I know it, I'm completely wrapped up in dancing with them and having the best time. Instead of pushing me, Shane watches me from the bar as I spend my first-ever girls' night dancing and carrying on with the world's most supportive people: unknown drunk girls at the club.

They are *wasted*. So much so that I'm sure they'll never remember me in the morning, though I will never forget them. I'm grateful for every giggle and sway. It's not until Shane puts my address into the GPS that the freedom and joy are replaced by crushing sadness.

"What's wrong?" he asks as he pulls onto my street.

"Nothing. That was the best night of my life." I don't just sound sad, I realize, but angry too.

"Why are you so upset about that?" He knows why, but he wants to make me acknowledge it.

"I'm married, Shane. One night dancing with my psychiatrist and a handful of strangers shouldn't have felt that good."

"But it did?" he asks me, and once again, I love and hate the direct way he guides me to the point of the issue.

"You know it did."

"Seraphina, if there's anything I've learned about you in the short time we've known each other, it's how incredibly small your world is. This was *nothing*. What you experienced today isn't one shred of the joy and excitement you should know. I need you to think long and hard about the type of life you want to lead and how you plan to get it."

I want to be hurt by his words, but part of me understands what he's saying all too well.

He can give me all of that and more.

"Come see me tomorrow. We'll have your next lesson in enjoying life."

His smile is small but smug. He knows I can't resist

anything he offers me. The only thing I was still strong enough to resist was crossing the boundaries of our physical relationship. Although his not pressing me for it only made me want him more.

I agree to come and see him as I step out of the car. I shut the door behind me, but I hear the window roll down.

"Two o'clock," he calls after me.

"Whenever you say," I answer, not realizing how true that statement is and how far it extends. Whenever, whatever, I'm not sure I *can* tell him no.

I look back as I walk up to the door. Shane is watching me but pulls away as I unlock and open the door. I assume he's trying to help me avoid an uncomfortable conversation, but my heart twinges with rejection. I step into the house, ignoring Tim sitting on the couch.

"Where were you?!" he shouts, lunging to his feet.

"Dancing. Are you going to choke me for it?" I spit back. If he's going to hurt me again then so be it. But he's injured and slow, and I'm not afraid like last time.

Tim's jaw hangs open and I walk away, leaving him standing there. I close my bedroom door behind me and lock it. I'm not waking up next to him again, and if he wants to get to me, he's going to have to break it down.

CHAPTER FOURTEEN
SERA

THE NEXT DAY I WAKE TO SUNLIGHT STREAMING THROUGH the curtains—I must have been exhausted because I never sleep in. Tim left me alone for the night, and for that, I'm relieved, though I'm dreading having to face him now. I quickly shower, dress, and sneak out of the house before I can figure out if he's home or not. He is, I realize as I dart past his truck and walk around the block to where I parked my car before I went out with Shane.

Fully aware of how bad this looks, I'm relieved Tim didn't notice where I parked or my escape. How am I going to handle the situation when I have to face him? If Tim knew of my intention to see Shane again, he would try to stop me. He's already made it clear he doesn't trust him. What would Tim think if he knew who I went dancing with and why?

Like my husband, these aren't problems I plan on facing now. There's a fancy café on the far side of town near Shane's office. I've never been there before but always wanted to, and now seems like the perfect time. So I drive over, park on the street, and head inside. A girl my age stands behind the counter, and I order a coffee and biscotti. I ask her for a job application, and while I doubt I'll ever turn it in, it's going to be a while before two o'clock rolls around.

I find a table near the window where I can watch people pass. It's not nearly as glamorous as they make it seem in movies, and I quickly wish I had a new phone like everyone else. Mine is clunky, outdated, and barely works even with free Wi-Fi. I thank my lucky stars when I spot a bookshelf in the corner full to the brim with well-worn titles. I head over and pick one before I head back up to the counter and order another coffee. I don't want to get kicked out.

It's about twelve forty-five, and I am deep into an old mystery novel when I hear the chair opposite mine pull out. My mouth pops open as I see Shane taking the seat. He's holding a paper mug like mine and a little plate with a muffin.

"Mind if I eat with you?" he asks after he's already settled.

"Hi," I squeak.

"Hi," he smiles back. "I was surprised to see you here. I come here almost every day, all different times, and I've never seen you."

"It's my first time."

I don't understand why he's looking at me like he wants to eat me alive.

"How lucky for me, then."

"Mm," I take a sip of my drink to keep from having to speak.

"Are you sure you're not following me?" There's a joking lilt to his voice, but anxiety sparks in my stomach.

He won't keep seeing me as a patient if he genuinely thinks that. I shake my head but say nothing. There's a long stretch of quiet between us where I get the impression he wants me to say something, but I have no idea what.

"Are you planning on coming to our appointment this afternoon?" he finally offers.

"Of course!" My brow wrinkles, and he laughs easily.

"Don't be so surprised. I wasn't sure after last night. I *thought* you had a fantastic time, but you didn't seem too happy when I left you."

He's looking me up and down, and while he sounds casual, I'm sure he's tense. Did I hurt his feelings last night with my melancholy? I sigh heavily. That can't be it. Despite the crossed lines, he hasn't done anything to make me believe he wants me in the same way I want him.

"I both had a fantastic time and wasn't happy when you left me, but I had every intention of coming to our appointment. That's why I'm here." I shrug.

"What do you mean? Our appointment is over an hour away, and *this* is a coffee shop, not my office."

"I've been waiting for our appointment. I can't stand being in the house with Tim," I shiver at the thought. "And this is close by. It seemed like a good time to hang out and drink coffee."

"Since when?" his breezy tone is gone, replaced by a curt chill.

"Since when what?"

"Since when have you been waiting here for *me*?"

My cheeks redden. "Oh, I, a while."

He reaches across the table, his fingers brushing the back of my knuckles.

"Hours?"

I bite my lip, trying to think of a way to deny it. He picks up the book I've been reading and judges from how far I've gotten.

"Seraphina, is this book from that shelf?" He points across the room to the shelf it came from.

What am I supposed to do? Lie? I say nothing.

"You've been here for hours."

I can't look at him.

His hand moves from my knuckles to my chin, forcing me to look up.

"I always have time for you, and I'll never make you wait. Next time, call me."

His blue eyes are so sincere and beautiful. The blue sweater he is wearing makes them look even more intense.

"You have other patients," I argue. He doesn't and can't *always* have time for me. I certainly can't always think he's a phone call away.

"And?"

"They require your time."

"Mm," he agrees but doesn't consider it a problem. "But I'll be the one to decide how much of it."

"I can't call you. I only have your office number."

"I'll give you my cell."

"But then I could call you anytime."

He laughs, as in actually laughs. The sound is so beautiful it hurts and hollows out my chest.

"So you see the point of me giving you my number."

He's teasing me, but I'm too stunned to care.

"Do you give your personal number to all of your patients?"

"No. I don't take them dancing either."

"Why me?"

The fingers on my chin move to my temple and then into my hair. "Because you're special, Angel. No more waiting for me. Drive over, and I'll meet you at the office now."

He gets up, and I stand after him.

He thinks I'm special. What am I supposed to do with that?

～

I'M NERVOUS AS I DRIVE OVER, PARK THE CAR, AND HEAD into the building. But when I hit the elevator, that nervousness turns into anticipation, and I want to be with him again so badly I wish the elevator moved faster.

Tasha isn't at her desk, and I thank Shane for bringing me in during her lunch break. I can't stand the girl, and I don't know if those feelings are fair. Probably not, but that doesn't take away from my relief. I head down the hall and find his office door open; he's still taking his coat off. I'm cold, but I do the same as I sit in my usual spot on the comfortable black leather and wait for him.

He sits across from me, and we just look at each other.

"Have you thought at all about our conversation last night?" he begins without any other preamble.

"Which one?"

He smiles as if he's been caught. "I was hoping you would tell me."

"I've been thinking about all of them, the whole night."

"And have you come to any conclusions?"

"None that aren't depressing," I say sarcastically.

His smile grows.

"I need to talk to you about a sensitive topic."

I nod, waiting for him to continue.

"Sex."

"Why do we need to talk about sex?" I sound terrified, but part of me is just as eager to hear what Doctor Shane has to say about sex.

"Sex is the primary reason you came to therapy, isn't it? And last night we were discussing all the things your life is lacking, all the things you can do for yourself, and this is one of them."

"Do for myself?" I repeat. "You can't have sex with yourself."

"Of course you can, Seraphina. Virginity is nothing more than a social construct. Sex is a million different things, a million different ways. The important thing with sex is how you feel about it. And you can make love to yourself, fuck yourself, or anything in between. Sexuality can be spiritual and enlightening, primal and debasing. It can be whatever is right for *you*."

"Right for *me*?"

"Yes. Exactly right for you whether you have no partner or many."

My face is so red it's painful.

"Many partners?"

He smirks. "You don't need to have many if you don't want to either. That's kind of the point."

"I mean, I don't know if sex is really that important."

I think I know how stupid I sound as I'm speaking, but if I have any doubt, it's cemented by his expression as he watches me minimize myself and my feelings.

"Have you ever orgasmed, Seraphina?"

My mouth drops open, and my cheeks flood with heat. *No*, but I don't say it. I'm breathing too loud, and I'm confident I've answered Shane's question without saying a word.

"Masturbation?"

"Doesn't work for me," I admit through dry lips.

"So, you've tried?"

"A few times, yes."

My fingers twist together, squeezing tight enough to keep me from bouncing in my seat.

"Can you tell me why it didn't work?"

I think about the fumbling times I touched myself. Twice in the shower and twice more lying in bed. Neither produced results that were particularly pleasurable. Everything about it felt awkward, from the idea and planning straight to the execution.

"It felt *wrong*," I decide because there are just too many complicated nuances to how awful I found the experience.

"So your issues are moral?"

I'm pink again, and my mouth is so dry it sticks to itself, "Not in the sense that I believe it's wrong, no."

"Then in what sense *are* they moral?"

I can't help the full-body tingles I get from his attention. Tim has never anticipated a thing about me, and Shane hearing the disclaimer in my words, tells me he knows me better than the man who married me.

"It's hard to feel sexy when a little voice inside you is screaming how sinful you are."

He nods, "Was it just the mental side you found problematic or the physical as well?"

"Honestly? Both. I've watched porn and read a lot of websites, but every time I've reached down there and tried, it just feels weird and wrong. I've never felt anything close to enjoyable, and I think I'm broken."

"You're not broken."

Tears sting my eyes, but I swallow them down. I stare at my fingers like they're the most interesting thing in the world. I'm so embarrassed and overwhelmed by everything I've admitted, everything I'm feeling.

"Seraphina, look at me."

I do as he says and meet the eyes that hold oceans.

"You are not broken. You are perfect."

I let out an irritated huff. "Perfect as I am? As God *made* me?" I taunt, shocked at my animosity. I always keep it so tightly under wraps.

"No, Seraphina."

I'm unsure if the heat in his eyes is anger or arousal, but it acts as a magnet, and I unconsciously lean toward him.

"You are perfect. Full stop. *Perfection*. No contingencies, no creators, just you."

My mouth is hanging open again, and I can't even force myself to close it.

"I am *not* perfect." I manage to refute him.

"That's a completely valid yet entirely wrong opinion, and you're entitled to it." I open my mouth to argue. "But I don't think your low opinion of yourself is the issue this time. And you *can* orgasm."

"How can you be so sure?"

"I can prove it." His tongue runs along his parted lips. "Do you trust me, Seraphina?"

CHAPTER
FIFTEEN
SERA

Do I trust him?

As far as doctor-patient exchanges go, I must admit that Shane's actions are far from ethical. But I also have to point out how complicit I have been in that. I asked him to hold me time and time again, agreed to dance with him, and watched him while he came. Those things trampled the lines between us, but I wanted it that way. I didn't have to come back here, but I did, and there's a reason for that.

Empirically, the answer is no. I shouldn't trust Shane. He is not behaving as someone should in his position. Yet, that reasonable part of my brain means nothing to the whole because my trust in Shane emanates from somewhere deep inside me that could not give less of a fuck about state boards.

"Yes," I answer, wide-eyed as I compare myself to Eve taking the apple from the serpent.

He smiles briefly, but the expression oozes such satisfaction that heat travels from my knees to my neck.

"I'd like to help you."

I'm fascinated by how his lips move and his throat dips as he swallows.

"I want that too."

"Then spread your legs."

I'm wearing leggings, and absolutely nothing is revealed by doing as he asks, but his gaze heats, and I freeze as I stare at my thighs.

"If you don't want to do this, say the word, and I'll stop. I will never bring it up again or ask to do anything more than what a psychiatrist should. But something tells me you don't just want my help. You need it, and you're much too good of a girl to ask for it."

I sit there speechless, not opening my legs, not arguing. Am I a good girl? I don't feel like one. But I can't deny I want to be one for him or how desperate, wet, and aching I am at the thought of pleasing him.

"Am I making you uncomfortable, Seraphina?"

I shake my head because he's not. But I'm uncomfortable from the deep and needy ache inside me. I'm *hollow* and as aroused by the idea of needing to be filled as I am disgusted with myself for thinking it.

"If you want my help, spread your legs. If not, I swear I'll lean back and never bring it up again."

Before he can press his back to the chair and close the door on my most depraved desires, my legs snap open. The wicked grin on Shane's face tells me I played into his mind games exactly how he expected.

Fuck, I'm going to hell.

"You should close your eyes. It will make this easier."

I should question him. At least *ask* how he plans to help get me off. But, instead, I let my eyes fall closed.

"I'm not watching you, Seraphina. You are safe. Why don't we start with some breathing exercises?"

I'm nervous, but I'm relieved. Breathing doesn't seem so scary. I listen as Shane instructs me to lean my head back while he takes me through a long series of breathing exercises. At first, I find them annoying, then kind of meditative. By the time he's led me through the fifth one, I'm more relaxed and looser than I have ever been, maybe, even a little drunk. My limbs float beside me, completely out of order. Shane's still talking, and my body responds to him as if his words are sinking in and becoming part of me.

When his deep, even voice says, "Rub your pussy through the fabric," I don't question it. Instead, I reach down tentatively, my fingers trailing the sensitive skin. My eyes stay closed as my fingers continue drifting up and down. There's a light tickle, and I feel much more aroused than the last time I tried to touch myself, but nothing spectacular is happening.

"How does that feel?"

It's the first question he's asked since he started taking me through this hypnotic relaxation process. I don't feel like myself, and while I try to form the words to tell him it's nice or okay, when nothing comes out, I shrug.

"Use your words, Seraphina."

His command unlocks something in me, and I open my mouth to speak.

"It's okay. It tingles a bit but isn't amazing."

"It's not supposed to feel amazing, Seraphina. It's supposed to tease you and make you want more. Do you want more?"

I try to think for a moment, but it takes longer than usual. I'm so attuned to my thoughts that I feel like I *am* them. I'm horny down to my fucking bones. I'm so wet my leggings are clinging to my thighs. I vaguely realize I swore in my thoughts, which is odd. Something about this *is* weird, yet I can't bring myself to care.

"Tell me what you want, Seraphina."

"I want more."

"Slip your fingers inside your leggings." I do, and even though I know exactly where they are supposed to go, my fingers are trapped and obediently waiting for him. "Find your clit."

I reach between my labia, trying to do as he said. I know where it is in theory. This should be easy. My fingers search, not finding it, and a sense of unease swells inside me. I want to do as he says, but I can't. This isn't working. I'm wrong. My shoulders tense, and in this supremely vulnerable place, I'm sure my failure will result in punishment.

"Seraphina, relax. Take a breath for me."

I obey immediately and completely. My fingers still, my shoulders fall, and I drift into an almost thoughtless sort of contentment.

"Tell me what's wrong."

"I can't find my clit, and it aches." I'm whining, and part of me knows I should be embarrassed by how desperately needy I am. Part of me knows I shouldn't be doing this at all, but I don't feel in control.

"Do you want me to help you find it?" Shane's smooth voice continues, guiding me through this odd experience.

"Yes and no,"

"Tell me in detail what's bothering you."

"I want to orgasm so bad it hurts, but I don't want to be a cheater."

"I won't touch you," he promises. "I'm just going to help you make yourself come."

"What should I do?"

"Get naked from the waist down, and spread your thighs. I need a good look at you."

His words fill my body with heat, and the spot between my thighs pools with arousal. I wonder if he'll be able to see it, and I'm both embarrassed and turned on by the idea.

My hands feel disconnected, I try to push my legging down, but I'm not getting it.

"Open your eyes."

I do, and for some reason, I couldn't do that without his say-so. Next, I remove my leggings and spread myself wide for Shane.

"As wide as you can, Seraphina, and then look at yourself."

Again, I comply.

"You're a very good girl, Seraphina. You take direction so well."

His praise washes over me like a steaming bubble bath. I have always been very obedient, but Shane has me feeling so much more than that. I feel pliable and suggestible. I'd do anything for him.

"Spread your cunt so I can see every inch of you and help you find that clit."

I reach down with both hands and spread myself wide, revealing every inch to him and me. I've never heard that word used in a sexual context, but instead of scandalized, I appreciate the hotness. I like how quick, sharp, and wrong it sounds.

I hear him stand and start to approach me. I want to look up and meet his eyes, but I can't do anything other than what he tells me. I stare at my parted cunt, because that's what he called it, and no other word seems to make sense anymore. My *cunt* is so wet I can see the liquid gathering at my entrance. I know he can see it too, and yet there is no shame. I'm only burning for what happens next.

He drops to his knees in front of me, and he's close enough to my cunt that I can finally see him without moving my eyes. He's concentrating on the pink flesh I'm showing him. His scrutiny is serious, and deep down, I know this depth of attention should make me nervous. In fact, I should squirm and blush and close my thighs rather than stare obediently.

"I think I see the problem," his voice is matter-of-fact, and rather than feeling terror at the word problem, I remain patient for his analysis. I wonder if Tim somehow knows there's something wrong with me without ever getting this close.

"What's the problem?" my voice sounds like it belongs to someone else.

"Your pretty little clit is tiny, Angel. I bet if I sucked it for you, I could get it nice and swollen and sensitive."

I don't respond. It's not a question.

"You would love the way that felt, wouldn't you, Angel?"

"I don't know." That's the truth. That name, he's called me Angel a few times before, but now it makes me tingle from head to toe.

"Your clit is little, Angel."

As he promised, he hasn't touched me, but I sense how much he wants to. His need is so potent that it's reaching me in my dreamlike state, and I cannot help but respond to it.

"Do you want me to suck on it for you? That way, you can find it easier while I teach you how to masturbate."

I don't answer because I still don't know.

"Tell me what's holding you back."

"Is having a small clit bad?" I ask, releasing my self-doubt. I'm watching myself as he instructs, and he's so close to my parted flesh I watch him lick his lips hungrily in my periphery.

"You're perfect, Angel. I swear."

"Please suck my clit for me, Doctor Shane."

In half a second, his mouth is on me. He's not licking me how I have seen and heard oral sex described. Instead, he's doing what he offered *precisely*. He's sucking on my clit, giving it a kind of pressure and attention I scarcely understand. The obscene pleasure registers in my brain, and I cry out only once before he releases me.

Dear God, I had a mouth on my cunt, and all I can think about is how badly I want more. Shane leans back, staying close so he can inspect my progress.

"Nice and swollen now, Angel. Touch yourself."

I reach down, and sure enough, the tiny pleasure center is swollen, engorged with blood, and so much easier to find. Shane stands and, I assume, goes to his desk. He returns with a compact makeup mirror, and I wonder who he got it from as he kneels in front of me.

"Look at the mirror."

My eyes flick to the reflection.

"Your cunt is small, Angel. Your clit is small, but the significant issue is that your hood covers it."

As I probe myself, he tilts the mirror so I can see what he means. It feels good, but it's nothing compared to when he latched his mouth to it.

"It might help if you pull your hood back while you touch it, or it might be too sensitive. Try it and see what you prefer."

I look at myself in the mirror, doing as he said and pulling back the skin covering my clitoris. I touch it with my fingertip, and *oh fuck*. It's so much more sensitive this way.

"Oh, God," a surprised moan escapes me.

He chuckles, "Everyone likes it in different ways, Angel. Try circles, side to side, up and down." I try each one, spending a few minutes giving them their proper due. I *really* like up and down. My hips start bouncing in time with my hand.

"You're doing so good. I bet you feel amazing right now. Your cunt is so pretty."

I *do* feel amazing. Shane's words are building me up to an impossible high, along with the sensations and weightlessness of the situation. I don't know why I'm not thinking straight, and I don't care. There's something wrong, though, and I can't place it.

"This feels good, but I don't think I'm going to come." I sound defeated, almost whimpering.

"Look at my face," I do, and there's a haziness around him as if his face is all I can see. He regards me with pity, like helping me is the only thing he wants in the world. "Can I help you, Angel? Only with my fingers and maybe my tongue. I promise I will only touch your pretty cunt. Just let me help you come."

"Please," I whine frantically, beyond thought. Shane leans forward, and he spreads me further. I let out a startled moan as his finger pushes into my entrance and stretches me out. He gets further in than I expected before he meets resistance. My hymen is still in place.

"This may sting."

"I need to come," I answer as I twitch my hips forward, coming just short of using his hand to take my own virginity.

"You're incredible. I'm so proud of you for taking what you want from my hand. Are you going to take your pleasure the same way, dirty Angel?"

I twitch my hips forward. The need is indescribable,

but I can't get past that stupid skin myself. I don't know how.

He smiles wickedly. "Don't worry, Angel. I've got you this time." He pushes into me. My hymen breaks under two of his fingers. He doesn't need much time to find a spot inside me that makes me see stars. "Keep rubbing that little clit. I'm teaching *you* how to do this, remember."

"Yes, Shane." Though it sounds more like a moan, it's the first time I've said his name, and he groans in response.

I keep rubbing my clit. He's stroking my insides, filling me, and pumping into me in a sublime rhythm I can't explain, and that's when I notice this pressure building inside of me.

"I'm going to pee!" I complain.

"No, you're not. Just relax."

The most intense wave of pleasure washes over me. I'm shaking, my body convulsing, and I'm peeing everywhere. The haze I've been under shatters with my orgasm, and I'm wrung out to my bones.

"I'm so sorry," I start apologizing when Shane dives face-first into my spread flesh, licking the liquid from my lips, thighs, and the leather couch. "Oh my God! Ew! What are you doing? I peed!"

He laughs as his tongue laves the puddle, "It's not pee, Seraphina. It's squirt." He looks up at me with a mischievous smile on his face. "Well, there's a little bit of pee in it, but it's mostly your cum. And it happens to be fucking *delicious.*"

"My cum?" I ask. My brain still hasn't engaged.

"That little cunt came hard," he shrugs as he stands. "If you don't want me to take your virginity, it's time for you to put your pants on."

The image of Tim pops into my head, and instead of

letting Shane take it, I put my leggings on and let the shame overwhelm me.

What the fuck did I do?

I don't look at him as I try to make myself presentable.

"Seraphina," my eyes flick up to his, "I'll see you for our next session. Please let Tim know he still has his appointment if he wants it."

"You'd still see him?"

"Of course." He looks insulted by the suggestion. "He's gone through a traumatic experience, and if I can help him process that, I'm more than happy to."

"Oh, okay."

I pick up my bag and head for the door, my cheeks hurt in embarrassment, and I have no clue what to do or say. Shane stands there, the picture of ease with his lips still wet from me. I'm hot and aching all over, and I hate myself so fucking much right now because the shame and the desire both burn equally. I don't even notice that I'm cursing in my thoughts more regularly.

My hand is on the knob when he says, "I'll see you next week, Seraphina." His voice is level, so perfectly even. I, on the other hand, am a complete mess.

"Mhm…"

I use all my self-control to walk out of the office rather than run full tilt.

He doesn't follow after me, and I'm grateful for it. I need to be alone. I need to be alone so fucking bad, but I'm out of time. My "errands" shouldn't take more than a couple of hours, and Tim will question where I've been. Surely he doesn't suspect the truth, though after last night, he may be closer than I want him to be. And I want to die for what I've done.

I don't think I've ever felt so low, and I've never hated myself this way. But, like the dirty slut I am, I enjoy the pulsing throb in my cunt, and I know I'm turned on by how wrong this is. Whatever Shane's done, it has broken a wall, and the word seems to fit now. I'm aroused by how ashamed I am. I long to return to whatever place he brought me, and I know he's the only one who can take me there since I've never been there before.

CHAPTER
SIXTEEN
SHANE

It's been two days since I gave Sera her first orgasm and sucked her clean of her cum. Sitting at my desk and indulging in fantasy, the phantom taste of her rolls on my tongue, teasing my mind and cock with how fucking good it was to have her, but also with how incomplete it was.

I didn't plan to put her under hypnosis and take advantage of her, but when thinking over the facts, I cannot deny what I did. I'm not a master hypnotist, and I couldn't make someone do something they didn't want to, but fuck, Seraphina is highly suggestible, and she wants it. The exercises were meant to relax her, not to put her in a trance.

The entire experience feels more like a dream than a reality. Seraphina was so perfect, with her pale eyes watching me in fascination. Her plush lips shaped into an "o" of shock and pleasure. Her chest flushed and heaved as I pumped my fingers into her.

I can't be in this office anymore without thinking about her. I swear I can still smell her sweetness in here, though I know it's only my imagination. I asked Tasha if she smelled something off yesterday, and she told me she didn't. I think she would've reacted in a different way if it smelled like stale sex when I asked her about it.

I'm a little embarrassed by how violently I beat my dick after Seraphina left. The smell of her *was* everywhere, never mind the taste of her exploding on my tongue. But, the most arousing part of all came as a surprise to me: her *shame*.

The terrified look in her eyes as her first-ever orgasm hit her, and the look of pain as she realized just how deep of a line she had crossed. Every flicker of emotion on her face turned me on, which is another matter that has me *divided*.

She's mine, and when she accepts that, she'll realize she's done nothing wrong. Tim is merely a placeholder, and there's no reason to feel guilty for falling into the pull of true love, especially when he is far from being a loving husband. But do I want to give up her flame-red cheeks or the little dip in her chest as she shudders in shame-filled ecstasy?

I consider all this as I stare at the couch. A desperate part of me wants to run my fingers over the spot she made and rub my dick, but I'm not that sad. Although it's been two days, and I'd like to say I've been a functioning member of society, I haven't. I have canceled all my appointments and instead spent that time following Seraphina, creeping into her room while she sleeps, and generally trying to relish her warmth.

Tim is being a prick to her, and If I'm honest, I'm tempted to repeat the hand exercise, but that would only make things harder for Seraphina, and that's the last thing I want to do.

I'm not sure he's coming in today, but Seraphina reminded Tim of the appointment. Knowing the intimate details of her life is worth subjecting myself to the undignified position of lurking beneath her hedges. The light blinks on my desk phone; Tasha's paging me to let me know my next patient is here. Well, Timmy, it's showtime.

The hall between reception and my office is long. I imagine myself in his head as he walks, trying to gauge when he will open that door, and I guess I have about ten seconds left before he walks in. I school my features, making them warm, open, and friendly. The kind of person people like opening up to, confiding in.

He doesn't knock before he walks right in, and that alone irks me; announcing your arrival is a simple courtesy. *What if I was rubbing my dick to the thought of your wife?* A small, sarcastic voice asks. For once, I agree with it. Although Seraphina being his wife is a technicality at best.

Tim is handsome, and I can see why an impressionable young girl would fall for him. His hair is in that odd stage of growth between short and long that looks like he has no clue what to do with it. His eyes are a vivid blue, but they're red-rimmed, not like he's been crying but drinking.

He regards me with a venomous look, and I deduce he's here because he knows what I did to his hand or what I did to his wife. Though, it doesn't take long for my suspicions to wane because even he isn't that much of a coward to only give me a dirty look if he had the faintest idea.

"Dr. Shane," he says as he walks in and takes a seat.

The cast on his arm is dirtier than it should be, but it matches his ratty work clothes. He doesn't stink or anything, but he looks unwashed.

"Tim, please," I say, gesturing toward the seat he's already taking. "Seraphina filled me in on the basic details of the injury but nothing specific. I hope you're not in too much pain."

The anger on his face flickers with a hint of doubt. My face is a picture of utter sincerity.

"It's not that bad," he answers me, sounding younger all of a sudden.

"Well, I didn't mean to bring it up if it's not what you're here to talk about today." I gesture toward him broadly. "I'll be honest with you, Tim. After our last meeting, I'm surprised to see you, especially with your injury. I presume you must have had a serious reason to come in alone."

He deflates like a popped beach ball while fear and bitterness replace his anger. "Yeah, things are really fucked up."

He runs his good hand through his hair, messing it up and making it look even more ill-kept.

"I am so fucking mad at Sera for bringing us here, but since she already opened that can of worms, maybe I can get something out of it."

It's a fair enough thought. A lot of people are dragged to therapy against their will by partners, and many of them gain a lot from the experience. Of course, many still break up anyway, but they learn a lot about themselves in the process, and while that's not the end goal when you enter a relationship, deep knowledge of who you are isn't something to ignore.

"What do you want to get out of it?"

He looks at me like I'm stupid, then makes an annoyed sound like he thinks *he's* stupid and tugs at his hair.

"I'm not smart like Sera, and I'm not good at talking about feelings."

"That's okay." He's either lying about that, or he's smarter than he realizes because he's an expert at playing Seraphina. "Our feelings are how we feel. They can be incredibly complicated, but there are simple roots for all of them. So how do you feel, Tim?"

He looks lost. "I don't know."

"So, confused, maybe?"

He sighs, deflating all over again. "Yeah, I'm confused."

"Any other big things you're feeling?"

"I'm so fucking sad, but I don't even know why."

I'm surprised by the tiny bolt of pity I feel for him, and a concrete plan forms. He doesn't *love* my soulmate. Not in any way that counts, and I pity him. As bad as he is for her, he is stuck with someone wrong for him as much as she is. What if Tim wants out more than anyone?

"Are you always sad, Tim?"

He looks up at me, his blue eyes going soft, and then I see a familiar flicker, shame. It's not delicious on him like it is on Seraphina. Instead, it's ridiculous.

"No, I'm not," he admits. "Only when I'm with Sera or thinking about the fact I'm married to her."

My eyebrows furrow in surprise, which is a normal response. But what I want to say is, how the fuck could you feel that way about the sun in human form?

"Do you know why you feel that way around her?"

He looks back and forth, trying to figure out a way to say what's so clear on his mind. "I'm not good with feelings and shit. I swear it sounds stupid, but sad and confused is more than I had before this appointment."

He's visibly upset and shaken. I know I can help all of us. I can steer us all exactly where we need to go.

"Can I, can I tell you about us? Maybe you can help me figure this shit out."

I smile at him with genuine warmth. I want nothing more than to hear the intimate details about how he and Sera came together and married so young. These are details that no amount of stalking can garner if no one is talking about it.

"Please do. I have the next hour clear if we need."

MIND TO BEND

"I met Sera when we were babies. Our dads are the best of friends, and our moms..." he trails off, looking into the corner like it's much further away. "Being in similar situations that they couldn't escape brought them together."

"Where are they now?" I already know the answer.

"Dead," he answers with a heavy breath. "Our dads weren't easy men to live with, and Sera and I leaned on each other a lot. After our moms died a year apart, we were inseparable."

He's quiet for a while.

"Did it become romantic between the two of you immediately upon your mothers dying?"

"I'm not sure it's ever been *romantic*."

It takes everything in me not to tell him he's a dick for saying it like the idea is absurd, but I know I've fucked up; he senses my displeasure.

"Don't get me wrong. Sera is beautiful, and I *do* love her, but I married her to get away, and that choice only trapped me further."

"Do you mean that you're trapped in your marriage?"

He shakes his head, "We were supposed to get married at eighteen. Sera's dad is the pastor, and we knew that was the only way he would ever let her go. My dad is a mean drunk bastard, but he's devout. The two of them are the best of friends."

"The two of you have only been married eighteen months. What happened if you were meant to be married years ago?

"When I told my father I was marrying Sera, he was drunker than I realized. He started screaming about sin, shame, and a whole bunch of stuff I didn't understand. He punched me in the face before I could even figure out why he was angry." He looks lost as he stares at the ground like the memory is too heavy and dark to see past.

"Why was he so angry, Tim?"

"He thought I had gotten her pregnant. He thought I took the virginity of his best friend's daughter. He thought we were eloping to protect her reputation. So he—" Tim swallows hard. "He beat me pretty bad, broke my leg in a couple of places. I wasn't destined for the major leagues or anything, but I played football and was good enough to at least play in college. Well, before he did that, anyway.

"I had a small football scholarship and another one that I won because of the circumstances of my mom's death. But without the football scholarship, I couldn't get out anymore."

"And *Sera*?" The nickname sticks in my throat.

"She felt like it was her fault, so she stayed with me even when I'd rather she went away. She's always been so goddamn good and sweet. How can you tell someone like that, that you hate them because they remind you of every shitty thing that's ever happened to you? How can I fuck her when most of the time I can barely look at her?"

I'm feeling a lot of things right now. "You hate her?"

"Yes!" he almost shouts, "No..." His head is in his hands. "I love her, but I'm not in love with her, and I never have been."

"It sounds like you both tied yourselves to each other out of obligation."

He lets out a low, miserable moan, confirming my suspicions.

"Tim, look at me." It takes him a minute, but he does. "I'm not supposed to tell you this, but I think I can make things a lot easier for you. Please try to listen to what I'm saying rather than getting emotional. Can you do that for me?"

He nods, looking a bit scared but also excited.

"Sera isn't happy with you either." Unfortunately, his response isn't as instantaneously happy as I hoped. He looks crushed.

"She's not!?" he sounds like a little kid. For all his blustering and bravado about his motivations with her, it's clear he depends on her.

"Honestly, Tim, think about it."

He does, taking his sweet time. At this point, we'll need the next hour and maybe the one after that, but it's worth it if this works.

"She can't be happy. We don't even have a real marriage. It's legal, but other than that, it's a sham. Sera is a smart girl." A tear slides down his cheek, and I'm shocked at the sight. "Is she leaving me?"

"No, Tim. You know she could never do that to you." He sucks in a gasp as if I've wounded him. Of course it was only a guess, but it seems to ring true.

"She would never leave me even if she was dying to. So is she dying to leave me?"

I could say yes, but manipulation that heavy-handed doesn't work. "No."

I crinkle my brow and shake my head, trying to soften whatever he's feeling. I don't want him to leave Sera in an angry fit. I want him to do it maturely and calmly so she can have closure.

"She loves you, Tim, but we all know neither of you is satisfied in this marriage. Tim, she's never had an orgasm."

The lie falls freely, but my cock gets so damn hard I resist the urge to fist it through my pants.

"Are you serious?" he asks with an expression that looks startlingly like pity, and the softening I felt for him dies in my chest. My angel doesn't need his pity.

"Very, Tim. Can you imagine how unsatisfied she is? Do you imagine she can't feel the lack of love?"

He sticks a finger in his mouth and chews at his nail bed. "It sounds like you're saying that staying with Sera is cruel."

"What do you think?"

"Sera is a better girl than I'm treating her like, and she probably feels like shit because I act like she's awful. Why can't I let this shit go?"

"Tim, you don't need to be upset with yourself for that. You went through an extremely traumatic series of abuse, and it is a pity Sera triggers memories of all that loss and pain. It's unfortunate, but it sounds like you are in a fundamentally doomed relationship."

"It was doomed before I married her," he agrees, and I resist the urge to punch him. He knew he didn't love her in the only way that mattered when he took those vows, and he shouldn't have done it. Those were my vows to make. I hate this prick, but I understand him now, which means I'll have no problem controlling him.

"Do you know what you need to do?"

"I don't even care about this shit with her anymore. I need to figure out who did this to my arm and get revenge. And I need to do that without Sera breathing down my fucking neck, so I'm going to tell her tonight. It's the only way."

I'm so satisfied I nearly grin, but I force myself to ask what I would under normal circumstances. "Your arm?"

"I don't want to talk about it." He reinforces what he said earlier, but I am curious to know what Tim thinks about his attacker and if he regrets touching what's mine. He hasn't mentioned the spousal abuse, and neither have I. He will leave her tonight, and it won't matter once she and I are living happily ever after.

"That's quite alright, Tim. A word of advice?"

"Please, anything." He puts up his hands in a pleading gesture.

"Pack your bag before you break the news. That way, you can leave quickly and let her have space to process. Then, you don't need to fight with one another."

He nods gravely.

"You're right. This is going to hurt her, but I don't need to do anything to make it worse. And with me out of her hair, I'm sure Sera'll see this is a good thing in no time."

"I think you're right." And because I'm a sick bastard, and I understand my mark, I tell him, "I'm proud of the work you've done today."

A light flush lifts into his cheek. As I guessed, his drunk fuck of a dad never gave him much praise. Male-on-male affection is a funny thing. It is frowned upon by so many, but it is so damn essential to every one of us. There isn't a man alive who has never needed the praise and approval of another man. A father's approval is one of the most basic things a boy can crave, and Tim is starved for positive male bonds.

He clears his throat. "Thanks, Shane. Uhm, can I come back on my own? You know it won't be couple's counseling after I end this, but maybe we can keep this thing going?"

He's so awkward it's almost sweet, and that's when I hear myself saying, "Sure, Tim. Sounds great to me." If he does as he's supposed to and leaves Sera, I will be more than happy to help him sort his life out. It will be his reward for making things easier for me.

"Thank you for today. I didn't realize how much I needed this."

"Of course, Tim. Anytime."

CHAPTER
SEVENTEEN
SERA

Tim left a little over three hours ago. I'm sitting on the couch, literally sweating at the thought of him coming home from his therapy appointment. After everything that happened, I never thought he would go, and my guilty conscience says it's because he already suspects my act of infidelity. Maybe he even knows for sure now.

We haven't spoken in days. Things are worse than ever, and that's saying something. I can't imagine what's going through Tim's head anymore. I like to tell myself that I used to, that it's not my judgment that's lacking, and that Tim has changed. Though I'm not so convinced by that line anymore, and I question if I have *ever* known my husband, despite having known him all my life.

The sun set a few minutes ago, but the sky is not in total darkness yet. I'm twitchy and ready to jump out of my skin. So much so that when the front door opens, I yelp. Tim looks at me, and the expression on his face has my heart sinking. Whatever it is, it's not good.

Tight lines accentuate his eyes. His brows furrow

together, and I notice he's been mercilessly dragging his hands through his too-long hair.

"Hey, Ser," he blurts the old nickname my mom used to call me, and all of my alarm bells blare. "You okay? I didn't mean to scare you." I struggle to recognize the sweet and gentle man in front of me.

"Yeah, I was lost in thought." That's an understatement. I was drowning in my thoughts.

He nods.

"That makes sense. I've been thinking a lot myself. Can we talk?"

My heart pounds so painfully that I strain to breathe. Forcing out the words, "Yeah, okay," is almost more than I can manage. My gut is sure Shane told him. Tim knows what I did.

Taking a seat on the couch beside me, he sighs long and hard while I, in contrast, hold my breath to the point of seeing floating lights. "I don't want to drag this out. I will always care about you, but I can't do this anymore."

He hasn't even offered me an explanation or an accusation. Instead, he's ending our marriage without any anger, not even a tear. I cheated on him, and he doesn't even care. Has he already replaced me with this other woman so entirely? How can he not have even a single question? He just *won't* do this anymore. And why should he? We've never been a real couple, never been anything more than two fucked-up kids clinging to each other to stay afloat. We've never even had sex, and I've never felt so small.

Now that I've had a sexual encounter, as confusing and shame-filled as it was, I understand how superficial our relationship has been. I thought I was closer to Tim than any other person on Earth, and maybe that's technically true because I don't have friends, but I can't ignore that I know nothing about him. I don't know how he tastes. I don't know how he feels beneath my tongue. I don't know the sound of him saying my name as he comes, and before I take my next breath, I understand how much I've lost.

But I don't want to hurt him, and now that he's leaving me, I'm not sure I like that either. I've always craved freedom, but the idea of having it is so frightening. I can't even think what I would do with myself if I had it. I want to be beholden to Tim because what am I if I'm not anchored to him?

And how can I blame him for any of this when I know there's so much more we could have been? It's not his fault his father took it from us. What if we had a real chance? If we were not children who had been beaten, battered, and abused so intensely, there was nothing left of us but pain to pour onto each other, could we have been a genuine couple? Could we have been in love rather than just having love for one another?

I stare at him for a few moments. The fear hasn't eased, but there's pain welling alongside it.

"*What* can't you do?"

He drags his good hand through his hair, and his eyes fall to the floor like he used all his courage telling me the first bit.

"I can't be married to you. I can't be your husband. It's not right."

"Not right," I repeat, trying to understand what he's saying. I expected this conversation to go in a very different way after what I did. I'm not surprised he's leaving me, but I am surprised by his civilized reasoning.

"It's never been right between us, and after what happened…" he trails off, and I'm shocked by how calm he is.

"He told you," the words slip from my numb lips.

"I will never forgive myself for hurting you, Sera, but I did it because I am so fucking unhappy I am going crazy, and neither of us deserves that." His gaze is distant. "I was so close to killing you. I'm not even sure what made me stop. I wanted to kill you, and I shouldn't have let this situation get that far."

A chill runs down my spine, violently shaking me. I take a deep breath. Does Tim really not know? Would he be talking about murdering me if he did? Queasy at the thought, I can't say it for sure.

"You're right. We shouldn't stay together if you want to cause me harm." Talking about my murder with the man I thought I loved, whom I promised my life and heart is an out-of-body experience

"Sera, I mean it. I do not want to hurt you. I have always cared for you, but I can't keep doing this. I'm terrified of the person I'm becoming."

"Me too," I admit.

"Okay," he seems relieved for a moment. "There are a lot of details to work out, but if we're not fighting each other, there's no reason this can't go smoothly."

"Of course not," I'm speaking at the correct times, but I swear I'm not deciding what to say ahead of time. Instead, I mimic Siri, responding to prompts.

"I'll leave for now, but I'd like to keep the house if you don't mind."

His words have a mean kick, "Of course I *mind*, Tim. *I* bought it. What else do you want me to just hand to you?"

"You have all that money from your mom's settlement. You can buy another one. I *can't*."

I want to argue with him, but my transgression points an ugly finger at me. The idea of giving him this house and starting over infuriates me. This money was left to me by *my* mother, and he has no right to take it from me. But

I'm a cheater, a liar, and I deserve whatever suffering comes my way.

"Okay, Tim. You can have the house."

He opens his mouth, prepared to argue his case. I've always curbed myself around him, but he knows my temper sometimes gets the best of me. Tim was sure I would fight him on this, and I engage in the pointless exercise of wondering what his end goal was. And that is when he turns to me with an odd expression.

"You said something strange before."

"I didn't say more than a couple of words."

"Yeah, but what did you mean you said he told me what happened?"

"That's not what I said," I answer too quickly.

"Yes. It. Is." he enunciates. "What did you mean by that?"

"I—"

"Is *he* that piece of shit, the head-scrambling *doctor*?"

"No!" I splutter, and I curse myself for not having developed better lying abilities by now.

Something clicks into place for him. He reaches out, and I think he's going to touch me gently for the first time in longer than I can remember, but instead, he grips my hair and twists me until I'm facing him.

"Tell. Me. What. You. Did." His eyes narrow, and there's genuine rage in them. If I thought he didn't care, I was wrong because he is ready to kill me, and he has to care at least a little to do that.

"I, we—"

"We?" he scoffs, "Did you fuck him, Sera?"

"No!" I shriek.

"But you did something with him, didn't you?"

What am I supposed to say? I already feel bad enough without lying too, not to mention it's written all over my face. He came home intending to leave me for some other reason than my infidelity, and somehow I turned what could have been a peaceful breakup into a Shakespearean drama.

"Are you fucking kidding me?" He seethes, tipping my head to the side and staring into my eyes.

My hair pulls against my scalp, and several strands break away. Tears fill my eyes, and I try my hardest to look away. I hate myself so much right now that a part of me feels like I deserve this. Suddenly, his eyes go cold, his hand drops, and he stands.

"We'll talk about this when I get back. Until then, try not to whore your way across the county."

He stands and leaves me sitting on the couch. As soon as I hear the front door close, the dam breaks and I sob. Honestly, what was I thinking, and what have I done with my life? Even after all that, the thought of what Shane did to me makes me hot and quivery, and knowing that about myself certainly doesn't help my ever-worsening self-image.

CHAPTER
EIGHTEEN
SHANE

I'm stunned when, almost two hours to the minute after Tim left my office, he comes storming back in, clearly enraged.

"What the fuck did you do to my wife?!" he shouts.

His long hair was already greasy when I saw him earlier, but now it's tangled and messed up as well. His broken hand hangs in his sling, but even that twitches toward me.

"Tim," I hold up my hands in a placating gesture. I don't want him to realize how hungry I am for this. The urge to smash my fist into his face and forget the caring psychiatrist act is intense. "I'm not sure what you are referring to, but why don't you have a seat, and we can discuss it."

He puffs up his chest, "I don't want to discuss anything with you. I want to know what you did to my wife!"

He's shouting at the top of his lungs, and I wonder where this territorial behavior came from. An hour ago, she was a curse placed upon him, one he intended to break. There is a chance he loves Sera more than he realizes, but most likely, his ego can't handle another man taking what he considers his.

Funny, he's the one who doesn't want her. I worship my Angel.

"Tim, why don't you tell me what you think I did? When you left here, it seemed you decided to end the relationship. Is that what happened when you got home? I understand if you're upset with me for encouraging you, but it seemed like what you truly wanted."

He blinks rapidly, my ignorant act landing just as I hoped it would. His blue eyes dart between me and the clock on the wall beside me, trying to decide if he believes me. His uninjured hand is back in his hair, and I can see how greasy it is, moving between his fingers in chunks rather than strands. For someone who fucked a woman other than his wife, he seems awfully upset with the idea of his wife cheating on him. He squares his shoulder, his jaw hardening.

"Wouldn't you like to fucking know if I ended it?!" he shouts again, and indeed I would. I'd love to go and comfort Seraphina while he has his temper tantrum elsewhere.

"Tim,"

He reaches out and grabs me by the collar. For a second, I do nothing.

"Let go and step back."

I smell alcohol on his breath, which I didn't smell during our appointment. My jaw ticks as I try to establish when he got drunk. Did he hurt Sera again?

"Or?"

"Or nothing. You and I both know this behavior is inappropriate. I'll call the police, and I don't need to explain how damaging the consequences could be to your life and business. Speaking of which, is Sera okay, Tim?"

I level him with my most compassionate yet unyielding stare. I have known the effect I have on people long before I came into this line of work. I only became a psychiatrist to hone my skills. Also, my interest in medically induced somnophilia certainly made the perks appealing. I stare into his eyes, waiting for him to decide while I envision Seraphina lying drugged on my desk, legs open, one hundred percent at my mercy, and the final piece of the fantasy? She asked for it.

He considers me before he releases my collar and steps back. He takes a couple more, his legs hitting the couch. He sits on instinct and in the same spot I licked up Seraphina's cum.

"Fine, you want to talk about it!? I know you did something with Sera, and you're going to tell me what."

His eyes are red, and his face is flushed. My gaze travels over him, trying to get a sense of his body language and if he's going to strike. That's when I see the outline of his cock in his pants.

"So that's what this is about?" I smirk, and he follows my gaze to his very hard cock. "You want to fuck me, Tim? Are you jealous?"

He splutters, seething mad and beyond the ability to form sentences.

"No," I shake my head, having much more fun than I should be. "You want to watch me fuck Sera. Do you think about her when you cheat on her?"

His mouth pops open in shock, and his angry, flushed cheeks grow even redder in his embarrassment.

"You know, Tim, I hear some fucked-up shit in my line of work, but that's something else. You won't fuck your wife, but you'll fantasize about other men with her. How long has this been going on?"

"I've never cheated on her." His fists are clenched tight

on his armrests, and I know I only need to prod him a few more times.

"Not even with Katrina?"

It's an educated guess, given Katrina is the most frequently featured woman on his social media, but I know I've hit my mark when he turns purple.

"She comments on all your posts, and leaves you little heart eyes and fire emojis. I bet she likes you enough to think you're serious." I'm encouraged by his silence and his darkening complexion. "She doesn't know you have a wife, does she?"

"You're not going to tell her." He mutters loud enough for me to hear him, and that's when it clicks: he's not just cheating. He cares about Katrina.

I give him my most innocent smile.

"That depends on you, doesn't it?"

"How so?"

He's scared now. He doesn't want to lose this girl, and I almost laugh. I've seen Katrina both online and in person while I kept an eye on Tim. She's a pretty girl despite her dull blonde hair and flat blue eyes. I will never understand how he could prefer her over sunlight and springtime. On the other hand, the intense male urge to fight for what's yours even if you don't want it makes perfect sense.

"Your hands are still balled up. Are you going to punch me, or are you going to back down?"

"Tell me what you and Sera did," he orders, his fists relaxing in an apparent show of submission.

I genuinely believe the sick fuck wants to know so he can take the image back to Katrina and fuck it out with her.

"What she and I did isn't important. What's important is that the two of you aren't happy, and you're ending your relationship so you can move on to brighter things."

There's nothing brighter in heaven or hell than Seraphina's fire, but let him try.

"So you did do something together?!" he snaps as he shoots to his feet. "I should have known she's a dirty fucking whore just like her mother."

"You want to know what we did? I sucked her clit until she squirted all over that couch." My eyes flick to the spot he was sitting. "Then I licked both of them clean. If you're wondering what your own wife's pussy smells like, bend over and see if I left any scraps for you."

Just as I thought he would, he lunges for me. His fist connects with my face, and the crunch is as satisfying as it is painful. Tim's strong, but he's drunk, sloppy, and working with one arm. It takes him a long time to hit me again, and I still do nothing.

The camera mounted in the corner points directly at us, and I'm not personally in control of it. There is no reason to check it, and the security office is empty, unless this cunt so happens to go to the police claiming I assaulted him. Except the images will tell a different tale: there's no doubt who is the offender.

I stand up, push him back a step, and throw my first punch. It's too easy with his one hand broken, and if I didn't hate him so much, I would consider this unsportsmanlike. My knuckles connect with his cheek, and his head kicks to the side. I hit him again. Primal satisfaction fills me, and something deep inside me, simple and violent, revels in fighting for what's mine.

I hit him a final time. The plan is to kick his ass a bit and call the cops. He's done enough to get himself out of the way, and I'm happy to shove him the rest of the way. But then he opens his mouth.

"Wanted to kill her. Should have just fucking killed her."

I pride myself on my self-control. More than that, it's a pathological need. I crave control. So when my brain disconnects from my body and rage takes over, I have no idea how to take it back. This has never happened to me before.

All I see is red, blood, haze, Sera's life fading beneath his fucking fingertips. I should have killed him when he touched her, but some of me doubted his intentions. Part of me wanted to avoid the hassle and complications of a more permanent disposal of Tim. Why bother when it should have been so easy to manipulate him out of the situation?

His eyes fall closed for a moment, and I take the opportunity to wrap my hands tightly around his throat. His lids flutter before his survival instinct kicks in and he begins to fight. Tim is strong, a football player, and I'm sure he assumes that, with what I do for a living, this will be easy for him to escape, certain he's outmatched me in a grapple.

He's wrong.

I position myself so that my leverage on him improves and reduces his to nothing. His face is a disgusting, distorted swirl of bruise-like color, and spit flies from his lips. He realizes he isn't gaining the upper hand, and genuine fear flashes in his eyes.

"Please," he mouths as my hands close even tighter.

"You should have killed her," I tell him as I feel his pulse slowing beneath my fingers. "Then, at least, it would have been worth dying for."

He doesn't have a chance to answer. He passes out from oxygen loss, but it'll be a bit longer before he's dead, and I hold on until I'm sure he is gone.

I let go of him, sit back on my heels, and look down at his limp body on the floor.

"Well, fuck, Tim. I really thought we had made some

progress this afternoon. Murphy was right all along: what can go wrong, will go wrong, huh?"

His eyes aren't yet closed, pale blue half-peeking through the dead slits.

"You shouldn't have touched what wasn't yours," I tell him solemnly and pat him on the shoulder before I deal with the most reckless decision I have ever made.

CHAPTER
NINETEEN
SHANE

Tim is dead, and despite the gruesome nature of the last several hours all I can think of is my Angel, and how I'm finally getting my hands on her. No matter how impossible it feels right now, I need to be patient. Covered in her late husband's blood, bits of his muscle tissue and fragments of bone cling to my sweater. I *don't* want her to see me like this. That's how I convince myself to go home first and properly cover my tracks.

I'm bloody, something I hoped to avoid, but Tim's disposal required some *disarticulation*. I'm not a murderer by trade or preference, but I must admit how satisfying it was to choke the life out of him and cut him into pieces after what he did to my Angel.

I remove my clothes, carefully bagging them to dispose of later. No one is going to find Tim, I'm sure of it. Deleting the footage was easier than I anticipated, the security office door wasn't even locked. I'll have to circle back to his truck but I'm certain it's hidden for now. If they ever come here looking, I don't want to give them any excuses to tie me to him, not when there's nothing left anywhere else.

I climb into my shower and meticulously wash every inch of my body. There's more blood in my hair than I realized. It's black, so I shouldn't be surprised it didn't stand out. Images of sawing Tim apart and dropping the pieces into vats of farming acid fill my mind. I don't feel guilty, perhaps a little irritated that it came to all of this when he could have, and should have, just left her.

No matter. There's no use crying over spilled milk.

I spend more time than I'd like on my fingernails before I settle on cutting them down so far they nearly bleed. I force myself to take my time cleaning myself, the shower, and the drain, ensuring I've covered all bases. When finished, I leave my apartment, climb into my car, and head over to Seraphina.

I don't bother parking down the street or with any other sneaking measures I've taken all the other times I've visited her home. Instead, I stride up the path to the red front door like I own the place, and for all intents and purposes, I do. It's Seraphina's home, and she is mine.

The door is unlocked, giving way easily beneath my hand. I push the front door open, and the familiar dessert smell that is Sera overtakes me. Her home is so thick with it, and my cock twitches with each breath.

There's music coming from the bedroom. It's angsty and loud. The lyrics are something hilariously maudlin about a wedding for dead people. She's something special, my Angel. But, beneath the melancholic notes, there's another sound, running water.

I hate fucking in water.

I race through the house to the master bedroom and find Seraphina standing in the ensuite with her bathrobe draped around her. Steam fills the room while she stares at the running shower but hasn't yet stepped inside. She looks awful. I never imagined I could think that about her, but there's no denying it. Her face is gaunt, her eyes hollow, eyelids red and puffy like she's been crying for hours. Her lips are a similar color with angry chapped lines.

I hate that I have played a hand in her being this upset, and I'm enraged that another man could have this effect on her. I don't give a fuck that he was her husband. I will be her *everything*.

She doesn't hear me as I creep up behind her. I'm not trying to be particularly stealthy, but her music is loud, and the water is running. I imagine her as a teen girl wailing along to this song and feeling more seen than she'd ever felt before. I don't think she heard it as a teen, though, not with what I know of her upbringing. So when did my little Angel develop this taste?

She screams as I wrap my arms around her. One hand goes to her mouth, cutting off her protests. The other moves to her waist and quickly slips beneath her robe as she struggles in my grip.

"Shh, it's okay. It's just me."

"Shane?!"

Seraphina whirls around, pushing free of my arms. I let her go and she presses the button to kill the music.

"What are you doing here?"

"Tim came to see me, and I was worried."

Her face falls, and a little tear gathers on the edge of her lashes.

"Oh. And?" She's miserably failing at sounding nonchalant.

"He was beyond upset. He told me he wasn't coming back after what he did to you the last time…"

Her face stills. "After the last time. So, you thought Tim might be planning to kill me," she supplies.

"I knocked, but since no one answered the door, I came in."

It's wrong to lie to her, but I haven't come up with many good answers, and the truth is a sticky situation at best.

"No, I'm not a corpse."

She's trying to diffuse the tension with self-deprecating humor. Something she often does and makes me angry every time. I won't have it.

"Are you okay?"

She turns to me, training those pale green and yellow eyes on me.

"You're the expert, Shane. What do you think?"

"I think you're suffering, and I can't *stand* it."

She pauses and drags in a noisy breath. I step into her, desperate to close that distance. Instead, she tries to take a step back.

That isn't going to work. I crowd her space, pushing her up against the counter. She looks up at me, and I can see the depth and complexity of her emotions. My Angel is in agony, but her pupils are wide, and I can see her fluttering pulse at her throat.

"What do you know or care about my suffering?" she bites out as she looks up at me. "You know what we did was wrong, and you still did it. I-I-"

"You what, Seraphina? You feel guilty because I did for you what he never could? Because you can feel how right this is, just like I can?" I press against her, my warmth pouring through the silk of her robe. She gasps at the contact, and before she can come up with any other arguments to upset herself or piss me off, I crash my lips to hers.

She makes a startled choking noise in the back of her throat, and I'm sure she has never been kissed like this before. She's tentative at first and then messy as she melts into me. She's unpracticed, but her raw enthusiasm makes up for what she lacks in skill.

She tastes sublime, and my cock is aching with each pass of her eager tongue over mine. I can taste the sweetness of her sorrow, the tang of her guilt. Every complicated or painful thing she's feeling is so delicious I want to eat them all out of her and leave her light and unburdened. I didn't lie when I said I hated her suffering, but to be the one who slays her dragons, they need to exist in the first place.

A woman like Seraphina doesn't need a man. She doesn't need anyone or anything. If she only believed in herself, she could take on the world. I want to see her that way. I want to watch her scorch the earth in her fire. The only catch is that I need to trick her into believing she needs me with the same intensity I need her. Because as much as she is *mine*, I am utterly *hers*.

I fist my fingers in her long blonde hair. It's so silky and soft. The smell of her shampoo permeates the air as I tighten my grip and tip her head back, deepening our kiss. She's moaning into my mouth, the robe falling open, exposing her parting thighs.

I slide my knee between her thighs to support her as she slumps. Her bare cunt catches on the rough denim of my jeans, and she cries into my mouth. My lips and tongue bat away the sound as she grinds her wet little pussy on me.

"I'm not even inside of you, Seraphina. Feel how right this is."

I grind my leg against her, and her eyes roll back.

"This doesn't feel right. It feels like I'm breaking every vow I've ever made. This is *wrong*."

I slip my fingers between her parted lips and find her clit, pressing the tiny nub firmly.

"Then why do you like it so much?" I roll my thumb, and she whimpers.

"Sin is supposed to feel good. That's how it tricks us into doing it." Her pretty white teeth press into her lower lip as I work her closer to the edge.

I pull away from her and watch her face, her fluttering pulse. Then I lean in and whisper in her ear.

"Do you think it's going to feel good when I lay you on that bed and take your virginity in a few minutes?"

"You can't."

"I'm going to, Seraphina. Now are you going to be a good girl and let me work you up to it, or am I going to have to take it?"

She startles.

"Take it?"

"Yes, Seraphina. Hold you down, shove your thighs open, and steal the virginity other men wouldn't let you *give* away."

She flinches, and I know my words are a slap to the face, but I'm not in my right mind tonight. I killed a man, for fuck's sake, and instead of building an alibi that has nothing to do with him, I'm here, about to fuck his wife and leave her virginity on the bedspread.

"I'm sick," she finally says.

"Why, Seraphina? Because you're wet for me, and I'm not your husband? Because you're a filthy little sinner?" I'm not trying to be a dick, but I can't help it. I want to degrade her as much as I want to build her up. I want her to depend on me as much as I want to see her strong and flourishing. Cognitive dissonance and I are old friends.

"No," she whines. Her hips buck into my hand as I

work her higher and higher. "Because I want you to take it, just like you said. I want you to force me."

Fuck me.

"Tell me a word, something to say if you want me to stop," I bite out, doing my damndest to keep my head when all I want to do is lose it and take, take, take.

"I don't need a safe word, and I don't want to consent. I want you to take what you want." Her pupils are blown wide with lust.

"What if I want more than you're willing to give?"

Her eyebrows raise, and I wonder if she has any idea of my wanting to own her body, mind, and soul.

"Then I'll know for sure that this only feels right because—"

I reach out and grip her throat, cutting off her words but not her oxygen.

"Let me make something clear," my voice is serene and contrasts with the way I hold her to remind her of my ownership. "I'm going to hurt you. I'm going to choke you, hit you, spit on you. I'm going to shove my cock between your thighs and take your virginity, and when I do, it will not be soft and sweet. It's going to be me claiming what's mine. And Seraphina, I will *never* let you go once I claim you."

She looks terrified, but she's incredibly aroused. Her cunt is gleaming in the light from the modern yet feminine chandelier.

"Why do you want to hurt me?"

"Because I know you're going to love it."

"I don't—"

She screams as my teeth sink into the sensitive skin on the side of her neck. It's brutal and vicious. Then, pretty much like I thought, she moans and writhes against me.

"Fuck," she utters, low and guttural, as I sweep my tongue over the injury and soothe the hurt.

"Don't tell me my hand around your throat isn't part of the reason you're wet, Seraphina. You're going to love every minute I force on you."

She says nothing.

"Admit it, or I won't fuck you."

"I want it, but please don't make me repeat it."

A single tear drips down her cheek, and I lick it off.

"Angel, I won't make you say you *want* it. I'm going to make you *beg* for it."

With that, I shove my fingers into her cunt.

Fuck, she's tight, and I feel what's left of her hymen breaking further. It's an odd little bit of skin people obsess over, though it is possible to have sex many times without entirely breaking it, just as it is possible to tear to shreds on horseback.

"Shane, oh my God!" she screams as I push in up to my knuckles. It's too much, too fast for her tight little cunt, but her muscles are twitching and pulsing around it, and she's gasping through a torrent of moans. As I thought, my Angel likes to play rough.

I pull my fingers out and turn her around with a hand in her hair. My fist forces her face against the cold countertop, not hard enough to hurt her but enough to remind her of the weakness of her position. She's trembling, and I'm sure this isn't the romantic deflowering she imagined she and Tim would share. But no matter how much I scrub, his blood will remain on my hands, just like hers will coat my cock. There's nothing romantic about this aside from the fact that I'm confident I'm meant to love her. This is a feral claiming.

I work my fingers back into her, and the noises she makes are a mix of pained cries and moans. Her eyes are screwed shut, and tears slip from the corners. My cock is a lot bigger than my fingers, and I need her ready.

"Look at me, Seraphina."

She opens her eyes and her lips form an "o" as she meets my gaze.

I pull my fingers out of her, but the hand in her hair doesn't loosen. Lining the crown of my cock up with her tight cunt, I apply the slightest pressure, and my sweet Angel doesn't look away.

"You are mine now, Seraphina. Nothing can change that."

There's a flash of fear in her gaze, and I'm glad for it. She should realize how serious the situation she's gotten herself into is, but I don't give her a chance to change her mind.

I push my hips forward while holding my cock steady. Seraphina is so goddamn tight that I see stars before I've managed to pop the fat head inside of her. I grunt at the distinct change in pressure as I work past her opening and sheath myself in her.

She's crying softly. I'm big, and though I fingered her until she was soft and ready, I didn't give the dirty girl time to adjust to my full length. She told me she wanted me to *take* her virginity, and I have. I sink into her inch by inch until her virgin cunt is entirely stretched over my cock.

"You look so pretty crying on my cock, Angel. Now let's see you come on it."

I drive my hips into her, listening to her moans, gasps, and pants. I find a rhythm she likes, and I consider playing with her clit until she makes a mess all over me, but I have a better idea for my dirty Angel's first time. The hand in her hair tightens as I pull her head back, revealing the length of her throat. I run my free hand along her lips, and my perfect slut opens her mouth for me.

Slipping two thick fingers to the back of her throat, she gags and tightens around my dick. My balls draw up, "Fuck", I hiss as I breathe through the sudden and overwhelming urge to come. *Not yet.*

Pumping in and out of her mouth, I test the tight ring of her throat. She's crying from the overstimulation, but her cunt is twitching like I'm electrocuting it, so I know she loves this. She gags, and I feel her throat working around my fingers.

"Breathe," I coach her as I shove my fingers deeper. She might puke, but not before she comes. She breathes through her nose while I continue my assault. I am aware of her clamping down on me and her not-so-subtle muscles tightening as her orgasm explodes through her. Her broken cries vibrate around my fingers, and I plaster her insides in thick white.

I've never come so hard. My balls are buzzing along with every inch of my skin. I feel more alive than I ever have.

I pull my fingers out of her throat, and she rushes to the sink like she thinks she's going to vomit. She dry heaves, but nothing comes up other than drool, and I couldn't be more proud.

"God, Angel, you're going to be my *perfect* dirty slut."

CHAPTER
TWENTY
SERA

My skin is buzzing, and every inch of me is lit up and *alive*. I feel so fucking good, euphoric, like being pushed past my limits broke some of the seemingly-permanent pain that lingered around my heart. My clit is pulsing between my legs, and my opening is stretched, swollen, and used. I am debased, and for some reason, the thought only makes me ready for him to do it again.

I'm not a virgin. I mean, I'm *really* not a virgin. I've read so many fumbling first-time stories, and I believed that would be the case for me. I thought it would be full of love but lacking in pleasure and finesse. What I experienced was nothing like I expected.

I've just finished dry heaving, and I'm staring at my reflection. My lips are red and puffy, and so are my eyes. The tears have dried on my cheeks, and I can see the salty lines. Shane watches me in the mirror. He's standing behind me, fully dressed, looking at me like I'm the sexiest thing he's ever seen. Like I've *thrilled* him.

I want to be the cause of that look. I want to be elated. Fuck! I *am* elated for half a second before the reality of what I've done sinks in. I cheated on Tim, and I lost my virginity to someone other than my husband. I am a cheater and a whore. It doesn't matter that Tim cheated first, that he choked me, or anything else because I *hate* myself, and none of his transgressions will undo what I did.

"What the fuck was that?" I'm swearing again. I vaguely remember doing that while he was making me orgasm harder than I imagined possible, but it sounds wrong coming from my lips. I've never been the type to curse. Even Tim told me it didn't work for me, and he regularly cursed after we left home. I wish I could pretend moaning Shane's name felt wrong too, but nothing has ever felt more right.

"That was me taking your virginity and making you come on my cock."

He's so blunt, and even after everything we did, I blush.

"Not that part!" I sound embarrassed, and the wolfish smile he gives me makes my skin prickle with fear and arousal.

"It takes training to deepthroat, Seraphina. You must have noticed I'm not particularly patient. I'm going to slide my cock so far down that throat of yours, your pretty chin is going to sit on my balls, and I need you ready when it happens."

"You want to…"

"Fuck your throat and watch you swallow my cum."

I'm red, blushing like never before. I can't believe what we just did or Shane's words. What bothers me the most is how much I loved it, how much it turned me on. Fuck, I am sick. What if Tim comes home and sees what we have done? Did Tim actually tell him he was leaving me? My mind is racing. I'm turning over how fucked I am in the head versus how fucked I am in life when something I have no control over slides down my legs: his cum.

"Oh my God. You didn't wear a condom." My voice is whisper quiet, but I want to scream.

"I'm clean."

My brain fizzles out, my mouth drops open, my jaw aches from how Shane stretched it, and my throat burns. I say a quick prayer asking for Tim not to come home.

"As comforting as that is, Shane, I'm *not* on birth control. You could have gotten me pregnant!"

He smiles, and the expression steals my breath. He is so fucking handsome when he's happy.

"That's the plan."

He is the picture of serenity, and suddenly I realize *I'm* not the crazy one. Shane is.

"The plan? What fucking plan?"

I'm standing stock-still, my pink silk robe is open, and my breasts are exposed, but I don't have the room to care after what we've done. Shane's gaze focuses on my nipples, and his tongue flicks over his lower lip.

"The one where I make you my wife, and you have my babies. Though, it doesn't have to be in that order, Seraphina."

"I am married. This should have never happened! You certainly can't get me pregnant. Are you crazy?" I'm verging on hysterics, so close to hyperventilating.

His voice is soft and placating. "He's leaving you, Seraphina. He told me so himself. He doesn't want you."

I wrap my arms around my naked self and manage to close the robe.

"Shane, I need to talk to him. Our relationship isn't about you. This is about my husband and me. Whatever this was, this should have never happened." I point to his cock covered in my blood and sob, "That wasn't meant for you!"

He steps into me, gripping me by my chin and forcing my eyes to his. "You have no idea what you're talking about, Seraphina. That was one hundred percent mine, and I have no regrets about claiming you or your cunt."

"I'm married!" I scream at the top of my lungs, shattering the previous quiet and making us both jump.

"Not anymore, you're not." He seethes as he shoves his cock back into his pants.

"What does that mean?"

"It means that you're not married in any way that matters, and I'm not going to let you do whatever you think you're doing right now."

I'm disgusted. The thrill from Shane ravaging my cunt and throat still tingles through me. Physically, I'm more satisfied than I imagined possible, but mentally, I want to die.

"Get the fuck out of my house, Shane. Get the fuck out of my house before I call the police."

"I'm sorry, Seraphina."

For a moment, I think he's apologizing for what he did, for fucking me even though I'm married. But he's not, and I realize that when he stalks toward me.

"What are you doing?"

He grabs my wrist and yanks me against his body. I fight as hard as possible, not because I don't want him but because I really think he's crazy. I'm wetter than I've ever been, and I want him so bad I ache. But what is he planning on doing?

I know I can't afford to find out, no matter how interested I am, so I kick and claw as Shane wrestles me through the door and down onto the bed. While I'm busy being ashamed by how fast my strength fails to his, he binds me in ropes I didn't know he had waiting. My screaming and fighting are to no avail.

"I thought you might be difficult, Angel."

He yanks something from his pocket, and I slam my mouth closed as I see his trajectory. He pries my mouth open and stuffs it with my panties before taping it off.

"I really am sorry about this."

It's hard to believe him with his rock-hard cock jabbing into my side. Otherwise preoccupied and still fighting as hard as possible, I am aware of his hands running all over me. I'm positively mortified when he slips his fingers between the robe and my labia.

He pushes his fingers inside me as he comments, "Your cum and mine feel different, Angel. There's almost none of mine left inside you, but you're so fucking wet still."

His thick and long fingers continue to caress me until I'm moaning for him.

"It's okay to want me as much as I want you. You're going to see that soon."

He pumps his fingers in and out of me until I orgasm around them. My nipples scrape against the silk as he thrusts, and the tingling careens me into a harder release. He's watching me with a look of pure lust.

"You know what? Fuck it! I need you too badly to wait. I'm giving you another load."

His hand collides with my ass cheek, and I yelp. It's nowhere near as hard as others have hit me, and the pain doesn't phase me. What shocks me into silence and submission is the heat and increased wetness. He takes the opportunity to line himself up with my entrance.

"If you don't want this, scream as loud as you can, and I promise I won't fuck you right now."

And because I'm a whore, just as Tim accused, I don't

make a sound until his oversized cock is back inside my battered cunt.

"You're so good for me, Angel, even when you misbehave. You didn't want me to tie you up and take you away. You fought so hard you drew blood, but your little cunt already knows who you belong to."

I moan into my panties. Shane's so big inside me it hurts. I'm sore all over, but fuck if I'm not also experiencing more pleasure than I thought possible. Too much. Too big. Too fast. Everything about him pushes my boundaries. Even the unforgivable shame adds a twist of pain to the experience, and I spark like a live wire as I come around him again.

"Fuck, look at you. You're stunning. That's right, Angel. Give it up. Let me feel you come." I let go of everything I am as I scream and coat his dick for the second time. Once I return to earth, I register how weak my body is.

Part of me hopes this was just a sex game and he's done. He's going to untie me and let me go to bed. The shame will likely kill me if he does, but I have to face the consequences of my actions.

An emotional release washes over me, removing every bit of remorse when my dark knight throws me over his shoulder and carries me away.

CHAPTER
TWENTY-ONE
SHANE

Seraphina sits in the passenger seat beside me. I keep the bindings around her arms and legs loose so that I can buckle her in. She lets me, neither complaining nor trying to reason with me as I retie her wrists. The sour tang to her ordinary sweet-smelling sweat is the scent of her fear—my new favorite fragrance. And it fills the cab around us.

She's not screaming, which I appreciate, but her pretty, full lips sit between a frown and a pout. I want to kiss the expression off her, but we need to get where we're going. My Angel isn't fighting, which makes things easier. She's bound, of course, but she could still hurt herself if inclined to.

She's crying a steady stream of tears, and as much as it hurts me to see her pain, I keep quiet. There is nothing I can give her right now that will make her feel better. I hoped she would embrace the freedom granted by Tim choosing to leave her, and the fact I killed him would have remained irrelevant. Though my little Angel doesn't know anything other than self-torture.

I'll break her away from that. She's going to learn to

treat herself appropriately as if she's too goddamn good for this world and anyone in it but me. Then *I'll* be the only one responsible for her torture, and I know how much my Angel will love that. Even now, her nipples are hard and straining against the silky fabric of her robe. I tied it closed for her before subjecting her to the chilly night air, but I can't pretend that her shivering against me didn't turn me on.

The heat has been blasting since we left the house, so I know she's not cold anymore. She's been quiet for so long that I decide ungagging her won't hurt anything. I want to hear her voice and smooth things over between us during our very long drive.

"Don't scream," I tell her as I reach over and rip the tape from her mouth.

She yelps.

"I'm sorry, Angel."

My fingers trail over her offended skin, and she gasps. I could have been gentle, but it wouldn't hurt any less. The significance of those panties is lost on her as she tries her best to spit them out. I took them the first night I came to her house, and I've been wrapping them around my cock every night since. Knowing how they've absorbed my cum and her screams only turns me on that much more.

"If you bite me, I will punish you. I don't want to, but I will."

I don't wait for her to respond. Instead, I reach between her teeth and pull out the panties while she gags her way to relief. My regret for being so forceful with her ends when I see her hard nipples and her blown-out pupils overtaking her impossibly light irises. She says nothing, too busy drawing ragged breaths in and out until she settles. Her tears slow with her breaths, and I'm proud of how she's calmed herself.

"Good girl," I pat her hair, and rather than flinching, she leans into my touch.

She's wordless, but I have a satisfied smirk on my face because it only took two fucks for this girl to crave me. From my peripheral vision, I spot her rubbing her thighs together, desperately trying to relieve the tension. My Angel enjoys the way she's bound, confirming my intentions to keep her tied while I pleasure her many times over once we're safe.

The city lights glow in the distance, fading to nothing as the black highway stretches before us. Her gaze flicks around the cab, and I try to anticipate what she's looking for while I split my attention between the road and her. We're heading toward the foothills of a nearby mountain range. In a few hours, the landscape will be unrecognizable. The road steadily increases in elevation. The trees grow denser, then thinner.

My ears pop right before Seraphina asks, "Where are you taking me?"

"My friend has a house in the mountains. We're going to stay there for a little while."

She scoffs, "Your friend knows you're abducting me and is still willing to give you a place to stay?"

"Something like that."

I'm amused, and I know she can hear it. Her pretty cheeks pinken, and she huffs right before she turns away from me to stare out the window. I take the turns in the road slowly, trying not to get pulled over or into an accident. I can afford to be patient now that I have everything I want. Seraphina's gaze touches me like the most gentle caress, and I would give anything to know what she's thinking.

"How long is a little while?"

"Hm?"

"You said 'a little while,' how long is that?" her voice breaks, and one of the tears she stemmed spills over her cheek.

Time *is* relative, clever Angel.

"That depends on you," I answer, leaving my left hand on the steering wheel as the right drifts over her thigh.

She does her best to bat me away with her tied hands.

"I don't think any of this is up to me."

"That part is not up to you, Seraphina, but things will go much easier for us if you stop pretending you don't like it. I can see the wet spot on your robe."

Her mouth drops open in shock, but I'm telling the truth.

"As for how long I'm keeping you in a private mansion in the mountains where I intend to lavish you with every bit of affection you've ever missed out on? To spoil you with every luxury you can imagine? It's entirely up to you. If you give me what I want, you can leave."

"And what do you want?" Is she trying to sound stern? The breathless quality of her voice gives her nervousness away. She's desperate to know what I have planned for her, but the anticipation will only make it sweeter.

"You'll find out soon."

She makes a dissatisfied noise in the back of her throat before falling silent. The road passes beneath us, the sky finally revealing bright stars. She's focusing on the sky, and despite her circumstances, she looks peaceful.

"My arms hurt," she tells me a while later. We've only passed two cars since we've been on the road, and even I have to admit it's eerie. Usually, this road is well traveled, but fate is trying to make this as easy for me as possible.

"Are you going to fight if I untie you?" I'm musing. I don't think she will, but it takes her a second to answer, so she must be considering her options quite seriously.

"What benefit would fighting you have?"

She tilts her head toward the window, and I must admit she's not surrounded by the most helpful of environments. Too bad that's not what she really thinks. Seraphina is a crappy actress.

"Are you planning to knock me unconscious and take the car back to your precious *Tim*?"

Her cheeks turn pink, but it's not anger. It's an admission of guilt.

"No!"

"I am sorry that your arms hurt, Angel, but we'll be there in a few hours. I'll untie you then. After that, I plan on making it up to you, provided you behave." She has no idea how many ways I plan to make her shake.

"Hours? You can't be planning to leave me tied up this entire time. What if I have to pee?" Her little jaw turns up at me defiantly, as if she thinks she's won something.

"Piss yourself."

She turns to look directly at me, which she's been trying to avoid. Her jaw hangs open as she gapes at me, and I'm overcome with the desire to teach her how to put that pretty mouth to good use.

"You're a bastard."

"Ask me again when you *actually* have to pee, Angel."

She wiggles toward the window, trying to put distance between us. It's an exercise in futility, but I'll let her have the illusion of space.

"You're *really* planning to leave me tied up for hours!?"

"I wasn't, but you sealed the deal. You know as well as I do you were thinking things that would get you in trouble."

"It would be stupid to try something when you know I was planning something. You might as well untie me."

Her eyes dart around the cab like she's thinking about

throwing herself out of it while I'm driving the speed limit on a state highway.

"Stupidity hasn't stopped you before, Seraphina." I'm insulting her, but my voice has an indulgent note. She doesn't hear the affection in her panic. Instead, she flinches as if I've slapped her.

"What does that mean, Shane? That I'm *stupid* for being in this position? That you abducting me is *my* fault? You're clearly not a great guy, but I didn't take you for a victim-blamer."

I laugh coldly, and I know the sound digs at her because she shrinks in on herself.

"You're not a victim, Seraphina. You haven't even asked me to take you home." I wait, giving her a chance to do that. I won't take her back regardless, but just like I thought, she keeps quiet.

"You're not stupid, Seraphina, and I'm doing *this* because you belong to me."

I reach over and palm her pretty cunt through the silk of the robe. It parts slightly, allowing my splayed fingers to rest partially on her flesh. She's wet for me, and I am so fucking hard for her.

"I know how smart and capable you are, but you'd still be mine, even if you were nothing but a cunt on legs."

I rub her clit through the silk, the slippery material working her into a near frenzy.

"You're *stupid* for marrying a man who didn't love you when the man you were meant for was waiting to worship you."

She moans, and the sound is equal parts pleasure and pain.

"You begged him to touch *my* cunt, Seraphina,"

I press my finger more firmly against her clit, drawing a moan.

"I can't tell you how angry that makes me. I want to punish you for it, even though I know it's unfair. I don't want to be fair when it comes to you."

I prove my point by picking up the tempo and dipping my finger lower, playing in the wetness at her entrance.

"You're feeling guilty about all the wrong things, Angel."

I shove one thick finger inside her.

"Shane,"

I work the next one into her.

"Don't feel guilty for how good this feels. I promise you, Tim left you. He's not coming back or waiting for you. He told me he didn't want you. What do you think he meant by choking you and cheating? He has never claimed you. But me? I can't get enough of you. I want to live under your skin and fuck my way into your soul."

Her tight cunt is clenching around my fingers. I want to trade the digits for my dick so badly I'm seeing stars. I've fucked her twice in as many hours, and I'm still achingly ready for her. The fact that I'm angry with her and want to prove a point only makes my need for her worse.

My hand tightens on the wheel while the other plunges in and out of her, drawing her closer to her fourth orgasm. Yes, I'm counting them, and I don't give a fuck. They're all mine.

I'm squeezing the wheel too fucking hard like the pressure might somehow transfer to my dick and take the edge off. I need to get a handle on myself, but I can't stand that she's still thinking about Tim, worried about him, when he wasn't worthy of a moment of her time, let alone being her husband.

I'm going to pull this car over and fuck her right now, or I need to hurt her like she's hurting me by denying us.

"He wouldn't tell his friends you were his wife. He wa—*is* ashamed of you."

I very nearly slip and use the past tense.

She sucks in a breath, and her brows press together, my words having the desired effect. I want to tell her that Tim can't be disappointed in the light of my life, he's fucking dead, but that would only upset her.

"I'm not like *Tim*, Angel." His name burns like acid on my tongue. "I'll tattoo your name on my skin. I'll marry you, fill you with so much cum you'll smell like me, and it'll be impossible to deny who you belong to. You'll give me children, and I'll show you off to every person we meet, not giving a fuck if they care or not. No one will ever doubt how I feel about you. Least of all, you."

She's panting, and her pretty lips parted as she licks frantically back and forth at the bottom one.

"Do you like that, Angel? Do you like that I need you?"

Her hips buck into my hands. She's chasing her release, even tied the way she is, and I'm proud of her for it.

Guess her arms don't hurt that badly.

I'm watching the road because I'm obsessed enough with the need to keep her safe, but my eyes can't stay off her for long. Her robe has worked open, her tits on full display for me. Her nipples are so pale. I desperately want to bite them, suck them, and turn them pink and red. My cock is so hard it's painful, and my foot pushes down on the gas like adrenaline is the cure to my discomfort.

"Would it scare you to learn all the things I've done to have you right here, or would it turn you on to know that from the moment I saw you, I knew exactly where you and I would end up?"

She doesn't say anything, her hips still bucking toward me, and I'm getting tired of this monologue.

"Answer me, or I'll stop finger fucking your needy cunt, Seraphina."

My fingers still, and she wails in aggravation.

"It scares me and turns me on…"

I keep them still, refusing to give her what she desperately needs.

"Please, Shane. Please!"

With that, I pick the pace back up.

"You don't ever need to be afraid of me, Angel. I will never do anything you won't ultimately love."

"Ultimately love?" she pants, sounding confused and close to her orgasm. The twitching pulses from her tight cunt lend to that suspicion.

"You won't like everything we do, but you'll love how I make you feel while doing it." I laugh as I imagine all the ways I plan to use her.

"Like anal?" she asks, and I'm so pleased by her bold question and the apparent way it excites her.

"*No, Angel.*" I tease her gently. "I can tell your ass is just as needy as your cunt. You'll love every minute of me taking your tight hole with my big cock."

She clamps down around me and screams through her release.

After her orgasm, she's quiet for a long time but not tearful like before. I can practically feel her thinking beside me, and I hope her thoughts lead her in a positive direction. The car smells of her, and I'm dying to eat her cum out of her and slide my cock home.

"Remember when you led me through those breathing exercises in your office?"

My heart speeds at her question, and my cock does the impossible and grows even harder. I'll never forget it. I didn't mean to hypnotize her that day, but I can't deny how I took advantage and dreamed of doing it again.

"I've never felt like that before." Her tone gives nothing away.

"Is that all you wanted to say, Seraphina?"

"I liked it." She swallows hard. "I think it was obvious how much I liked it." She's referring to the puddle she left after her orgasm. "I'm not sure exactly what you did, but I want you to do it again."

"Oh?"

"I felt so free, fucking amazing. I don't want to be in control, Shane."

"Anything for you, Angel."

I press my thumb into her earlobe, gently massaging her tension away.

"Close your eyes, Seraphina. I'm going to take care of everything."

CHAPTER
TWENTY-TWO
SERA

The door beside me opens, and comforting masculine hands unbuckle my belt and lift me from the seat. Shane smells amazing as he pulls me to his chest and crushes my face against the fine wool of his sweater. His feet crunch on the gravel as he carries me away from the car and toward what I can only assume is the mansion. I struggle against him, trying my hardest to get a look, but he doesn't lighten up.

"Seraphina," he grunts in an admonishing tone, and I stop struggling, but I see a flash of palatial gray stone.

My bound hands lay pressed between us, aching from the pressure and the chafing ropes, but I'm sick enough that the pain turns me on. I didn't realize how messed up in the head I was until I met Shane. Sure, I needed therapy. I've always recognized myself as lightly traumatized, but the things I'd done and accepted since meeting him? I don't think I know myself at all.

But I do know that, no matter what he's guilty of, he's not responsible for how much I like all these wicked things. He's a criminal, and I have every right to hate him. He's taken my virginity, bound, ravished, and abducted me, but the feelings I have for him are so far from hate. I'm terrified of the warmth blossoming in my chest.

I should be afraid of him. Instead, I am allowing him to give me everything I want and eliminate all my problems in the process. These bindings should feel horrifying and constrictive rather than comforting and committed. I *am* afraid of him. The man is crazy. God only knows what Shane plans to do with me, but I know I am as messed up as he is. If I weren't, I wouldn't be wet and desperate to see what he does next.

Shane's so gentle as we reach the stairs. I look up and see a hint of the pinkening sky. He carries me up the stairs, and a cold wind sweeps past us. I shiver against him, it's colder here in the mountains, and my silk robe feels especially cruel. The murky twilight clears as we approach the front door, creaking open ahead of us. I try hard to turn my head and look at the person opening it, but Shane shoves me into his chest with force, obscuring my view.

"What's the problem, Shane? Afraid I'll see how pretty she is and want her for myself?" A deep, slightly accented voice teases from the doorway.

"I'm afraid she'll see how pretty *you* are and tell the authorities about the mansion where she was held." Shane's voice mocks. He doesn't believe I would go to the authorities and a sliver of fear spikes inside me. Is that because he intends to kill me before that's possible?

"You don't believe that," the man says, echoing my thoughts.

"Let me in, Pax." Shane's annoyance leaks into the chilly night air, only seeming to amuse our *host*, who chuckles at his expense.

"*Only* because your girl has a marvelous ass and a wet spot on her crotch."

I would gladly die.

I wish I could see this *Pax* as much as I'm relieved I can't. He sounds like someone who considers himself handsome. Or maybe he's so rich and powerful that his looks don't matter. He has that "I own the world" vibe. Plus, he's unbothered by Shane bringing a bound and barely dressed woman here.

More light pours over us, and Pax must have stepped aside because Shane carries me up a few steps and into the house. It's colder than I hoped, but I still can't see much. Shane takes a few more steps before finally releasing my face. I realize we're in a tight wooden foyer, it's odd, but my expression morphs from confusion to awe as we enter the main space.

The ceiling arches at least twenty feet into the air, maybe more. But everything is a pale gray stone like the outside. The damned place is a castle built into the mountain with modern, chic furnishings. The windows stretch from floor to the spot the ceiling begins to curve. With my own wide eyes reflected at us, this night feels especially sinister.

"The girl's ass is mine, by the way," Shane tells Pax as he sets me on my still-tied-up feet.

I can see *Pax* now; part of me wishes I hadn't put a face to the name. His hair is dark like Shane's, but the lengths curl on top of his head and the sides are buzzed short. He doesn't have blue eyes but a startling green, and where Shane is pale, he's tan. Their lips and chin are close to identical, and something in those jewel-toned sets of eyes is startlingly similar. They *could* be brothers.

The silk robe I wear leaves little to the imagination, and never in my life have I felt more like a whore on display than I do for the two of them. My latest orgasm still coats my thighs, and God only knows what Shane did to me when I asked him to play around in my head. Memories of his voice and his stroking fingers return to me, and I throw up a wall to block them. My mind obeys immediately, leaving me in the dark, exactly where I want to be.

He could have made me come a dozen more times. It's possible with how sore I am, and the idea that he *did* despite me not remembering, has me frantic and desperately horny. I'm so damn ashamed of myself for everything I've allowed to happen, but I'm soaking wet. I can feel it gathering at my entrance like nothing would please me more than him taking me in front of this stranger who happens to scare me.

I have to force myself to think of Tim, *my husband*. I know he cheated and hurt me, but I can't escape knowing that two wrongs don't make a right. I'm a *whore*, and even the epithet turns me on. I don't want to be with Tim. Our marriage is over; that much is obvious, but I hate myself for letting things happen this way. And I hate that I haven't asked Shane to let me go or take me home, even when he pointed it out.

"Fine," Pax agrees. He pulls his bottom lip between his teeth, sucking it far enough for his top teeth to run over the stubble. "I guess I'll just have to steal my own pretty virgin, Cousin."

"Are you only in the market for virgins now?" he asks with a disgusted note in his voice.

"I suppose I could say my interest is in virginity, but I'd be lying if I told you someone special hasn't *already* struck my interest."

On the spot, I become nervous for this girl. My stomach aches at the thought of what he might do to her. But I don't dare ask, and neither does Shane. I should probably be more worried about myself.

"Is the place stocked?" he asks, bending to unbind my feet. His hand is soothing at my back as he guides us further into the space.

Pax shifts toward the door, and I'm grateful he's not staying. Something about him terrifies me much more than the man who abducted me.

"Of course," Pax answers as if it's the ultimate given.

"And the staff?"

"Have been dismissed."

There goes any touch of hope I had that someone would be here if things got too out of hand.

"Perfect," Shane turns to me with a bone-chilling, panty-melting smile. "I have you all to myself."

"Let me know if you need anything," Pax says as he waves and strides out the front door, slamming it shut behind him.

I'd never heard quiet like this before. I feel like I'm in a museum, but this place is more than that. It's a castle, and if Pax is to be believed, we're the only ones here. This space is monumentally too large to be occupied by only two souls.

Shane looking me up and down brings me back to my predicament. My bare feet ache on the freezing marble as I shift from foot to foot. The intensity of his scrutiny unnerves me, and I'm once again ashamed of my body's response to him: hard nipples, slick thighs, and desire beyond control—a ready whore.

"Kneel, Angel."

I do as he commands without question. The action is reflexive rather than a conscious decision, and my face crumples in confusion as I look up at him. The chandelier behind him holds about a hundred bulbs, and they burn my eyes as I'm forced to give him my rapt attention. I take stock of my body, shocked at how I've lewdly spread my knees. My cunt is out, and that word pops out the same way I dropped to my knees, on compulsion. What other fun tricks did he leave inside me?

"Eyes down, Angel."

My eyes immediately hit the floor, and I gasp in relief. They burn as I squeeze them shut, and tears slide down my cheeks. Bright spots stain my vision, and the different sensations overcome me. Lifting my hands, I rub my eyes, realizing that while I've obeyed Shane's commands, I'm not ultimately under his control.

"Do you remember our session in the car?" his voice is smooth and coaxes the deepest, most fragile parts of me as if he's personally touched them and taught them how to respond to him.

I don't remember, and I don't want to.

Not if he's talking about what happened when he brought me to that new and profound place. The place where he teaches me to use words like cunt and drop to my knees at nothing more than a command.

His ocean-blue eyes are pulling me in. His lips are so damn plush I need to taste him. I'm unsure of a lot, but I know this feeling isn't part of those dreamlike lessons. I don't know why I'm on my knees, but I'm sure he's proving a point.

"When you, you…" My thoughts get tangled up in the years of conditioning, and it's impossible to continue.

"Speak freely, Angel. No one is judging you."

I speak as if I've never known a moment of shame or hesitation. "I remember you played with my clit and fingered my cunt until I orgasmed for you."

"Look at me." My gaze flicks up to his. "I did do that, but I meant after."

Certain the confusion shows on my face as I wade through those memories, I recall the feeling of weightlessness and freedom, light in ways I can't explain, and then... So many orgasms. My cheeks flame.

"I asked you to take me through those breathing exercises?" I don't know why I'm asking.

"Yes, Seraphina." The wolf smiles at me like he's wearing this grandma costume only for my comfort and the benefit of my denial. "Do you remember what happened next?"

"I remember it when I try."

"And if you don't?"

"Nothing."

He smiles at me like that pleases him before he continues, "We worked on some of the things I want to teach you, such as words that I want you to use and ways that I want you to show off for me."

My pulse races. The idea that Shane implanted commands into my brain to use me for his pleasure is the single most sickening and arousing thing I've ever contemplated. He smirks as if he knows what I'm thinking.

"Now, little Angel, relax and tell me about your body."

Again I have that disconnected sensation where the response he wants comes out before I even consider it. Yet, I know what I'm doing and get great satisfaction from responding as his whore should. Where is that ever-present burning guilt in all of this? Because I feel free and alive.

"It's all made for you, mouth, tits, cunt, and ass." After the words are free, I'm shocked by what I've said, so much so I squeak and cover my mouth. I've never spoken like that, and the idea that I mindlessly let him teach me to refer to myself that way is...

Unsettling.

And it makes me so goddamn wet I need him right now.

"We also talked about asking for the things we want.

Do you remember the next two orgasms you had on my fingers while we drove here?"

"I do now."

He smiles, like this is as he expected and wanted. "Do you feel them in your needy cunt?"

I think about it, feeling for subtle differences. I was already so well used, but I do feel it. "Yes."

"But you still want more? Even though you can feel you've come more times than you can count tonight."

He gazes down at me with a haughty superiority, and I want to melt.

"Yes."

"Use your words, Angel."

"I want your cock in my cunt. I want to come on it, and I want to taste it."

He groans and palms his cock through his pants. "In that order, Angel? You want to taste yourself on me?"

"I didn't... I wasn't thinking."

I didn't mean to say it in that order, but I know it's too late. The excited gleam in Shane's eyes tells me everything. In an instant, his hand is in my hair. He pushes my head down, forcing my ass into the air, and presses my face against the hard marble floor. It doesn't hurt, but it's demeaning, and I whine for him.

He's positioned me so that I'm ass up and face down, perfectly presented to him. My bound hands are folded beneath me, and I wiggle as the ropes burn and cut. His smooth hand fondles each cheek and then pushes the robe over my back. He spends no more than a minute pinching and groping, the rough treatment making me whimper. With no further preamble, he enters me.

I shout, unable to adjust to how he's stretched my cunt. I just lost my virginity, and he's using me like it's my damn job. Like I'm a whore, his whore. I'm so full, stretched to my limits. I should be embarrassed when only a minute or two later, I'm orgasming on him, but goddamn, is it intense, and I'm still in that half-real place. Liquid gushes out of me and drips down our thighs.

"Shane!" I wail, begging and thanking him all at once.

He fucks me through my orgasm and waits for my cunt to settle around him before he rips out of me. He grabs me by my hair once again, turns me around, and shoves his thick, long cock straight down my throat as he did with his fingers. And pretty much like that time, the feeling of him stretching me too far and pushing me past my limits makes me feel alive in ways I never have. I want to choke on his cock and have him revive me infinitely, and for right now, that's what I plan to do.

CHAPTER TWENTY-THREE

SERA

My head is blissfully clear when I wake up the next day. Thinking of nothing but the feel of the sheets on my skin, the weight of the duvet on my back, and the stream of sunlight filtering in through the windows of the wide french doors, I don't feel guilty, ashamed, or worried. All I know is that I'm waking up like the world is wonderful, and I'm blessed to be in it.

This feeling of contentment and happiness is so foreign to me that I forget my name. But then, everything comes crashing down on me.

I shoot to my feet, looking around the room. I'm alone, but I can still smell Shane in here: his cologne, the musky and delicious scent of his skin. The bed beside me is rumpled, and I wonder if he slept beside me or laid there after he'd had his filthy way with me.

What have I done?

My head spins, and I drop back to the bed, trying to get a hold of myself before I pass out.

"In through the nose, out through the mouth," I coach myself.

Finally, after a few minutes of breathing, and the door remaining shut, everything holds still. I look around, understanding I need a plan.

The sheets are white and crisp. I guess any virgin blood I might have shed was left behind on the sheets Tim and I shared. For a moment, I consider his reaction, and I want to die. Pushing the thought aside, I catalog the room, which is larger and more spacious than my entire house. Given this is a literal *castle*, that shouldn't surprise me.

The decor here is warmer than the floor below, wooden and rustic, like being in a log cabin. Fire burns in the fireplace, and french doors open onto a terrace with the most fantastic mountain view. I'm breathless again; it's not panic this time but rather the vista sprawling before me.

After a stunned few minutes of enjoying nature's beauty, I turn back toward the room and notice my phone on the nightstand. I run to it on stumbling feet, and my fingers shake as if it's a bomb rather than an old Galaxy. Surprisingly, it's charged, and I have no texts or missed calls. Maybe Tim hasn't been home yet. Perhaps he left me as Shane said he would.

That would be an incredible relief, but I don't believe I've gotten that lucky.

I've been at the hands of violent men enough to know how a small misstep can set them off. But I still open my phone and try to search for my location. Rather predictable, it's turned off and I can't get into my settings. Much to my surprise, I have full service, although my contacts list has never looked so short. Calling the police is an option. Unfortunately or fortunately, depending on your view of the situation, I'm confident Shane could have me out of here long before they reached me.

I think about calling *anyone* for a minute. My dad is the

only person other than Tim that would even consider picking me up. But the price of that is way too high. And with what I would have to tell him happened, I'd rather die. There's no one for me to call, nothing for me to say. Even I can't deny that while Shane did force himself on me and kidnap me, I never said no, and deep down, I wanted every minute of it. So I'm holding this phone and hesitating as if I expect it to explode in my face. And I believe that's because I don't want to call anyone.

What this phone represents seems too good to be true. It feels like a test designed for me to fail, so tell me why some fucked-up little bitch inside me wants to please Shane anyway. It occurs to me that I'm swearing without the associated guilt, and while I don't remember, I know Shane is responsible. So instead of taking the obvious bait the phone offers, I call his cell.

His secretary picks up, and my jaw drops at her chipper voice. *What the fuck?* I thought I was calling his personal line, but that's not the case. I hide my shock as best I can and tell her I need to speak to Dr. Shane. All that pep deflates when she hears my name. *Fuck you too, Tasha.* I expect her to tell me that Shane's not in or out for a few days, but when she says I'll transfer you, I snap.

"Seraphina," he purrs down the line a moment later.

My body responds to the sound of his voice like he's been bringing me to mind-altering orgasm repeatedly for years, like it knows him and his command better than anything else. I'm wet and ready for him, desperate to feel that too-tight stretch that comes with taking him all the way. The image of his trimmed hair tickling my clit as he pumped into me last night, fills my mind. But none of that matters right now.

"Are you really at your office?" I'm seething mad. Angrier than I've ever been. "Did you really kidnap me, drive me out here, fuck me senseless and drive back to the city to offer *psychiatric care?*"

"Can you really say you were '*kidnapped*' when you are left alone in a comfortable bed with your phone? Because if that were the case, I'd call the police, not my kidnapper," he sounds so fucking smug.

"I could, you know…" I'm bluffing, but he's so damn smug.

"Could what?"

"Call the police," I taunt.

"Then who would make you come?"

"I can do that myself."

His chuckle reaches down the line, tingling my spine. "Go ahead, Angel. Do it right now. I'll wait."

"Make myself come or call the police?"

"After our lessons, you have a much better chance of the first, but—"

I hang up on the bastard and dial nine-one-one. It rings, but I hear footsteps in the hallway instead of someone answering.

"Hello," Shane's smooth voice greets me through the phone as he throws back the door. He laughs, and it echoes through both our phones. I end the call, hoping to save what's left of my ears as the feedback punishes me for my actions. "You called the police on me? That's very naughty."

I swallow hard, watching his position. He's not moving yet, but I don't trust that.

"You told me to. I thought you liked it when I'm obedient."

He gives me a sexy half-smirk. "I also told you to make yourself come, Angel, but that phone was a test, and you failed."

I huff in outrage.

"How could I have failed?! I called you first!"

"You did, but you also called the police on me."

"You kidnapped me!" I shoot back, "And why did your secretary say you're in the office? Clearly, you're not!"

He smiles softly at me.

"I'm taking clients virtually, Angel. A lot of people rely on me."

He steps toward me, and I slap at the hand that traces my cheek. He ignores me and moves to my lips next.

"I thought you were mad about what happened between us, not me giving my patients attention."

I roll my eyes at that and turn away from him.

"What happened between us is the problem. If you're giving your attention to your other patients, that's *fine* by me."

"Someone is feeling bratty this morning." I'm unsure if he's teasing or trying to soothe me, but the statement is true enough. "Come here, Angel. Let me make you feel better."

"Shane, I don't want to do any more of that. We've done that too many times, and I already feel like garbage." I turn toward the closet, hoping I can find some clean clothes and take a shower. He came inside me more than a few times, and it's coating my thighs.

"I don't need to fuck you to make you feel better. How about I draw you a bath? I promise no funny business. I hate fucking in water."

My cheeks immediately turn pink, but I giggle. I look Shane over from head to toe now that I'm not fuming mad anymore. His black hair is sleep rumpled. Those stunning blue eyes rove over me like I'm the sexiest thing he's ever seen. His incredible body is coiled ever so slightly, and I nod.

"Get naked. I'll get everything ready."

About ten minutes later, he stalks out of the bathroom, and his eyes find mine. There's heat there and anger.

"I told you to get naked."

"I can't just get naked in front of you. I'm married, Shane." The argument is knee-jerk, and it doesn't hold up at this point.

He's in my face, his hand is around my throat, and I think he's going to choke me half to death as Tim did. His hand tightens slightly, and I'm shaking, but the squeezing never comes. He's *not* choking me. Instead, he's restraining me, collaring me. His fingers find my jaw, tipping it up, forcing me to face him.

"Listen to me, Seraphina. He left you. You are not his wife. You are *mine*. I don't want to hear another word about him. Do you understand me?"

My cheeks are hot, and I'm unsure if it's the blood rushing to my face or my tears. "Please, don't hurt me." I assume I need a lot of effort to gasp the words out, but it's easy. He's not hurting me.

"I would never hurt you, Seraphina, but I will prove a point to you every damn time if I have to. I will do whatever I must to convince you that you're mine and nothing else matters."

"I want that to be true so badly, Shane, but it's *not*. I want to give in to this more than anything, but I can't. This is wrong."

My tears are running over the hand around my throat, but he holds me in place.

"This is not wrong, Seraphina. No one is judging you."

His words relieve the worst of my suffering, but I'm still hesitant and keeping my distance as best I can while he holds my throat.

"I know you're afraid, but do you know what else you are?"

"What are you talking about?"

"You're turned on, Seraphina. It's time you stop letting that piece of shit ruin your life. Now, take off your fucking clothes and get in the bath before I make you."

A smile slides over my lips, and a crazed little giggle slips out. Shane's eyes shine with frenzied light.

"You are so perfect for me, my dirty little Angel."

He pushes me back until my knees hit the bed and then lays me down. Starting with my top, he slowly peels off my clothes. I'm naked and panting when he lowers and sucks my breast into his mouth.

I moan long and loud. "I thought you weren't going to try to have sex with me."

"I'm not. I'm sucking your tits."

He switches to the other, then bites the tip of each nipple. I'm moaning and writhing. He pops off with a wet sucking sound and flips me over. He fondles my ass before bending my arms behind my back and forcing me to my feet. Pathetic mewling sounds slip from my lips as he pushes me forward and trails his lips across my neck.

"I'm glad you waited for me, Angel, but the more I think about what a needy slut you are, the worse I feel for leaving you unattended for so long."

I flush from my hairline to my breasts, and my aching nipples harden further.

"You said this wasn't about sex," I complain as he pushes me toward the ensuite.

"This is about me apologizing for neglecting what's mine. And I hate that I neglected your needy cunt when I could have made your life better, happier, and more relaxed a long time ago."

"You think highly of yourself, don't you?"

"I do."

His lips skim along my neck as we enter the bathroom. The steam raises goosebumps along my skin.

"But it's more so that I know how therapeutic sex is and how badly *you* need to feel wanted."

Shane releases my arms as we stand at the edge of the tub.

"Climb in, Angel. You're sore from being tied up for hours yesterday. I'm going to rub every inch of your body until you're soft as putty, and we're going to have another session."

I shiver as I pick up my foot and dip it into the hot water, allowing my body to adjust to the temperature difference.

"Another session?"

"If you let me, we'll do this every day. I'll spend the rest of our lives pushing you to the edge, freeing you of pain and self-doubt. I'll make you feel better than you thought possible, and do you know what else?"

"What?"

"As long as I'm in it, I'll ensure you have whatever life you want."

CHAPTER
TWENTY-FOUR
SHANE

Sera dips her luscious body into the bath, and the soft foam eats up every inch until the water in the oversized tub covers her. The sweet scents of vanilla and Egyptian musk float off the water, and I can't wait to rub them into her skin. She shivers as she adjusts to the heat, and I watch in fascination as her breasts bob.

"How's the temperature?"

She leans her head back against the porcelain before offering me a lazy smile.

"You know it's a little too hot, right?" Tendrils of golden blonde hair float beside her and stick to her breasts, the darkened ends looking brown.

"I do," I admit as I destroy the distance between us and kneel behind her. "I like when you're a little bit past comfortable."

I run my finger over the curve of her shoulder and along her breast. She tenses until I press a sweet kiss against her neck and hum into the space. I smile, remembering our conversation about physical touch and her taking comfort from it. There's no doubt that she responds beautifully to physical affection. She's starved for it. I hit a few buttons hidden beneath a panel, and she squeals in shock as jets come to life.

"This place is insane," she comments with awe and frustration as she moves her fingers through the artificial swells. "What other tricks are waiting?"

"More than you can imagine, I'm afraid, and only some of them are as sexy as jacuzzi tubs." These walls hold many secrets, and if things go as I plan, she and I won't be here long enough to let them dampen her light.

"Should that scare me?"

I bite back my grin. I do like it when she's afraid. "Healthy skepticism was invented to keep you alive."

She shivers but relaxes into my touch when my hands slide over her body.

"You've always made me nervous, you know?"

"You've done an excellent job of hiding it."

She snorts, "Yeah, right. You taught me how to orgasm because I was so subtle about your effect on me."

Her eyes meet mine in the mirror in front of us, and I wink. "Did you ever think it was because of your effect on me rather than the other way around?"

"No, I never considered that."

The steaming glass partially obscures our reflection, and I turn my attention to her smooth and silky skin. The animal part of me enjoys how slick and wet she feels. Her nipples stand, reddened from the heat, and they sway with each pass of my fingers. I start massaging her neck and shoulders, enjoying her little gasps and the splashes of her tits.

I work out her tension, inch by inch, but the spot she likes most are the muscles directly above her breasts. Whether they're that sore or my little slut is hoping I'll dip lower, I'm not sure.

"Oh my God," she gasps.

"You hold a lot of tension right here." I roll my thumbs over the round caps of her shoulders, digging into a spot that makes her whimper. "Do you ever get tired of torturing yourself?"

I kiss and suck at her neck, and she sighs.

"I'm not supposed to feel good about what we're doing, Shane."

"Does torturing yourself get tiring? Will rearranging the words win me a real answer?"

She flicks the back of my hand, and I relish the playful gesture.

"I guess I am tired of it. But how do I stop?" The tension I squeezed out of her is already creeping back in, and my hands clamp down to keep her shoulders from hitting her ears.

"First step? Enjoy this. It will be good for your muscles and your sweet cunt. I know how sore you must be, Angel. Let *me* take care of *you*."

She moans at my words as much as my touch. My hands roam her body, taking their time on every bit of her. A deep but subtle excitement runs through me at the prospect of spending my life learning her body and the places it holds tension, of eliminating every problem and worry until she's nothing but radiant happiness. When I slip my fingers into her slickness, she whimpers softly.

"Please, m'sore," she grumbles, not quite awake.

"That's okay, Angel. This will feel good."

If she doesn't want my hands washing her, the jets can do the job for me. I place a hand beneath each thigh, lifting and spreading them. She squeals, but her firmly planted shoulders keep her in place.

"Wha—" she starts to complain, but a pulsating jet hits her clit, and she lets out a long, low moan instead. Her hips buck, and I press my face against hers to keep her from thrashing away. My fingers tighten against the soft flesh of her thighs and she whimpers at the pain.

"Harder,"

"Slow down, Seraphina." This isn't that kind of game. "This will get you nice and clean and won't make you any sorer." I use my detached, professional tone. "Orgasms are good for you."

She doesn't get to say another word. She's too busy shaking and grunting like she's never felt anything so intense. Within a minute, she's orgasming, screaming, and crying my name as she comes. Water splashes me as I suck her neck, leaving a fat hickey. I can't get enough of her taste. The urge to bite down, drink her blood and cum is overwhelming. I wish I had another mouth and set of arms for everything I want to touch and do to her, though it still wouldn't be enough. Once she's crying for me to let her down, I lower her thighs, turn off the jets, and let her rest.

I kiss her neck softly, soothing away the damage I did to her tender skin. Now that she's calm and happy, I talk her through the breathing exercises that only work on those already willing and susceptible. My Angel wants the release I give her so severely she throws her subconscious open and begs me to come in. I don't intend to leave her disappointed in any facet of her life.

"Seraphina, are you with me?"

"Mm,"

It doesn't take long until she's in that impressionable place where I can mold her how she *needs*. I love seeing her like this, desperate for anything I might teach or give her. She's like this all the time underneath her timid exterior, but all that self-imposed torment gets in the way of the little slut she wants to be. My cock is so hard from the control she's gifted me, and combined with touching her body, I am in physical pain.

"Little Angel,"

"Shane," she coos back, and I pull my cock out of my pants.

Running my hand up and down the length, I relish the sight of her. Her eyes stay closed but her chin tips in my direction. The bubbles have fallen flat with the jets off, revealing the slightly distorted view of Seraphina's beautifully open body. She came so hard, and with the hot water, her muscles are as soft as her mind. I'm sure I could slip into her tight ass without any pain if I could find a way under her without disturbing her.

God, I want to claim her ass.

I grip my cock tightly and run a gentle hand over her.

"What do you think of yourself, pretty Angel?"

She sighs softly.

"I'm a whore. A cheater who is running around on my husband, all because I'm falling in love with my therapist. I'm dumb and—"

"That's enough of that," I interrupt her tirade. Exploring those feelings is important, but I won't allow her to berate herself, especially after she's just admitted she loves me. I love her too, but I know full well it doesn't count until she decides to tell me herself.

Her hands rest against her chest and grab at her heart like she ripped the admission from it, and I know I can't hold her to it. Her cheeks are pink, and I hate that I've allowed her to become distressed in this place that should only relax her.

"Don't worry, Angel. You didn't say too much. You're not embarrassed."

She softens again, and I'm torn between incredible joy and rage. I am also falling in love with her, and hearing

Seraphina feels the same is exhilarating. My cock twitches in my hand, leaking precum at the thought. I could blow my load right now.

But the rest? To say her words anger me is a profound understatement. It takes all my self-control not to wrap my hand around her neck and fuck her throat as punishment, especially given the intensity I'm craving her with. But I wouldn't do that to her. I may be a sick bastard, but even I have my limits. I'll never punish her for anything I learn in these sessions.

"You're not *a* whore, Angel. You are *my* whore."

"Your whore."

"And my whore is smart and worthy, the most beautiful and precious."

She doesn't answer.

"Did you hear me, Seraphina?"

"Your whore," she confirms.

"My pretty whore, *my* perfect slut, and you don't belong to Tim."

"I married him, though."

I clench my fist and take a deep breath.

"I know this lesson is hard for you but repeat after me, Angel. I don't belong to Tim."

She pauses as if what I'm saying is so contrary to her internal monologue that reaching her takes a long time.

"I don't belong to Tim," I repeat.

Her brow furrows but eventually relaxes, her eyes never opening.

"I don't belong to Tim." Her chin dips into the water, the water kissing her lush bottom lip.

"You're right, Angel."

"I don't belong to Tim."

Her long legs are floating and fully spread, revealing

her pretty pink pussy. I nearly cum but squeeze myself hard in time to stop the eruption.

I know that lesson will take time. This isn't my first time giving it, but Seraphina's feelings surrounding Tim are deep and complicated. They will take a lot of time to unpack. But that doesn't change how much it turns me on when she admits the truth.

"Angel, are you smart?" I grunt, trying to ignore how fucking hot it is to have her right in front of me, talking to me, and not even realize I'm stroking my cock for her.

"No," she answers swiftly. This is another point we're struggling with, but she got "kneel" right the first time. She's a stubborn little bitch. Go figure.

"Angel, you are smart. Say it." I'm so close, and I need her to admit it before I come.

"I'm smart."

She pouts, and I take a calculated guess at how hard she's fighting against the praise in that beautiful, brilliant head of hers.

"You can do anything you set your mind to."

"I can do anything," she repeats, and I smile at how easy that one was. This is going better than the last time.

"Okay, Angel. Do you remember the most important thing?" My balls are buzzing, and the base of my spine is tingling. Jerking off has never been so satisfying.

"The most important thing?" she questions numbly.

"Yes, Angel. What do you need to live?"

"I need *Shane* to live."

"That's right. You are my perfect, pretty slut. You are so smart, so capable. You can do anything in the world *except* be without Shane."

She nods as she says, "I need Shane."

And I explode, coming so hard my back bows, and I see stars.

CHAPTER
TWENTY-FIVE
SERAPHINA

"Seraphina?" His smooth voice pulls me out of the relaxing trance I'd slipped into while lazing on the plush couch in the *salon*.

My gaze trails over the stunning landscape portraits before finding the center of my world.

"Shane," I coo back, thrilled to be the object of his attention.

After our session the night before and an amazing night's sleep, Shane cooked me breakfast in bed and cued a film on a pull-down projector screen that took up the entire wall. I'd spent the morning watching myself orgasm and learning how to ride dick.

The experience left me rubbery but satisfied. Then, Shane talked me through another session. I napped, let the sun warm my face, and napped again. Even after I woke, I lingered, enjoying myself. I had never felt so *unburdened*.

Shane leans over the couch, grabs my face, and kisses me with sweet deep presses.

"Get dressed, pretty Angel. I have plans for the two of us."

I flush at the compliment but don't bother questioning his command. Thus far, I've *loved* his surprises, and he's never asked for more than I'm capable of. I rise to my feet and stretch my body for his inspection. My cheeks heat as he looks me up and down and says, "Very good, now put on something pretty but warm before I smack that ass."

I squeak, a little too excited by the prospect. I won't misbehave, though. I'd rather he spank me because I asked. Taking the initiative I know he wants, I head back to the room I've been staying in. He follows a step behind.

We step into the room, and I gesture broadly. The fine silk robe he gave me last night hangs around my shoulders, and as I spread my arms, I also display my breasts. His heated gaze warms me, and I have an errant thought about that being bad, but it doesn't stick around.

"What am I supposed to wear? You didn't give me a chance to pack." We both know that he stole me away and that I wanted it. There's no use arguing our path.

"Take a look." He nods toward the closet, and I follow his lead. I'm a little nervous that the whole thing is going to be full, but he proves how suited we are to one another when I see the moderate selection of clothing. I finger the rack, appreciating the sensible options and the elaborate ones.

"Thank you," I hum as I touch all the beautiful textures.

"You are most welcome."

A long black dress with a bright floral pattern catches my eye, and I pick it up. "Can I wear this?"

"Do you like it?"

"I *love* it."

"Then I insist."

He waves for me to continue, and I'm unbothered as I drop the robe and allow him a full view of my body. The dress is softer than anything I've ever owned and tingles my skin as it slips over me. He hands me a pair of matching silk slippers. With a strong yet gentle grip, he turns me to the mirror.

"What do you think?" he asks me with a feline smile.

"What do *you* think?" I counter. His approval means everything to me.

"I picked everything in this closet, Seraphina. Nothing in it will displease me." He chuckles. "And today is all about what *you* think."

"I'm beautiful," I murmur.

He kisses my shoulder.

"Yes, you are."

Once I'm dressed, he walks me back through the house and out onto an elaborate stone patio.

"Wow," I breathe.

There must be a hundred candles illuminating the space, as well as a round brick contraption with a chimney and flames dancing inside. A small lagoon-shaped pool sits beside a hot tub with luxurious furniture surrounding it.

"Do you like it?" He offers me a sweet smile, lacking his usual calm assuredness.

"I love it," I correct. "There's a pool?"

"Three, actually. This is the smallest, but that's not why we're here." He points to what must be a barbecue of some kind. "It's too cold for outdoor swimming, but we can check out the indoor pool later if you like."

I think about it for a minute, trying to assimilate the idea that this one gorgeous pool wasn't the impressive one.

"I haven't been swimming since I was a kid. I love the water." The realization is almost shocking. There are things I *love*.

"Later, then," he promises easily as he leads over to a table I hadn't seen.

He flips a switch, and an outdoor light turns on, revealing the contents. Dough, tomato sauce, and more toppings than I can imagine. In fact, I have no clue what several of them are. There are weird things like candy and chunks of cake, and bottles of syrups. I run my hand along the table, taking it all in.

"Have you ever made brick oven pizza?"

"I've never even *had* it."

"Even better."

He steps up behind me, pressing himself against me and pulling the last hint of chill out of my skin. His hands come to rest next to mine on the table, and he helps me through the process of stretching the dough, applying the sauce, and choosing toppings.

"Tim likes pepperoni," I comment, forgetting how much mentions of *him* irritate Shane.

He picks up the bowl of pepperoni and chucks it off the patio and into the woods. The jump or yelp I expect never comes, and I realize it's because I'm not afraid of Shane and know he's not threatening to throw me next. When Tim starts punching walls, it's only a matter of time before his aggression works it's way out on me.

"Fuck Tim, Angel!" Shane grabs my cheeks in his hands, turning me to him and pulling me out of my depressing thoughts. "We'll make as many pizzas as we need to until we figure out what *you* like."

I giggle at that and turn my face to kiss his thumb.

"I definitely can't eat enough to try *all* of them."

"I might have something that can help with that." There's a teasing glint in his gaze.

"Oh?"

"You'll see."

We're adding some fancy french sounding mushrooms

and a sausage that's way too old to be good for you when I ask, "What are the sweet toppings for?"

"Dessert pizza."

"Is that a *thing*?" I gasp in true delight.

"It's a thing, and after *this*, you're going to lose your mind."

He pulls something out from behind his ear. At first, I think it's a cigarette, but he sparks it against the fireplace, and I instantly realize that it's not tobacco. He takes a deep drag, holds it for a moment, then blows it out. The smoke coils up and away from us.

"You want me to smoke weed!?" I squeak, sounding exactly like I did when I was sixteen, and one of the kids from town offered.

"If it makes you feel any better, it's not only legal but has plenty of medicinal uses. I *am* your doctor."

"You're my psychiatrist," I correct. "And I'm starting to think there may be a conflict of interest."

"You can fire me if you like, but I'm still going to smoke this, and you can join me if you like."

It only takes a few minutes for the pizza to cook. I'm watching him turn it with the giant paddle and smoke, trying to decide if I should take the plunge or not. I'm lacking all of my normal baggage, freer than I've ever been, and rationally, I can't think of a single reason why I should turn down trying pot and eating fancy pizza.

When the pizza is ready, he places it on the counter to cool. I'm salivating at the scent of it, but it's still bubbling and would burn the heck out of my mouth. Shane chooses one of the lawn chairs and lays back, kicking up his legs and taking another hit.

"Come on, pretty Angel, let's see if you like weed. Then, we're going to eat pizza."

I roll my eyes as I climb on and straddle him. I'm still

undecided, but I'm not about to refuse his touch. The moment I'm in his lap, the smell is almost overwhelming but not bad. I'd always heard weed smelled like skunks, and it does a bit, but I'm surprised by the almost lemon-like brightness and freshness.

"It smells good."

"Mm," he agrees, "I like this strain."

"Do you smoke often?"

"Once every couple of months? It's nice to get out of your head sometimes."

That does sound nice. I've never even had alcohol. We're not catholic, so I've never tasted wine. Despite Tim drinking, it enrages him if I suggest *I* might. There's so much I haven't done. So much I don't know.

Shane holds it up in front of me. "Are you ready?"

"I don't know."

"What's holding you back? If you really don't want to, it's not a big deal."

He pulls it back to his lips.

"It's kind of stupid."

"Not a single thing about you is stupid, Angel. Now, tell me what's on your mind."

I sigh. "I'm thinking about my father and the things he used to tell me about the Devil and…" I stare off into the distance, not continuing and hoping he will make everything better for me like he always does.

"Do you believe in God, Angel?"

His free hand toys with the lengths of my hair, and I stare at the sky as I consider my answer.

"I'm not sure anymore, but sometimes I do." *When I'm looking at the stars and sitting on your lap.*

He pauses, taking another drag. It's getting toward the end, but I'd guess I have another few minutes to decide.

"Do you believe the Devil creates?"

His perfect lips form a circle as he exhales.

That was a much simpler question to answer, "No, he corrupts."

"Then *this* isn't the problem," he waves the joint in front of us. "It's just one more thing for you to decide if you enjoy."

I'm relieved by his answer and nod, more eager than I thought I'd be. He takes a deep puff before pressing his lips to mine and exhaling slowly. I follow his lead and breathe in whatever he wants to give me, so much more than a little smoke.

We try every topping on that table, laughing like crazy people. I've never felt like this, and it's not just the weed. I'm only a little out of it, a little silly. I thought this was going to be insane and transformative, but really it's just nice. Is there anything my father and Tim aren't wrong about?

Shane goes inside at one point and grabs a blanket to drape around my shoulders. I'm lying on a couch looking up at the stars when a handsome face pops into my line of sight.

"Pax!" I startle, too stoned to make any sense of why he's standing above me.

"Shush, I'm only here to check he hasn't killed you yet." He places a finger to his lips, bidding me to be silent. I blink once, and he's gone. By the time I sit up and look around me, I'm not sure I ever saw him at all.

CHAPTER
TWENTY-SIX
SHANE

It's been two weeks since I brought Seraphina here, and I must admit, I had no idea it would be *this* blissful. I showed her the video of our session that first morning, and no surprise, my filthy girl loved it. So much so that she's thrown herself into it this time with me as best she could.

Her mindless devotion is the most satisfying submission she could offer me, but this is only a vacation. The real Seraphina will come out when she's ready. Once I know it's safe for her.

I take her sweet cunt at least three times a day, but often more. I am so incensed by her smell, taste, and feel I can't think straight. I've called in sick for two weeks since the first day I took online appointments. I told them I have mono, and while it's a blatant lie, I'd call it the least of my sins. Though, I will have to come up with something else soon.

I covered my crimes, and Tim had a history of alcoholism and spousal abuse, this situation is navigable. I could make our lives work back in that tiny city if she *really* wanted to, but we would be better off moving on. This peaceful setup won't work forever. Already, the signs of neglect around the house and grounds are evident; I'm going to have to bring the staff back soon.

So far, things with Seraphina are amazing, but I can tell we're not ready for the real world yet. Between the mind-blowing sex, hypnosis sessions, and bonding we've been doing, she's still crying, and, in my professional opinion, she mourns the life she's leaving behind.

She doesn't know Tim is dead. I had hoped to have told her the truth about everything by this point, but that hasn't been possible yet. We can stay here as long as we want to, but I relied on us not needing to spend months to get to where she needs to be, and I also didn't want to have to pay the millions it takes to keep the whole staff silent.

I haven't told her everything, and part of the reason is sitting in front of my desk: Pax. He comes to this house far too often for my comfort. Our moms were identical twins, meaning we share a little more in common than your average cousins do. Genetically, we're half-siblings.

His hair is as black as mine, and he's artfully gelled it back like he's going to the fucking prom. His wool suit costs a small fortune, and while I could easily afford the same, I've never felt the need to drip wealth.

His grin looks too similar to mine as he looks me up and down. I don't want to know his thoughts, but Pax has never given anyone that luxury.

"You look delighted, Shane. I can't say I've ever seen you in such high spirits."

"I'm alarmed to admit you look happy too, Cousin." I'm not always the most normal guy. I admit that my infatuation with Seraphina isn't typical, but Pax is a little more, let's call it, eccentric than I am, and that wicked glint in his eyes spells trouble.

"I've found a pretty little thing to keep my interest, just like my big cousin. A nun. And God, is she sweet."

Pax and I are both spoiled brats. We've been given everything we wanted in life and taken the rest. I don't have a leg to stand on regarding women or moral pursuits, but me being scared for the woman he's set his sights on is saying something. Pax *isn't* like me.

"An actual fucking nun, Pax, or are you speaking metaphorically?"

"Wouldn't you like to know, Cousin?" he teases me with an even more wicked smile.

"You're not planning on killing her, are you?" I can't deny the genuine concern in my tone. I don't typically give a shit about his antics, but after what I did to Tim, the last thing I need is more heat in our direction. I wouldn't put it past Pax to try and pin it on me if he did kill someone since we look alike enough to confuse a witness. And it wouldn't be the first time he killed someone young and pretty out of jealousy.

"*Cousin*, it's not very forgiving of you to keep bringing up the one time that I *accidentally*—"

"Murdered your nanny?" I finish for him, thinking of the bloody mess he'd made of the nineteen-year-old girl when he was thirteen.

He scoffs at me like I'm the world's biggest idiot. "You know Matilda had it coming." He brushes me off like I've said nothing of particular importance. But that girl was not his to punish, and he knows it. "Are *you* planning to kill Seraphina?"

I nearly hit him for the mere suggestion, and he sees the reaction all over my face.

"I'll take that as a *no*," he laughs. "Don't say stupid shit, Shanc. I could never hurt my Snapdragon."

I drop my head into my hands, wondering if he's even

spoken to her as well as what this poor woman of God did to garner his attention.

"Fucking Christ, Pax. Please don't do anything so extreme you can't dig yourself out."

"*You're* one to talk. You know Seraphina and her dead husband are all over the news, right? How long do you think it will take for her to notice?"

I give him a stern look before my gaze flicks to the door. It's open a crack. I stand and move toward it, shutting it before returning to him.

"I know it's going to happen sooner or later, but I was hoping for later." I scratch my jaw in thought. "I underestimated her loyalty to that piece of shit. She won't forgive me if she finds out too soon."

"What will you do if she doesn't forgive you? Will you let her go?" He gives me a wicked smile like he finds my pain tantalizing.

"No, I'll toss your shit in the yard and take this house for us. You know it's mine anyway, don't you, Pax?" And it is mine. He isn't the next in line to it either. I just don't feel the need to live in a castle.

"Of course I remember, *Cousin*. No need to be a dick about it. I would never keep you from any of my *properties*, and some of them may interest you with your newfound proclivities. Don't think I missed the rope."

"Of course you wouldn't," I answer dryly.

"Well, I ought to be going." He slaps his knees and stands like a midwesterner, politely dismissing me.

"You never even got to the point of this little visit." I'm observing him because I'm confident the slippery fuck is up to something.

"Sure I did." He winks. "Until next time."

He walks out of my office whistling, and I take a deep

breath, deciding against following him. The sooner he's out of this house, the better.

I stay at my desk for a few minutes. In the back of my mind, I'm worrying over Seraphina and hoping Pax doesn't do anything too terrible to this girl who's caught his attention. But I'm not going to stop him either way. We have always agreed to look the other way regarding each other's businesses. Neither of us has typical tastes, and the last thing we need is familial judgment on top of the legal implications of our actions.

Matilda, the nanny he killed, is the one exception. She was my girlfriend, and she fucked my thirteen-year-old cousin. According to Pax, she even told him she loved him. So yeah, she had it coming, but that's one sore spot I'll never completely let go.

CHAPTER
TWENTY-SEVEN
SERA

I knew Shane didn't want me to overhear his conversation, and the part of me that wanted to please him was almost powerful enough to keep me moving. I was only in the hall because I was hungry and heading to the kitchen for a piece of fruit or something I could mindlessly snack on while I flitted around, recovering from the night's antics. But when I heard them discussing me, I had to listen.

He killed Tim.

They said many things that should scare me, things I should be focusing on, but those words ring over and over in my head. My thoughts spin as I try to piece together how fucked my life is—how fucked I am. Tim is *dead*. It's my fault, and no matter what he told Pax, I'm next.

Unsure of how I'm not in a full-blown panic attack, I run down the hall toward the foyer and away from Shane's office. My only saving grace is that Shane didn't see me, but I know Pax did. I listened behind the door only long enough to be sure of what I heard, but I ran when those reptilian green eyes connected with mine. I listened to the critical parts: the man I've been screwing these past weeks, living in sin-soaked ecstasy with, killed my husband and kidnapped me. It takes everything in me not to hurl my guts up.

The door to the office kicks open, and I tuck myself behind a ridiculous marble statue at the last possible second. Convinced I've succeeded, I let out a breath as Pax moves past me, but when he gets to the door, he looks right at me, and he fucking winks. Pax continues, leaving said door open behind him. He didn't say a word, but I could hear him in my head beckoning me to run.

I'm not stupid enough to think this guy wants to help me. He wants to complicate matters for his cousin, but it's my best chance. I already know the clothes Shane provided me with are refined and luxurious and unsuitable for any outdoor exhibition. I have a soft pair of slippers on my feet, but they're the only footwear I have, except for the other colors to match the silky slips and shifts Shane prefers me to wear.

It's spring but still early, and we're in the mountains. I've been outside a few times for fresh air, and it's never been warm. Shane wrapped a blanket around my shoulders and held my hand each time. While it was happening, it felt romantic; now, it feels frightening and possessive.

He killed Tim.

Shane has left me nothing to make my escape likely or probable. *This is as good as it gets*, and with that thought, I bound out of the house and run for my life.

It's colder than I feared outside. The day is gray and overcast, lacking any extra warmth that might come from the sun rays. It's fine. I feel so cold inside I might as well be dead. At that thought, I fly down the incredible staircase, praying to a God I've forsaken that I don't go tumbling ass over teakettle.

If Shane catches me, he will figure out why I ran, and I have no clue how long he plans to let me live once we both know he killed Tim. There's a massive difference between feeling dead and *being* dead.

I manage to keep my slippers as I dart through the manicured lawn and garden, but that doesn't last long. We're even higher up on the mountain than I realized. I hoped the incredible views from my window were overstating things a little—they weren't. The terrain is rough. I'm not used to running on an incline or scaling mountains, and the landscape here is steep and rocky. I lose the slippers before I've gone a hundred yards.

I'm fast because I ran track in high school. But that was a long time ago, and I was never known for the more intense displays of strength that comes with the sport. I'm not pole vaulting anytime soon. Panting, out of shape, and wheezing, I curse myself for not running anymore. How did I let Tim take something so simple from me?

Someone could see you and tell them *where we live.*

Pine trees stick up, forcing me to dodge them, but their thin branches still scratch and tear at my skin. I'm crying, but the tears are drying on my cheeks with the wind whipping at my face.

My foot catches a sharp rock, the jagged stone breaking through my skin. I cry out, unable to stop myself from the sudden pain. The rock doesn't dislodge, and each panicked step is agony. My hot blood flows, slickening each of my steps and removing my traction, making my stride even less sure than it was before. I'm slowing, exhausted, agonized, and miserable. But then Shane shouts my name.

His outraged voice rips down the side of the mountain, and I'm stunned by how it vibrates around me. I push myself despite the pain because I'm confident the last thing I want is for him to find me.

My tears pour as I move through the trees and rocks. I'm slowing, and I know I can't keep this up for much longer. The pain is intense. Rocks, debris, and only God knows what else is packed inside the injury by the force of my steps. I need to hide, find a place to rest, and let him calm down enough to slow his search before I have a chance to get out of here.

But I never get the chance.

His body collides with mine, out of nowhere. I would have heard him coming if it weren't for my panting and mewling, pained noises. If I thought for a moment the time we spent together would make him soft on me, Shane forcibly removes that illusion as my body collides with the hard stone.

My head spins from the impact, but his hand braces the worst of the force on my skull. The protective gesture doesn't last. That same hand moves to the back of my hair, gripping tight and forcing my face even harder into the rough and sharp stone. He's on top of me, feral noises spilling from his mouth. The entirety of his weight presses into my back like a death sentence.

My thin nightgown clings to my sweat-soaked body, and now that I've stopped running, I'm freezing. The only warm parts of me are the points of contact between us. Shane gasps, not saying anything as he watches me. I can see his face, but I can't look at him, which doesn't matter since his incensed eyes soak up my tears as surely as the stone beneath me.

He still hasn't said anything as he moves the hand on my hair to my neck and squeezes. I look at him now, terrified by this turn of events, except I don't find the kind of blind rage on his face that I saw when Tim choked me. His ocean-blue eyes consume me, and a silent snarl twists his features. Everything about this is so unlike Shane. He's always speaking, always guiding me through what's happening, and I am sure that even if he killed me, he would describe his actions as I died. I wonder if this is how Tim died.

I don't have the breath to ask, and he doesn't seem inclined to answer my unspoken questions. Instead, he's silent as he squeezes until I see stars. I've never been so afraid, never felt so small and helpless, and that's saying something. I'm mortifyingly wet, and I can't even begin to understand why my life being in danger arouses me, but fuck, it does.

This world is not worth it. *None* of this is worth it. I've never seen quite so clearly how fucking redundant my existence is.

Shane loosens his grip, and I breathe in a rush of oxygen. My nipples harden, and I'm tingling from head to toe, buzzing like I'm high, and aching for relief from this unbearable tension coiling inside me. My stupid body thinks if he fucks me, I'll be safe. Or maybe I am that messed up.

I have enough sanity and breath to choke out, "Just kill me, just kill me like you killed Tim."

My words dig at him, I can see it on his face, and I think he will end me. I'm not going to face myself or the way I hate the things I've done and the person I became. I don't think about the afterlife, I spent most of my actual life doing that, and I figure I will find out soon enough.

Even though I'm fucking terrified, I've accepted my death.

Except, he doesn't kill me.

He closes his hand again and brings me to the edge of unconsciousness. When I'm about to pass out, he lets me breathe. This time he shoves his tongue roughly against mine and tastes my panicked breaths. The next time he chokes me, his tongue finds my ear, and his teeth clamp tightly around the lobe.

A humiliating slew of noises tumbles out of me while he's still silent. His disgusted expression looks closer to hatred than lust, which is devastating, but he's using my body, and I can't help its response to him. My hips are bucking, and I don't want to stop myself. They still as he steals enough of my air for things to start going black.

I can't take this. My nerves are shattering while Shane controls my breath and repeatedly takes me to the edge of unconsciousness. I'm sopping wet, almost unconscious, and in the seconds I can think, I hate us both so goddamn much.

I do pass out, and when I wake up, I'm still on the cutting rocks. Only a minute or two must have passed, but Shane's got my soaked nightgown up around my hips and propped my knees up. The stones dig into my knees, but he doesn't even pause at the pathetic sounds I make. I feel the cold breeze on my cunt, and I'm not surprised he's going to fuck me one more time before he kills me.

Maybe he'll fuck you after too. A small, insidious voice whispers from the back of my mind.

I'm afraid of dying, but who isn't? I'm so scared of Shane. What I'm not afraid of is his cock inside me, and I find myself responding to the conditioning. I grind myself against him. I might as well come one more time before I go, and that fucked-up part of me that loves danger knows it will be the best of my limited experience.

"I'm relieved you still want me to take that cunt, Angel. But that won't do for your punishment."

The sound of his voice almost breaks me. First, I'm so relieved I almost cry, but then his words sink in.

Punishment, not death.

A finger probes my tight ass, and I shiver as his spit

slips between my cheeks. That finger dips inside, gently at first, and I'm not in pain so much as humiliated by my position and the saliva dripping over me. When he shoves his entire finger in, I moan—I like what he's doing to me.

But that doesn't last.

Shane spreads my ass cheeks, spits once more on my last virgin hole, and plunges his much too-large cock deep inside me. Burning agony doesn't begin to describe it. It hurts so bad that my vision blackens around the edges as it did when he choked me. My strangled screams turn my stomach worse than the pain.

"Exactly, Angel. That's exactly how I felt when I realized you ran from me."

His fingers dig into my hips, leaving bruises as he forcefully stuffs his cock deep into my ass. That swell of relief at his voice crashes into me again, and I curse my stupid heart for trusting him.

"Please, stop!" I scream. It hurts so fucking bad I want to die. It hurts so fucking bad I regret running. It hurts so bad that when I register my own juices dripping down my thighs, I know I am broken.

His hips still, but he's deep inside me, stretching me further than ever.

"You told me you didn't want a safe word. You told me you didn't want consent. Now you're going to learn your lesson."

I did say those things after he told me he planned to *take* my virginity. And that turned me on so badly I didn't even consider the consequences; I just fucked him.

"Shane, it hurts, please."

"Do you want a safeword, after all, Angel?"

"Stop!" I scream at the top of my lungs. Part of me wants him to, and the other can't bear to establish the boundary of a safeword with him. I want Shane to abuse my boundaries.

"Seraphina, you need this. You need to understand who you belong to and what happens to you when you run."

He's sheathed inside me, and he starts moving again. The smacking sound of his balls colliding with my cunt humiliates and arouses me, but the pain is intense.

"It hurts!" I wail, wishing more than anything I had avoided this, even if that meant staying in the house while trying to bide my time. Hell, even if that meant staying with the man who killed Tim. And why couldn't I say I wanted a safeword?

Because you don't want one.

I'm crying hard, tears pouring down my cheeks, and he's pumping himself into my ass. I don't even know if he's enjoying it. He's not grunting how he usually does, and he's not filling my ears with his pretty filth.

"I hate that you made me do this to you," he says, answering my unspoken question. "I'm not going to come from this, Seraphina, but you are. You're going to come so hard, you'll see God right before I rip my cock out of your ass and remind you that I'm the Devil and *you're* in hell."

I can't believe his control as he does what he said he would. His cock is as hard as the rocks beneath me, but he doesn't even look at me. I'm so tight around him that it's agony, and even though I know who he is now, his indifference hurts the worst.

I'm his perfect, pretty slut. I'm his whore.

Another voice screams in the back of my mind—the voice he put there during our twisted sessions.

You need to please him! The desperate voice wails, and it feels like I'm dying when I glance over my shoulder and see how little he cares for this, for me.

Shane tilts my hips so that his cock doesn't go as deep. Of course it still aches, but in this position, his cock rubs at something pleasurable deep inside me.

Oh fuck.

At the same time, he reaches around the front of me and plays with my clit. The pleasure is intense, mixed with all the pain. My body is desperate for the relief an orgasm will bring, and my mind is desperate to please him even though I hate myself with every fiber of my being. Just like the well-trained whore I am, I go off like a rocket, my empty cunt pulsing desperately, wishing his fingers were inside while my overstuffed ass clenches around him.

True to his words, Shane doesn't come; he brings me to see God before ripping his cock out of my ass and reminding me that *he's* the Devil and *I'm* in hell.

CHAPTER
TWENTY-EIGHT

SERA

I don't know where I am as Shane throws me over his shoulder and carries me back to the castle on top of the mountain. I know where my body is, but my soul is far off. I wish I could say it's wandering after Tim, the man I pledged my love and life to. The man who died because I couldn't keep it in my pants.

But it's not.

It's mourning everything I thought Shane and I could be. I hate to admit it even now that I see who he is and what he's capable of, but in these last weeks, he had convinced me we could have a life together—one where I'm wanted and needed, lusted after deeply, and cherished. The loss of that dream cuts so deep that my bleeding soul hurts more than my numerous new wounds. A bird cries overhead, and I wonder if it's mistaken me for a carrion.

Shane's arm bands around my knees. I'm his prize, and even if a crow or something were big enough to take me, he wouldn't let me go. I lie draped over his back, and he doesn't bother stabilizing me. As a result, my face smacks against him with each step up the incline.

Shane's boots crunch and his breaths are labored, but he doesn't make a sound. Blood rushes to my head, and my eyes and fingertips feel about to explode. I wonder if he would warn me if I became too heavy and he needed to drop me. I'd smash my face on the rocks and roll down the whole way. It might kill me, but it might not, and the unknown keeps me from attempting to fight.

I also wonder if he hates me now, and that thought crushes me. Why does it hurt so much? Why do I want this man to love me even when I know what he's done? I've been crying since I learned he killed Tim, but my sobs come louder, bouncing off the unforgiving stone.

He says nothing to soothe me. Instead, he holds me tight and drags me up the mountain. My sobs and his labored steps are the only sounds we hear upon our return. They bounce off the stairs leading to the front door and echo in the giant entryway. When he closes the door behind us, I yelp. There's finality in that action, and my entrapment hurts like physical pain. I know that I'll never be able to get out of here in my current state.

I try to accept the fact that this is my life now. While I'm heartbroken over Tim and angry about what Shane did to me, I don't have the correct level of reluctance. Part of me still believes I might love it in this mountaintop castle, provided he doesn't kill me. I'm angry about being demeaned, debased, and used, but I fucking loved it. I hate myself more than I could ever hate Shane, and maybe that's why I can't muster the proper outrage.

Or maybe you think Tim deserved to die for what he did to you.

I nearly puke at the thought.

Still, that naïve person expects Shane to take me back to the room I've stayed in, the plush place full of pillows and books, looking out over a picturesque valley, clawfoot tub, and everything. He has consistently spoiled me, and even if he plans to kill me once we're there, I expect him to take me back. So, when he goes left toward a wing I've never seen, I kick and claw, trying my hardest to escape. *This could be so much worse than death.*

He opens a door, and I'm shaking with how cold it is. The air smells different than the rest of the house, and I'm curious if there's even heat. His hand finds the switch, illuminating the long old hallway with a pale yellow light. The walls are painted in a thick Robin's egg blue, fading and yellowing in places. My vision blurs around the edges from the pressure on my eyes, but I need to see as much as I can of where he's taking me.

Looking around at the much smaller halls and doorways, I can only conclude he's brought me to the servants' quarters. I'm terrified this is where the staff Pax said he dismissed actually lives. Shane confirms my suspicions about the servants' quarters when he opens a door and tosses me onto a threadbare single bed. I bounce off the mattress, which is so hard it can barely be called such. My fingers encounter scratchy wool with a thick, grimy coating.

He pulls a cord, and a single bulb flashes overhead. The room is a horrid green and dusty. There's a window, which I didn't expect, revealing a sliver of light above the ground. Of course no one could fit through it anyway, but it's nailed shut to ensure you can't breathe. The nails are rusty, and I silently thank God it's been a long time since people have stayed here.

You are *people, Seraphina.*

Shane drops to his knees before me, his fine dress pants smudging the dirt and dust on the floor. Scooting back from him, I encounter the wall before I get far. He snatches my more injured foot and pulls, dropping me onto my back so he can inspect the wound. Instead of letting him, I fight, kicking him as hard as possible. My foot connects with his nose, and I hear a crunch before I wail in agony.

Oh shit, oh fuck.

I regret my decision immediately, but not because I'm in horrible pain. I hate myself for hurting Shane. I hate myself for striking out against the only person I need. *Jesus Christ, I fucking love him.*

Blood drips from his nose, over his lips, and down his chin. His tongue darts out and licks away the trail on his lower lip, and I stop fighting. Our breaths are the only noise between us as I figure out where I got that idea. Why do I need Shane after such a short time? Why do I love him?

The answer rings in my head, clear as a bell.

Hypnosis.

With that one word, everything left of me breaks. The eyes I thought would drown me have finally succeeded, and I slump against the bed. All vestiges of my fight leave me as surely as Tim lost his life.

"None of it was real," I whisper, and if I thought Shane looked mad because I broke his nose, I was wrong.

That single stream of blood continues to trickle as he looks at me like I am dirt beneath his shoes. His blue eyes are blackening already, and their pain threatens to swallow me in their depths and erase even the memory of my existence.

"It was all real."

"You hypnotized me."

"And you remember every single session, Seraphina. I didn't *erase* your memories; you're not a goddamn puppet! Whether you want to think about what we did together is up to you, but you don't have amnesia. And the *hypnosis* didn't force you to do anything you didn't already want."

Shane watches my face. Maybe he wants me to

respond or thinks he can read the thoughts out of my head. Whatever he sees there doesn't satisfy him. Shane pushes off the ground, and I flinch as he reaches for me. He smiles as he grabs the tattered silk shift still covering me even after everything. Sure he's going to hurt me, instead, he wipes the blood from his lip off on the crusted fabric. Once his lips are slightly cleaner, he gently presses them to mine.

Despite my best intentions, I meet his tongue when he licks his way into my mouth.

"For now, let the pain in your ass remind you what will happen if you try to leave me again. I'll be back to clean your feet as soon as you let me." He points at the camera in the corner, and I notice the red light blinking at me for the first time. He stands and turns, closing my cell door and leaving me without another word.

I look at the wounds on my feet. They're jagged, filthy, and awful—I'll die before I let Shane clean them.

CHAPTER
TWENTY-NINE
SHANE

I'M SITTING IN MY STUDY, POURING OVER EVERY DETAIL, BIG or small, I ever learned about Seraphina and Tim. My head is throbbing, and I take another pill to stem the pulsing behind my eyes. My little Angel seriously broke my fucking nose. Big black bruises surround my eyes, and there's a definite crooked line of bone I decide against resetting. I deserve the pain.

In addition to the tear she left in my heart when she ran and my busted nose, there are long, jagged cuts on the bottom of my feet to match hers. I refuse to bandage them until she lets me clean her damn feet.

If there is one thing I can comfort myself with is that Seraphina hasn't lost her fight. During the shower she took yesterday, she tried to wash her feet in the old tub. The attempt was pathetic but proved I haven't broken her, and for that I'm elated. The sounds she made while picking at the dirt and stones played in the background when I cut my feet to match hers.

She's more upset than I assumed she would be. I knew she would be sad about Tim's passing and angry with me for killing him. But I also believed we had established enough of a foundation that she wouldn't lose it like this. There is more to her situation with him. Something that goes beyond her nature to punish herself relentlessly for every ungodly desire she has. I intend to find out what it is.

I love her for her strength and fire.

But I'm worrying over her like a fucking mother hen, which is making it hard to prove my point. My phone is propped up on my desk, playing my love for me. Occasionally, she mutters a few words aloud, and while I haven't learned anything from them yet, they're much too precious to miss.

I haven't gone to her in hours, but I'm desperate to tend to her and ensure she's okay. I know she's not great, but we can fix this. Watching her is hollow as she flips back and forth on the threadbare bed.

Bloody and fuming, I stomp across the marble floor as I call Pax, inviting him over in a few days expressly so I could kick his ass. My bloody footprints remain on the floor and will stay there until I can get the staff back in here.

When I realized Seraphina had run, I knew what she had heard and who was responsible for letting her go. My biggest regret is letting him get away while dealing with her. I can imagine him cackling his way down the drive with the windows open, listening to her screams, *my screams*.

I haven't found anything beyond what I already knew. Tim is dead, so I can't ask him, and that leaves my Angel. Going to see her isn't a hardship, considering I've been dying to run back to her the minute I left her, and that's even taking my nose into account. I get up from my desk and leave the office, locking the door behind me.

My feet burn and sting as I head to the kitchen. It's a gorgeous space, better suited for a high-end restaurant or a family of fifteen. Our family is insanely wealthy but ultimately relatively small. It's just myself, Pax, another few cousins, and an aunt. It's absurd for so few people to have so much, and that's a big part of why I chose a career and moved away from home. I never *wanted* many of the things I own, but Seraphina is always the exception.

I prove that to myself as I make her a sandwich the way I know she likes because I've paid attention since I met the woman. I'm hopeful it's tempting enough that even if she won't eat in front of me, she'll have it once I'm gone. A chill runs over my skin as I pull the lettuce out of the crisper and look around. I hope I haven't been negligent about allowing Pax here. I flip through the cameras on my phone and assure myself that even if he can get in, I'll know.

Dismissing my thoughts, I grab her a glass of juice right before I head out of the kitchen. I know she's angry with me, but we can work past it. Stopping at a hall closet beside one of the many first-floor guest bathrooms, I also grab first aid supplies.

Despite the dwindling branches of my family tree, generations of them stare back at me from oil paintings lining the wall. I'd love to be the last surviving member of my family and burn the whole legacy. Instead, the watchful eyes of my forefathers judge me harshly while I head toward the room where I'm keeping Sera, as if they hadn't abused and fucked their way through the servants' quarters often enough.

What I did was crude and brutal, but I was fucking angry. I'm prepared to make things better today, starting with letting Seraphina out and putting her back in her room. That's if *she's* prepared to be reasonable. I juggle the items as I pull a key from my pocket and unlock the door. The towel from her feeble attempt at a shower is crumpled beneath the door, and it takes me a few seconds to shove the door open. She's done it on purpose to get a rise out of me, and I almost smile, but then I see the bloodstains and the look on her face.

The camera doesn't accurately show how she's suffered. Lines of pain carve deeply into her sallow skin. She looks up at me from her spot on the tiny bed for only a moment before her eyes drop back to the ground. I haven't impressed her, but I can change that. I can be the perfect partner.

"Seraphina, I brought you something to eat, and I need you to let me clean your feet," I speak as softly as I would if she were a small child. She says nothing. Encouraged by her silence, I place all of my things on the table beside the bed. Then, pulling out antiseptic wipes and bandages, I see her looking over the turkey sandwich with avocado and orange juice. But when I step toward her, whatever calm kept her anger inside shatters without warning.

"Get away from me! Don't you dare touch me!" The venomous words dripping from her pretty mouth sting.

I could say many unhelpful things in this situation, but I keep them to myself as I sit on the edge of the bed, careful not to touch her.

She told me she didn't want consent. She told me she wanted me to take, and that's what I did. I've only ever given her what she's asked of me, no matter what was required of me. I am a monster, but not the one she's trying to convince herself.

"Your feet are going to get infected," I answer, leaving as much emotion as I can out of my voice.

"I don't care."

"You could lose them, Angel. All I want to do is clean them and make you feel better."

She laughs, but it turns into a sob. "Is that what you want? To make me feel better! Is that why you *killed* my husband?"

She's not fucking baiting me.

"Yes, making you feel better is what I want."

"So you killed my husband to make *me* feel *better!?*"

"No. I convinced Tim to leave you to improve every aspect of *your* life. I only killed him because after everything he did to you, he told me he regretted not killing you. He said he wished he had."

I stare into her yellow-green eyes, expecting her to understand. I'm a psychiatrist and understand the human mind exceedingly well, but no one is exempt from letting their hopes and expectations cloud their judgment. At this moment, I can see my mistake.

"You killed Tim because he made some stupid comment while I was alive and perfectly well?" her voice is small, stunned, and disbelieving. The pain in her eyes is so raw and honest, so unlike anything I've seen in her before. "He's dead because he was a smart-mouth dick?"

I'm shaking my head, doing everything to stop myself from reaching toward her. I want to grab her by her throat and tell her exactly how it is, but I stay where I am and meet her eyes.

"I crushed his arm because he hurt you."

Her eyes widen, and her mouth drops open as she gasps.

"He's dead because he didn't learn his lesson. But I've learned mine, and I'll do the same to anyone who dares to touch you."

My admission and vow only make her more nervous.

"A lot of people have hurt me, Shane. Are you going to kill all of them? Are you going to kill yourself?"

"I will kill every last person who has hurt you, and if

you count me among them, I'll take my life too. Just say the word, Seraphina."

Her cheeks turn red, but she doesn't answer.

"I ruined his life!" she wails instead, her breaths coming in wild gasps. "You shattered his arm because of me. His father shattered his legs because of me."

She won't tell me I hurt her because she doesn't believe I did, but she's seeing my actions more clearly. She's not ready to accept the cost of this life of ours, or loving what I did to her, mainly because she's scared. She wanted me to cleave her in half and prove how much I need her. Well, I did. Kinks develop in many ways, and I know my girl needs me to take it because she spent so long unable to give it away. Tim did that to her, and he suffered for it, but I'll never let her feel undesired.

"Let me clean your feet, Angel." Starting over has worked for us in the past.

"I loved him, and I *ruined* his life."

Her head falls into her hands, and the part of me that loves her more than anything wants to comfort her, but the jealous part that wishes Tim's memory didn't exist is offended by her pain.

I reach forward and twine my hand in her hair, forcing her to look at me. I can't stand this distance she's putting between us, or the fact she's in pain and refuses to let me help her.

"He ruined *your* life, Seraphina, and I took *his* for it,"

I press my face against hers, forehead to forehead, and she squeals in response. The act is somewhere between dominance and affection, and I feel myself toeing that wild line I often do with her.

"You ruined my life. You, Shane, not Tim. Now get away from me!"

"You'd rather die from an infection than let me clean your feet?"

"Yes," she says, leaving no room for doubts.

"Fine, Seraphina. It seems I have a point to prove."

I leave her there, slamming the door behind me. I'm too angry not to be petulant. I do not regret what I did anymore. I fucking hated having to punish her, and I hate leaving her in this room far away from me, but I will prove my point.

My fury feels like a separate entity as I think about her running. I must calm down before seeing her again, but I care too much to leave her with nothing. I head to the kitchen and make her an elaborate dinner before leaving it inside her door.

I return to her room the following day with breakfast, a gallon of water, and medical supplies. I have no clue how long I'll be gone, but she can get more water from the tap if she needs it. She will be hungry, though; turning dinner down last night was her damn choice. She's going to learn to pick her battles one of these days.

But, for now, my Angel is lying in bed again and refusing to look at me.

"Let me take care of your feet." I won't offer twice; if she rejects my help, that's fine. She'll have brought whatever happens next upon herself.

"Fuck you," she answers.

"I'm going to be gone for a few days. Would you like me to before I go?"

In response, she makes a disgusted noise in the back of her throat and still makes no move to let me clean her feet.

"Fine, Angel. You want a monster? I'll give you a monster."

I leave her there, hoping she won't be too sick when I return.

CHAPTER
THIRTY
SERA

I'm so angry I am about to explode, and despite all the injustices of my life, I have never known such rage.

"God damn it, Shane! Fuck you! I fucking hate you!" I'm shouting again as I have numerous times, and that's how I'm confident Shane has left me alone.

I drop on the unforgiving mattress and beat my fists against it. My stomach grumbles loud enough to hear over my assault, and I whine pitifully. When Shane still doesn't come, I throw a plate against the wall and realize my mistake a second too late; I will cut my feet further on the broken shards.

I didn't eat the sandwich he brought me for lunch or the elaborate steak and whipped potatoes he made for dinner, which felt much more like groveling than I expected. By breakfast the following day, both dishes were disgusting and dried out, and I was still too angry to eat. He presented me with the loveliest eggs benedict, and I didn't eat that either.

Stupidly, I'd grown confident he would keep spoiling me. I almost looked forward to turning my nose at whatever he slaved over for lunch. It felt amazing to have the power for once, to know how badly he wanted to please me. But that midday meal never came. Leaving me wondering when did I become so spoiled? And how can the man who's given me all that leave me now?

I regretted my decision by that evening when it was clear no more food was coming. I peeled the dried-out egg off the English muffin and ate that. Twelve hours later, I ate the rest of the food he left. The steak stuck in my throat on the way down, the cold potato made me gag, but I forced it down with water. All I do is cry, but I cried again when I realized Shane wasn't lying about going.

I have a bathroom, so at least he hasn't left me to wallow in literal filth and shit; it is the figurative kind that haunts my every thought. There is nothing here to keep me occupied, nothing to do or ponder other than my own thoughts. I find myself ripping up a napkin to keep myself entertained.

I'm hungry, my head hurts, my stomach aches, and with all this time, I have no reprieve from myself.

I think about Tim and all the years we spent together. I grieve him so fiercely, and as his loss rips at me, I'm forced to ask myself where that pain originates from. And the truth is, it's not from the loss of romantic love. It's because I lost the only person who ever believed me. I owed Tim better than what I gave him in life and in the death I caused. I wish we could have been better for each other.

But as those thoughts assail me, there are others too. I think of the way he used to make me feel before he even became outright abusive. Tim made me feel stupid and small, unlikeable. He never acted as if he wanted me. Even when we were young, he said all the right things, but his actions never backed up his words.

I don't know why he picked me because I'm now sure he never truly wanted me.

I know why I picked him though. He was cute and sweet when he wanted to be. But, more than anything else, I saw his pain, and he saw mine. I thought our pain would bond us, but it only made me loyal to him and him resentful of me. I was wrong for assuming the giving nature of my heart extended to other people and thinking he would love all of my broken pieces just because I was willing to love his.

Then his dad broke his legs.

Even if things were wrong between us, how on earth could I have left him after that? There were days I prayed he would leave me to spare us both, but that deliverance never came. So by the time, I said yes to marrying him again, to helping him escape, I had to give our relationship a chance.

I have been lying to myself for so long.

I think back to our childhood when we met before our moms died. Usually, it's difficult for me to remember much of anything from that time, but my mind feels clearer than ever. Finally, a memory from a few months before my mom died comes back to me, hard and fast.

My mother sits at her dressing table and stares at herself in the mirror. The dark bruise on her cheek isn't so nasty now that she's covered it in makeup. A tear rolls down her cheek, and she grabs a tissue to dab it away.

"Mama, why are you crying?"

My father hurt her, but it was a few days ago, and she doesn't usually cry this long.

"I'm just feeling guilty, Seraphina."

"Why, Mama, what did you do wrong?"

"If I were a better wife and mother, your father wouldn't need to strike me. I want to be better, Seraphina."

"You don't need to be better!" I argue a little too loudly. "You're perfect the way you are, and I love you."

She looks up at me, my yellow-green eyes staring back at me. "Did they tell you that at school? You know that no one but God is perfect, right?"

"But you're perfect the way God made you! That's what they said in church!" I'm hysterical. I hate the way she's making this all her fault.

"Don't get upset, Sera." Her tone is brusque now, and her eyes dart back and forth like she's checking to ensure *he hasn't heard us. "Be a better wife than I am. Tim's always loved you. Tim will make an excellent husband."*

Maybe in her opinion he did. Have I been sacrificing my happiness to please a dead woman? Did I let Tim ruin my life and his because my mother, who never understood anything about love, told me he was good for me? I know that's a big part of it. I'm devastated that his life was cut short, especially because of me, but I'm lying to myself if I pretend I will miss Timothy Baker.

One of the most frightening things I realize while I'm alone is that I remember everything. Every minute I believed to have slipped away to the hypnosis was right where Shane assured me they would be. But, true to his words, he didn't do anything to me I didn't want. That knowledge is more painful than Tim's loss.

I'm too emotionally drained to feel as guilty and ashamed as usual. So pushing past the point of physical discomfort, I've fallen into a meditative place where I can reflect on my actions without as much self-hatred. I'm not a good person, but I see myself for the first time in my life.

I can see a hint of the sun through the half window. That's how I know it's been three days since Shane left. I've watched the sun track across the sky throughout the morning and mourn when it's too high over the house to see. Day two was cloudy, and I thought I'd gone insane. Instead, I'm at the *edge* of my sanity and so fucking hungry. I hope he comes back soon so I can tell him I see how right he was.

I nearly sob in relief when I hear his footsteps in the hall. I have to remind myself that Shane left me without food for days and that the agony I'm suffering is at least ninety percent his fault. Even though I had eaten what he left me, it wasn't enough for how long he was gone, but good luck trying to tell that to my heart that's racing away and dying to jump into his arms.

Before the door opens, a delicious savory scent tightens my salivary glands and cramps my stomach in painful desire. The key twists in the lock, and Shane's standing there with a bowl of soup like my personal savior.

His black hair is messier than I've ever seen, and his typical five o'clock shadow has grown into a very short beard. His eyes are hollow and gaunt, and still black but yellowing in places from when I kicked him, making that deep blue look even more startling. His nose has a significant bump, and I regret hurting him. But even looking like he's been through hell, he's so handsome it hurts.

I try to think of Tim, the shape of his mouth, remember the color of his eyes, and I can't. I saw him two weeks ago, and I can't remember his eyes after only a few days without food.

I don't have the energy to cry or the salt in my body to produce tears. But I feel myself breaking open. I'm lying on the bed and do my best to pull myself up into a sitting position.

I'm so damn weak.

"Will you let me take care of your feet?"

It's the same question I so stubbornly refused before. My feet are in agony. I'm sure they're infected, and I've

MIND TO BEND

noticed signs of fever. I should have let Shane clean my damn feet. I know better than to cut off my nose to spite my face, and somehow, I got so swept up in him that I forgot that.

"Please…"

I go to stretch out, but he stops me.

"Eat first."

I can't argue with that. I'm so hungry and grateful that Shane brought something my tender stomach can handle. Struggling to sit up, I wait for him to hand me the food or tell me where he wants me. Instead, he sits beside me and offers me a spoonful. I hate him a little bit, but I can't deny that he paces me a lot slower than I want to eat, and that's likely why I don't vomit. He says nothing to me as he feeds me the entire bowl.

Once it's gone, he stands again.

"Lay down, Seraphina."

At his command, a shiver runs through me, but I obey. The next hour is one of the most painful of my life, much worse than the anal sex against the rocks, which ultimately makes me warm and tingly when I think of it.

"You tried to clean them yourself," he comments as he's bandaging my feet.

"Yeah, it hurt too much to get very far."

"You did a good job, Seraphina. The infection could have been a lot worse. I think you saved yourself from serious damage."

I flush under his praise. I know he could tell me how stubborn and petulant I've been and how much I cost myself for it, but I already know it, and he seems to understand his silence will always say more. Once he finishes wrapping my feet, he gently holds them, and as stupid as it sounds, I can feel how much he wants them to heal. It soothes the pain, the same way a mother's kiss does on a child's grazed knee. I don't understand how the same hands that took my husband's life can feel like that, but they do.

I'm full, exhausted, and in tremendous pain. His hands move from my feet slowly up my legs. I think he will fuck me, and a sick part of me is desperate for it. I'm wet and hungry at the idea, but that's not what he's doing. Instead, he checks my entire body. Finding the cuts on my knees, he carefully cleans and bandages them. Next, he finds the spot on my cheek where the stone scraped my skin raw. That doesn't need a bandage, but he cleans it all. He tends to and covers every single wound.

We still haven't spoken, and rather than awkward and tense, there's a sweetness to the reunion. His dexterous fingers work into my muscles, and Shane massages the tension out of every part of me. I'm soft and molten by the time he's rubbing the tips of my fingers.

"What do you want, Seraphina?"

"I want it to be like it was before." No matter what he's done to me, he's cared for me in a way that I can't ignore, and I'm melting into a puddle for him.

He smiles, then his expression drops.

"What's wrong?" My heart is pounding in my chest.

"I'm glad you've come around, Angel. And I'm so sorry about this, but I'm a man of my word, and you still haven't been punished yet."

"What do you mean? How could I have not been punished enough? What more is there?"

"I didn't leave you here *to* punish you. I left you here to *get* your punishment."

CHAPTER
THIRTY-ONE
SHANE

I push Seraphina's hair off her face and wipe my hand across her brow. She's sweaty and feverish. I'm awestricken by her radiant smile but wary as I lift her into my arms. The last time I thought she allowed me to help her without a fight, I was surprised by a foot crushing my nose. Could a little soup mend fences like that? Doubtful.

There's a wet spot on the bed beneath her, and I can tell from the damp shift that she's been sweating terribly. She will need antibiotics, but shouldn't need to be hospitalized. She weighs nothing, and my chest pangs in response. Looking around the derelict room, I'm forced to admit I'm another person who caused my Angel pain. I'll need to better handle my temper after this and ensure it never happens again.

Seraphina wraps her arms around my neck, her fingers tangling in my hair as she clings to me. Her nose burrows into the crook of my neck, and she inhales my scent. She smells like sweat and fear, but that sweetness that's distinctly hers persists. She's so tiny in my arms, so precious, and I feel the overwhelming urge to kiss every inch of her body and make everything right. My chest is so warm I struggle to keep standing. I want to lay us both on that shitty bed and hold her.

Holy shit, what have I done?

"This is a warmer reception than I expected," I admit as she kisses my neck and we leave the abandoned wing. I doubt I'll even send someone here to clean up after her. Maybe, I'll have it permanently blocked off.

She hums, and the vibrations tingle more around the stubble on my neck. "You were right about most things, and I missed you, even though you're an ass."

I laugh as I tip her chin up so that she has to look at me. How is she so lovely, even as sickly as she seems? Her eyes remind me of spring flowers despite the bags beneath them, and her lips are plush pink petals, even cracked and sore.

"You swearing at me is new. Though I was watching the cameras the whole time, and you did an awful lot of that while I was gone."

"Yeah, we're at the point in our relationship where I'm going to tell you when you're being an asshole, dick—"

I cut her off with a hand over her mouth.

"Are you sure you're not being affectionate because you were hungry and needed me to feed you?"

"Well, seeing as you left me alone for three days and are the *cause* of my hunger, I think you canceled out your *good deed*." Despite the acid in her tone, she nuzzles more deeply against my skin, like the separation was really the hardest part for her.

She sounds more irritated than outright angry, and I'm tired of the panicked feeling in my chest.

"Seraphina, I'm serious!"

She bites her lip as she stares at mine. A little smirk forms around the edges of her lips.

"It was lovely that you fed me." She cocks her head to the side. Is she flirting with me?

"That's not an answer."

"After three days alone in that shitty room, you're lucky I'm *answering* you at all."

"Seraphina,"

She sighs. "Shane, I'm not going to pretend anything you've done is okay, but I love you, and I don't care anymore. I've never been happier than when I'm with you. There's no one left to explain my choices to, and I choose you." She takes a deep breath. "It will take me time to get over what you did to Tim, but I suppose I can understand it. I-I don't know what I would do to someone who was hurting you."

I pause in the hallway letting her words sink in.

She loves me, chooses me, and understands?

"I hope you're not telling me what I want to hear in hopes of avoiding your punishment, Angel. That would be especially cruel of you." I sound angry, and I realize it's because I'm fucking scared.

"And why would it be cruel?"

"Because I love you so fucking much that when you left me, you ripped my heart out. And if you would say you loved me without meaning it…" I can't finish. There aren't words for the feeling.

"I would never do that to you, Shane." She grabs my cheeks and pulls my lips briefly to hers. "You were right. I remember everything, and no matter what it says about me, I wanted everything. I'm sick and fucked-up, but I love you."

"No, Angel, you have kinks, and you love a sick and fucked-up man. But you are perfect."

She's quiet for a minute as I carry her through the house.

"About my punishment…"

"I'm sorry, Angel. I wish I could take it back, but I'm a man of my word, and what's done is done." I want to keep talking and explain away what I'm about to do, but I know there's no justification, and there's no going back now. Hell, even if I didn't make a production out of it, I couldn't just let him go.

"What do you mean?" She stiffens in my arms as we enter the sunken lounge at the back of the house. "What did you do that you can't take back?"

"Seraphina?" A deep and gravel-filled voice asks from the couch on the other side of the room.

Seraphina pulls her face out of my neck, her mouth popping open in shock. Her head turns toward him with comic slowness, and a little sound rips from her throat when her eyes land on him. Her hands drop from around my neck, and she grabs onto her own.

"Dad? What are you doing here!?"

She pushes against my hold to get a closer look. Despite how weak she is, I let her down. She sways on her feet, and I help her to a chair. She sits because she's not strong enough to do anything else. Since she verified it was her father, she hasn't looked back, and her eyes stay on the floor.

"What is he doing here, Shane?" Red blotches stain her cheeks, and it's not the pretty flush I'm so fond of. She's distraught.

"He's your punishment," I answer, waving to the balding man watching us from the corner.

He's wearing a bloodied tan shirt and jeans. I found him in his living room reading a paper about homosexuality and sin and how the pope was playing a dangerous game by not openly condemning homosexuals. It was particularly satisfying to punch him in the face at that moment. In addition to hurting my Angel, I can't stand a bigot.

The offending middle-aged man sits bound, but I haven't needed to gag him. The worst thing he's done since I broke into Seraphina's childhood home and abducted him was punching me once in the cheek and quoting scripture. That was annoying, but ultimately any information he gave me would be more valuable than his silence. Of course he didn't tell me much in the day-and-a-half-long drive here, but what he gave me is enough to learn he's a nastier monster than I am. The kind that takes pleasure in hurting his own child.

Seraphina's face falls, big fat tears spilling over her eyes. I'm shocked by how quickly she understands what I have planned. She's malnourished and sick, so I expected to explain the situation.

"You're this mad at me!?" she bawls, her bottom lip quaking. "You brought him here so he could see what a disappointment I am? You needed to humiliate me even more!?"

She drops her face into her hands, her entire body shaking, and I regret what I've done. How could I underestimate the depths of her self-hatred?

"That's not what's happening here. You are not a disappointment, Angel."

I reach out to touch her, but she smacks my hand away.

Her father makes a disgusted sound from across the room. "Who is this man calling you 'Angel,' Seraphina?"

"My psychiatrist, Sir," she answers without missing a beat, and the hands hiding her face drop to her sides.

"And why would he be calling you something so familiar?" The man is seething mad, and I can only smile. "Why would you let him call you that?"

"Is there a reason I shouldn't?" I cock my head to the side.

When Jensen doesn't answer, I turn to his daughter. "Well?"

"That's what he used to call me."

"Naughty Angel. You never told me that." She is something special.

"Why, Seraphina?" The ropes holding him creak as he fights against them, and I wonder what he would do to her if he could get loose.

"I'm a whore, Dad! Are you happy!? Just like you always accused Mom of being, the only difference is she never was!" her voice rips through multiple octaves, and I realize she wasn't exaggerating her pain over Tim. This is what Seraphina looks like in grief. Seeing this man is agony for her.

Jensen's face turns a similar shade of red to his daughter's, and I notice that's where she got her fair skin and golden blonde hair from.

"Seraphina, stop crying right this minute and answer me. Where is your husband? Where is Timothy, and who is this man besides your psychiatrist?" The Pastor's voice carries over her tears, and with an efficiency far more significant than my hypnotism, Seraphina's back snaps ramrod straight, and her tears stop.

"I don't know, Sir." She sniffles miserably, but the tears stop. He's completely tied up, there's no way for him to hurt her, but he shifts toward her aggressively, awaiting the chance. She's so submissive to him that I bet she'd untie him if he asked.

This just became even more personal. There won't be another man with that type of power in her life. Anyone who hurts her dies, and this man has hurt her far worse than I imagined.

"He's dead, Pastor." I step in between them, blocking his line of sight to her. She's had enough of his hateful stares, enough time fearing the aggressive way he acts around her.

"Dear God," he gasps. "And what happened to him?"

"He was beating your daughter, so I killed him."

He closes his eyes, tips his head back, and prays. I let him get out a few words before I walk up to him and slap him across the face as hard as possible. He doesn't react beyond a soft "oof" and cracking his jaw after.

"You don't even care that he abused her, do you? Par for the course?" I smack him again. "You're praying for the dead piece of shit who beat your own flesh and blood."

"She was his wife. Therefore, his right was to punish her as he saw fit!" he shouts in pure rage, and I see Seraphina's home life crystal clear.

I turn away from him, letting him have my back as he mutters prayers that won't save him. I keep myself between them so he won't have a chance to see her again. Then, grabbing my Angel's chin, I force her to look at me. She sniffles as her reddened eyes meet mine.

"You seem to be under a misunderstanding, Seraphina. I didn't bring him here to hurt you with his shitty words and opinions. I couldn't give a fuck less what he thinks, and neither should you. The reason I brought him here is to kill him for hurting you. I needed to prove a point to you about what you mean to me, and this was the only way."

I expect more tears at the grand reveal of my wicked plans, but Seraphina remains silent, her eyes glazing over. I turn around to check the Pastor's face. He's stopped praying, and he's watching the place his daughter's voice came from with stoicism that shifts to horror as she doesn't object.

"You brought him here to kill him?" The hopeful lilt of her voice takes my breath.

Fully facing her, I pretend it's just the two of us in the room.

"Yes, Angel, I did." I take her hand and wind my fingers through hers, trying to understand her thoughts and feelings.

Tears spill from her eyes, but they're not hysterical.

"Thank you, Shane."

She lifts my hand to her lips and kisses the back of it.

"You're happy!?"

"I'm relieved. I'm so fucking relieved that I don't have to be afraid of him anymore. For years, I thought he was going to find me and hurt me. Because of you, he's never going to."

"No, he's not."

I stroke her hair, assuring her that I'll keep her safe.

"What did he do, Angel? Why were you so afraid?"

"She's always been a liar." Jensen interrupts from the couch. "I never did anything to that girl but raise her the way the good Lord commands."

He's not praying anymore because the good pastor act wasn't working for him, and now he's pulling out his other tricks. I stepped out of their line of sight, and she stares at him, eyes wide and frightened. The pulse on her neck flutters and I regret giving him a chance to speak to her. I should have slain this dragon for her and not made a spectacle of it.

"They were fighting, and he pushed my mom down a flight of stairs in one of the county buildings. That's why she died."

"Shut your mouth, Seraphina. Your mother fell."

"He said it was an accident, and they had to settle with him. That's where all my money came from. He got more than me, but I got a lot too." She's sobbing. "It's blood money."

"Is that how you bought the house?"

She nods.

"You're sick as you've always been, Seraphina. The Devil has gotten his claws even deeper into you than I feared. You're a lost cause, and I can only hope he calls you home before you disgrace yourself further."

She doesn't look at him as she speaks, "I remember you pushing her, Dad. She fell down those stairs because of you. It wasn't the building's fault, and Tim was the only one who believed me."

"Tim's mother slit her wrists to get away from him. Do you think I care what he believed? God knows my soul, Seraphina, and I have nothing to fear."

"No wonder you have so much baggage." I place my hand under her chin and look her over. "I'm done listening to this shit. No one gets to talk about you that way, Angel."

"Okay." She nods, and I smile.

"Are you sure this is what you want?"

She smiles back, "No, Shane, this is a punishment, remember?"

I kiss her swiftly, reminding her she's loved, before turning to her father.

"You should leave, Seraphina." I'm not facing her, but her defiance is thick in the air.

"I'm not going to watch, but I'm not leaving either."

"I don't want this to be another thing you feel guilty about." I caution her.

"I finally understand that it's not my place to judge."

"No, Angel. It's not." I'm beyond proud of her as I address her father.

"Any last words?"

I step toward him, making sure I'm blocking the scene from his daughter.

"May God strike you down."

"You first," I answer as I pull the knife out of my pocket and plunge it into his neck.

The End

EPILOGUE
SERAPHINA

20 YEARS LATER

I hum as I dig through the kitchen cabinets, pulling out all the items I need to bake for the party this afternoon. The long black island gleams with the rising sun, and I carefully lay each item out. I used to bake with the girls every chance I got, but Lydia is turning thirteen this year, and baking with Mom isn't cool anymore.

She still wants to eat a double chocolate cake though, and while Shane and I can afford any party she wants, my girl wants something low-key. Well, low-key for a well-off girl who attends an excellent private school.

The backyard of our estate is decorated to perfection, and the gardens and topiaries are trimmed and ready for the dunking booth and games we plan to bring in this afternoon. Despite what our sixteen-year-old Elodie says about it, it will be a great time.

Like always, I think of Tim as I look around. He would have thought this was great work, and I feel that old pang of regret and sadness. I still hate that his life paid for my happiness, but my God, I am happy. I wish I could say I had the same regrets about my father, but I don't. He deserved what he got. And while there was some heat afterward, Shane had enough money and connections to keep us out of trouble.

After my father and Tim's missing persons cases died down, Shane and I chose a rocky peak for our home, reminiscent of the castle estate where we fell in love but homier. We built this place from the ground up, and every inch of it is infused with my likes and wants. There isn't a single place in my life where I feel unfulfilled.

I love so many things other than my husband and daughters. My garden is overflowing with fruits and vegetables, and I know how to grow each right. The August sun is hot and tiring, but I love that too. The sting of sunburn on my cheeks from long days spent enjoying myself is one of the simplest joys in my life.

We're on summer break at school, and while I miss my kindergarteners, I love having this time with my husband and children when they'll have me.

I always thought I hated school, but it turns out I hated theology and the feeling of indoctrination. I love learning in a way I could never guess and sharing that with young minds. Shane quit his career as a psychiatrist at my request. I thought the temptation was too much for him, and he needed to apply his talents elsewhere. Shane went back to school with me while I got my master's of education, and he earned a tech degree. Meaning now he's a cyberstalker instead of a regular one. It allows him to be a productive member of society and a bit of a creep.

Lydia and Elodie are remarkably well-adjusted kids, and I'm proud we've managed a total power exchange relationship their entire lives without them noticing. I never did ask for that safeword, and the way Shane fucks me, to this day, is brutal. Regardless of our unconventional start, we're a happy family.

I'm whipping up the frosting when Shane walks into the kitchen, looking handsome as ever, maybe more so now that his black hair is sprinkled with grays. A few soft lines crinkle his eyes and the corners of his mouth, proof of our happy life. He steps up behind me, pressing my back to his front. His arms wind around my middle, and I hum with happiness.

"Angel, you've made a mess," he tells me as he dips his finger into the bowl, wipes the topping off on me, and licks the side of my neck. He finishes with a bite, and I shimmy against him and groan.

"GROSS!" Elodie shouts as she walks into the kitchen.

Her sister bounds behind her, hoping to catch a little attention from the coolest girl in the world.

"Mom, I'm thirteen. Tell Elodie I'm old enough to go to the concert with her!" The whine in her voice doesn't go far in selling the mature thing.

"You are not old enough to go to the concert with her," Shane answers before I can say anything. "Ellie isn't either."

"Dad! We already talked about this. Don't try to distract me from the fact that you were mauling Mom! You guys are old, and it's just disgusting. I am going to that concert!"

"I'm forty-four," I tell the little brat who insists on making me feel ancient.

"Yeah, Mom, you're old! You guys have been doing it for twenty years. Can you stop?!"

I start to scoop the frosting into the piping bag and plan the design in my head.

"Your father and I are in love, Ellie. You don't want

that to change, do you? There are too many unhappy families out there."

She groans. "No, I guess I wouldn't want to change that."

"Mom, Dad, can you tell us how you met again? It's so romantic." Lydia looks up at me, and I point at her father with a meaningful glare as if to say, "you made this shit up; you deal with it."

"Okay, okay. Well, it was the first day on campus, and your Mom and I were way older than the kids going there. We were late bloomers."

"Ugh, Dad, the dramatics," Ellie complains.

"Fine, fine! Well, we had our first class together and I said to her, 'Are you free after this? I have an idea.'"

ALSO BY AURELIA KNIGHT

Vow to Sever

Stolen Obsessions Book 2

Coming late 2023

The preorder date is only a placeholder and will be moved up.

Fool me Twice and Shame on Me

Dark Double Duet with Coauthor Stephanie Hurst

August and September 2023

The Illicit Library Collection books 1-3

Complete and free to read in Kindle Unlimited!

ACKNOWLEDGMENTS

There are so many people who have helped this book come to fruition but I'd like to make a few specials mentions.

My best author friend, Stephanie Hurst, thanks for always being there to listen to my story problems and help me through a tough spot.

My alpha readers Sonia and Teresa, you guys are the best and I can't thank you enough. Your encouragement was everything to me in finishing this book. I couldn't have done it without you!

To all my readers, thank you for the enthusiasm you showed this book before it even came out. I couldn't do this without you.

ABOUT AURELIA

Aurelia Knight is a hot mess, doing her best to keep it together most days. Words are the greatest love of her life second only to her husband and sons. If she's not typing away, getting lost in her own world, she's reading and slipping away into the worlds of other writers. A caffeine addict who believes sleep is secondary to the endless promise of "just one more chapter".

For the most up to date information join Aurelia's reader group on Facebook, Aurelia's Illicit Library, and subscribe to her mailing list at www.AureliaKnight.com

Printed in Great Britain
by Amazon